The CARLA Conspiracy

THE CARLA CONSPIRACY

DEREK HART

iUniverse, Inc.
Bloomington

The CARLA Conspiracy

This is a work of fiction. All of the characters, names, incidents, organizations, and dialogue in this novel are either the products of the author's imagination or are used fictitiously.

iUniverse books may be ordered through booksellers or by contacting:

iUniverse
1663 Liberty Drive
Bloomington, IN 47403
www.iuniverse.com
1-800-Authors (1-800-288-4677)

Because of the dynamic nature of the Internet, any web addresses or links contained in this book may have changed since publication and may no longer be valid. The views expressed in this work are solely those of the author and do not necessarily reflect the views of the publisher, and the publisher hereby disclaims any responsibility for them.

Any people depicted in stock imagery provided by Thinkstock are models, and such images are being used for illustrative purposes only.

Certain stock imagery © Thinkstock.

ISBN: 978-1-4759-4722-9 (sc)
ISBN: 978-1-4759-4723-6 (e)

Printed in the United States of America

iUniverse rev. date: 8/27/2012

What's in a Name?

The name **Carla** is Teutonic in origin, commonly found in Italian, Portuguese, Spanish, English, and German cultures, meaning strong woman. Derived from the German Karla - meaning "free woman," but its common use was first documented starting in the 8th century in the Latinized form Carola, in memory of the venerable Carola Gerhardinger of Regensburg.

In numerology, **Carla** is signified by the numbers 911, the internationally recognized call sign for requesting emergency assistance. For students of the relationships between certain numbers and letters, this would indicate that anyone named Carla would be of tremendous value during times of trouble.

The common attributes associated with the name **Carla** are:

-Meaning-
Strong woman.
-Motivation-
Desire to succeed.
-Character-
Confident with what she does.
-Feelings-
Passionate.
-Intelligence-
Possesses an inquiring mind.
-Spiritual-
Happy with personal beliefs.
-Nature-
Fun loving.
-Inherent-
A love of freedom.

DEDICATION

Dedicated to Alice Simon, who throughout the years, has
proven to be not only a great friend, but also a confidant and
ally. The author readily acknowledges her contribution to his
writing success and words can never repay her generosity.

Conspiracy:
1. An agreement to perform together an illegal, wrongful, or subversive act.
2. A group of conspirators.
3. *Law:* An agreement between two or more persons to commit a crime or accomplish a legal purpose through illegal action.
4. A joining or acting together, as if by sinister design: *a conspiracy of wind and tide that devastated coastal areas.*

PREFACE

FOUNDED IN 1889, THE University of New Mexico now occupies 600 acres along old Route 66 in the heart of Albuquerque, a city of half a million people. From the magnificent mesas to the west, past the banks of the historic Rio Grande, to the Sandia Mountains to the east, Albuquerque is a blend of culture and cuisine, styles and stories, people, pursuits and panoramas.

The University of New Mexico offers a unique campus environment with a Pueblo Revival architectural theme that echoes the buildings of the nearby Pueblo Indian villages. The nationally recognized Campus Arboretum offers an outstanding botanical experience in the midst of one of New Mexico's great public open spaces.

The University represents a wide cross-section of cultures and backgrounds. Over 24,700 students attend the main campus and another 7,100 attend branch campuses and education centers. The average student at the University is 27 years old.

The University of New Mexico boasts outstanding faculty members, including a Nobel Laureate, a MacArthur Fellow and several members of the national academies. Many faculty members have been published in various professional journals, including *Scientific American, New England Journal of Medicine* and *Nature.* University professors have been quoted in *Newsweek, Seattle Times, Business Week, People Magazine, Parade Magazine, US News and World Report,* and the *New Yorker,* among others. UNM professors have shared their expertise on *CNN, Today Show, Good Morning America, Nova* and other news shows.

The University employs 19,443 people statewide, including employees of the University Hospital. Alumni numbers more than 110,000 worldwide, while nearly half remain in the state.

UNM's main and branch campuses offer 88 certificates, 97 associate degrees, 145 bachelor's degrees, 83 master's degrees, 42 doctorate degrees, three professional degrees, 11 post-master's certificates and eight education specialists. Several UNM programs consistently rank among the best nationwide. *U.S. News & World Report* listed three programs in the UNM School of Medicine that ranked in the top 10. For eight consecutive years, the school's rural medicine program held the number two spot in the nation. UNM's primary-care curriculum ranked fourth, UNM's family medicine program ranked in fifth place. The UNM clinical law training program is in the top 10. The law school was recognized with the most racially diverse student bodies. UNM's law school remains among the top 100 law schools in the nation. UNM's School of Engineering was among the top 50 engineering schools in the country. In addition, UNM's anthropology, biology, flamenco dance and Latin American and Western history programs have respected national reputations.

Annual giving to the University exceeds $40 million. Total budget revenue for UNM was $1,267,900,000. UNM research injects millions of dollars into New Mexico's economy, augments teaching, by giving students valuable hands-on training in state-of-the-art laboratories, and funds new advancements in healthcare. The Health Sciences Center is the state's largest integrated health care treatment, research and education organization. Among the university's outstanding research units are the High Performance Computing Center, Cancer Center, New Mexico Engineering Research Institute, Center for High Technology Materials, Design Planning Assistance Center, Environmental Law and Policy, and the Center for Non-Invasive Diagnosis.

The University has branch campuses in Gallup, Los Alamos, Taos and Valencia County. In addition, UNM offers graduate and upper division programs in Los Alamos and Santa Fe and throughout the state. UNM's libraries, museums, galleries and Center for the Arts are a rich cultural resource for the state. UNM's Tamarind Institute is one of the premier printmaking workshops in the world. UNM is home to the Lobos and is part of the Mountain West conference. Lobo athletics draw fans from all over, and the University Arena or "The Pit" was ranked 13th by *Sports Illustrated* as one of the top 20 sports venues of the century.

If you have never been the state of New Mexico, then you are truly missing a wonderful adventure. Inside her borders are ancient cultures, unique cuisine, varied wildlife and breathtaking landscapes. There are mountains, lakes, deserts, and vast forests, combined with people who are vibrant, fascinating and as diverse as their history.

New Mexico is indeed the Land of Enchantment.

THE HANDS OF DEATH

AFTER A FEW HOURS of idly walking around several Albuquerque attractions, Garrett Brody, along with fellow University of New Mexico English professors Todd Everett and Alice Coleman, decided to go backpacking over the weekend. Since Bandelier National Monument was located such a short distance away, they agreed to make the park their final destination. While most of the driving was on winding scenic mountain roads, Bandelier still only took about 90 minutes to reach.

The primary attraction at Bandelier was the cliff dwelling ruins where pueblo ancestors lived for nearly 500 years. The trio initially strolled along the popular 1.4-mile introduction trail to stretch their legs after the drive. They really enjoyed climbing up the short ladders to the cliff dwellings and poking their heads into the small holes leading to where the Indians lived from the 11th to 16th century.

Eventually feeling more adventurous, they followed the trail as it extended another ½ mile to the Indian Ceremonial Cave. Here, they climbed straight up the cliff via a series of steep ladders, 140 vertical feet. The view from the large half-domed ceremonial cave was spectacular and looked out over the gorge and a bubbling creek. Inside the cave was a kiva, where special religious ceremonies were still allowed to take place. After climbing up to the cave, Brody received permission to scale down a steep ladder through a hole in the floor into the kiva, where he tried to imagine being a member of the pueblo during a simpler time of human existence. Afterwards they pitched their tents in the Park campground, barbequing steaks in an approved, fire-control grill.

The next morning, Brody, along with his two University of New Mexico academic friends, began their serious hiking to Painted Cave, then along the Frijoles Rim Trail, and finally past the Yapashi Ruins. The forty-mile round-trip journey was considered strenuous, as they would traverse mesas, explore sheer-walled canyons, search the large unexcavated pueblo called Yapashi, and negotiate the steep descent from the San Miguel Mountains into Capulin Canyon, where fantastic prehistoric and historic pictographs decorated the walls of a large alcove.

A popular misconception of New Mexico was it consists of nothing but desert. While it was true that a portion of desert extended up from Mexico into southern New Mexico, the state's scenery was beautiful and diverse. The Rocky Mountains thrust into the north-central portion from Colorado, reaching an altitude of just over 13,000 feet near Taos. The vast Colorado Plateau, a region of high tablelands serrated by canyons cut deeply through red sandstone and shale, covers the northwest section of the State.

Although not truly a desert, the Southwest was quite arid and New Mexico received less than 20 inches of precipitation a year, so most crops require supplementary irrigation. However, Northern New Mexico enjoyed a temperate mountain climate with four distinct seasons, and was relatively green and well watered. Even though April was almost over, springtime often came late to the Rockies. It was windy and wet snowstorms occurred even in late May. March had ended with warm, dry conditions, but was followed by a two-month rainy season. Even on many summer days, rain would pour down by early afternoon, accompanied by lightning and sometimes hail. Then the skies would clear and the evenings were almost invariably delightful and cool, filled with magnificent twinkling stars.

Bandelier National Monument contained 23,267 acres of designated wilderness, with more than 70 miles of backcountry trails. The terrain was challenging and the scenery spectacular. Elevations ranged from 5,000 to 10,000 feet, while lush, narrow canyons alternated with sweeping mesa-top vistas.

After a half-hour drive down bumpy forest service roads, fog and light drizzle greeted the trio at the end of St. Peter's Dome Road. In the distance was Boundary Peak, which marked the west border of Bandelier National Monument. They unpacked their gear and headed off into the wilderness.

The fog and rain dried up quickly, and they discovered an amazing view of the canyons below. The first part of the hike took them down from

8000 feet to 6100 feet and into Capulin Canyon. Part way down, the trees disappeared and were replaced by scrub-brush.

They took a long break at Painted Cave and ate lunch. Alice and Todd sat for a long time in complete silence, contemplating the hundreds of petroglyphs.

Some of the drawings are Anasazi, who inhabited the area around AD 1300. Others were much more recent. Near the center were carved a Star of David, a church with steeple, and a lizard poking his head above a mountain range, about to devour the church. There were also many abstract symbols, blown-paint hand reliefs, deer, birds and other strange animals.

After Painted Cave, they hiked down to a bluff overlooking the Rio Grande, near the southern boundary of Bandelier. This was where they agreed to pitch tents and make a campsite looking northeast.

Alice and Todd negotiated their way down the bluff to check out the river. Their plan was to get drinking water out of the river, with suitable treatment, of course. However, the water was very muddy and smelled horrible, so they passed on that idea.

The backpackers had carried everything they would need, with four days worth of food. This also included tents, sleeping bags, clothing, and water, the most precious commodity of all. Each hiker carried six quarts at any given time. None of the backcountry camps were staffed, but most had a water source, although hikers had to purify it with an Iodine solution. The elevation started out over 8000 feet above sea level and went up from there. The three of them had to get used to the thinner air, which they slowly adjusted to over the several days hiking. It did not help that they were carrying backpacks weighing close to 58 pounds each. However, the beautiful surroundings were well worth the physical exertion.

The area abounded with Mule Deer, Jack Rabbits and lots of unusual vegetation, like huge Douglas Firs, Aspen Trees, and blooming cactus. One of the hassles of backpacking in the area was the need to follow strict bear safety procedures. There were plenty of brown bears and a few mountain lions in the area, but no Grizzlies. The hikers had to put up all of their odor-producing items, such as food, cameras and film, toothpaste, and garbage into "bear bags." These were hoisted up onto a cable each night. They had also been advised to not wear any underarm deodorant either.

This led to a lot of body odor after a few days with no shower. However, outhouses were strategically placed at points in or near camps. Some of them were simply boxes with seats mounted on top, out in the open. The nicest facilities were enclosed, and were known affectionately as red roof inns, for their brightly painted crimson tops.

The first night the trio had a beautiful clear sky. The moon was so bright that the hikers cast crisp shadows. They stayed up very late and watched shooting stars, while sprawled around a small campfire. Garrett remained awake long after the others had drifted off to sleep, as he often suffered from rest-robbing nightmares. An incident from his recent past regularly haunted him. He hadn't brought his laptop computer, of course, so his typical nocturnal writing habits were interrupted. Instead, he just stared up at the heavens and pondered all sorts of grand and sometime ridiculous thoughts.

The next morning Brody hiked down the bluff to the river to try his hand at getting water. The level had dropped during the night, so it was even less appetizing than the previous evening. The water Garrett was able to find looked and smelled like an emulsion of mud and rotting flesh.

"Do we really have to drink this?" Alice asked, curling her nose from the smell.

Even after treatment, it was still undrinkable. Their nearest fresh-water supply was seven miles and several canyons away.

They packed up their gear and started the hike. Reaching the mesa overlooking Alamo Canyon, everyone realized how thirsty they were. Somehow, they also kept losing the trail. It seemed like countless miles, in the scorching midday heat, but the hikers finally reached the Yapashi Pueblo Ruins. Ancient people lived here in the 13th century, but now there were just fallen walls and pottery shards.

After resting in the shade for a while, Brody spurred his companions to continue. They then reached Stone Lions Shrine. In the center of a circle of rocks were two lions carved from stone. They were quite weathered, but the rough outline of the big cats was still discernable.

After another thirty minutes of hiking, the Ranger's station finally came into sight and everyone sighed with relief.

Salvation!

A hand-pump delivered clear, fresh water. Waiting the ten minutes for the water treatment to work was very difficult for such thirsty people. Then a park ranger showed up and tried to make passing conversation, but even Brody was too grumpy and tired to be very friendly.

After drinking a couple of quarts of water apiece, they sat at one of the picnic tables and made a leisurely lunch.

"Next trip, let's pick a trail which starts uphill and ends downhill," Alice announced emphatically.

Both Garrett and Todd laughed aloud.

"Next time, let's take more canteens," Todd suggested instead.

Everyone agreed.

Once they felt refreshed and properly hydrated, the hikers set out again, hoping to return to the parking lot before dusk. The trail was mostly downhill from that spot, which pleased Alice immensely. Garrett took up the lead position and set an aggressive pace. However, with such captivating scenery and abundant wildlife nearby, they just naturally slowed down to take it all in.

Suddenly, Brody came to an abrupt halt.

He held up his hand to stop the others.

"What's wrong?" Todd asked.

"I don't know," Garret replied. "There's something lying in the middle of the trail and it looks like an injured animal. I'm going closer to investigate."

"Be careful, Garrett," Alice warned. "It might attack you."

Brody waved her off. "Believe me, I will be. You two stay there and if I start running for my life, don't hang around to watch."

Todd laughed nervously. "Don't worry, we won't."

Garrett approached slowly, trying not to make any sudden movements or noise. Alice was mesmerized by Brody's approach, slinking forward as if he was a predator on the hunt. She had ever seen anyone behave in such a manner.

As Garret got closer, however, his curiosity turned to horror.

It wasn't an animal at all.

It was a human being.

"Oh, my God," Brody said.

The dead person was completely naked, lying face down, with four bullet holes punched into his upper torso. None of the shots had been fatal on their own, but the victim probably had bled to death.

"What is it, Garrett?" Alice called out.

"It's a dead man," Brody replied.

Alice almost got sick to her stomach and as Todd put his arms around her, he called back, "Are you sure?"

"Yes, I'm quite sure," Garrett replied. "Just stay where you are."

"*Gracias*, Maria," he tried his hand at Spanish, butchering it completely.

Maria giggled and went off to place his order.

A cup of hot coffee arrived just a few moments later.

The service was fast, and the delicious spicy food, along with the good coffee, perked up his spirits. The eggs were smothered with green chili sauce, which provided heat but not fire. Crispy fried potatoes and soupy refried beans complimented the eggs. Brody cleaned up his plate with soft, fresh tortillas.

However, even the awesome meal failed to erase the gruesome discovery from the day before. In all of Garrett's vast experience, he never got used to watching anything die. That was a good thing, of course, but holding a man's hand as that life ebbed away was something Brody would never forget.

Still more disturbing were the dying man's only words.

"Carla is the key."

Now what exactly was that supposed to mean?

How many thousands of women, in the United States alone, were named Carla? Even with the most basic laws of probability, the scope seemed too monumental to even consider. Brody didn't envy the police in this matter, especially since there were no apparent clues readily available to help identify the victim.

The waitress brought the check.

"*Gracias, Maria,*" Brody said, once more trying his hand at Spanish.

"*De nada,*" she replied, giggling again.

He handed her cash with the receipt. "Keep the change. It was excellent."

Maria was pleasantly surprised at his generosity. "Thank you so much, *señor*. You are very kind."

As Garrett departed, she called after him, "Please come again."

"I will," he replied sheepishly, still feeling woefully inadequate with his use of Spanish.

Perhaps he should take up formal lessons.

Even with the tragic memory of a man's death still fresh in his mind, Brody couldn't deny it was a beautiful day. With the start of the summer semester, the period of study lasting approximately 16 weeks, or one-third the academic year, he was really looking forward to a fresh batch of students. Garrett had uncovered some real talent amongst the previous classes. Discovering budding authors, while still maintaining contact with most of them, kept his motivation active and perhaps kept their publishing hopes alive.

Brody decided to proofread his course syllabus one more time, before class started on Monday, so he drove directly back to his condominium. However, he was still having difficulty concentrating. Instead of wasting time, he filled the dishwasher, threw a load of dirty laundry in the washing machine, and completed a few other domestic chores. Just as he got the vacuum cleaner out of the closet, the doorbell rang.

Garrett went to the front door and peeked through the security peephole.

He opened it.

Standing there was a man in his late 30's, with a notebook under his left arm and a very serious and business-like expression on his face.

"Good morning," Garrett said. "May I help you?"

"I'm Detective Rameriz," the man introduced himself, displaying his badge. "I'm with the Albuquerque Police Homicide Division. I wonder if I might ask you a few questions?"

Brody swung the door open wider and said, "Of course, Detective, come on in."

"Thank you," Rameriz said, stepping inside.

"If you don't mind, would you please take your shoes off?" Brody asked. "It keeps the carpet cleaner."

Detective Rameriz looked only mildly irritated at the request, before slipping out of his shoes.

"Thank you," Garrett said, leading the investigator into the den. "Can I get you something to drink or eat?"

"No, thank you," Rameriz said. "This should only take a few minutes."

"Okay, make yourself comfortable," Garrett said, pointing towards the sofa.

The two men sat across from each other.

"So I assume you're here to talk about the dying man we found in Bandelier?" Brody asked.

Rameriz nodded. "Yes."

"Have you identified him yet?"

"His name was Dr. Flavius Newman," the detective stated after looking at his homicide report. "He was employed at the Los Alamos National Laboratory."

know me and for me to know you. Make an appointment to see me once you've been through a few classes. Feel free to make appointments before or after class or over the telephone. If for some reason you must cancel, be sure to call me. Remember, teaching is not my only responsibility, since I also have a literary agent and book publisher to answer to. I can also be available on the weekends and certain evenings, so just ask. I'll try to be as accommodating as possible.

"The purpose of meeting with me, regardless of your level of interest in the course, is to enhance your understanding of what is going on in class. Besides, getting to know me can have other benefits as well. Most of the time, I can be fairly interesting."

This time, one female student chuckled and Garrett immediately noticed her, for she was very good looking. He smiled back, while regaining his train of thought.

"We may discover that we have common interests, which can be the basis for a good relationship long after you've finished the course," Brody went on, but was now directing his comments to the beautiful woman in the second row. "You may also find that a particular subject is much more interesting to you than you previously thought. It is not unusual for decisions about college majors to originate with a good student-professor relationship. Finally, I may have information about special opportunities that you may find useful. Of course, a single office visit won't change your life, but it could lead to opportunities you hadn't previously considered. In fact, I'm looking for a research assistant, so you might land that coveted position."

Brody could see there was plenty of interest regarding that announcement.

"Please get assignments in on time," Brody went on. "Unless there's an earthquake, fire, flood, or some catastrophic illness strikes you, you've got the same time to complete an assignment as everyone else. This class meets three days a week, Monday, Wednesday and Friday, so don't forget. You want me to know who you are for the right reasons.

"One last item. Being courteous in class doesn't mean you have to agree with everything I say. While I'm considered an expert in my field, that doesn't mean you can't teach me a thing or two and I hope you'll engage me in constructive dialogue. A good argument, without anger or hostility, can really be a wonderful teaching tool. Be specific, positive, and constructive with your feedback and we'll enjoy the perfect learning situation."

Brody waited for a moment to see if any hands went up.

"Any questions?" he prompted.

Apparently there were none.

"All right then, let's get started," Brody was ready to begin his opening discussion. "It has commonly been said that a writer should write about what he or she knows. This is true, but the definition of what a person knows has been left open for interpretation. For instance, how many of you think I was ever employed by the CIA?"

Only a few tentative hands went up, but most of the students just laughed.

Garrett smiled broadly, showing his perfectly capped white teeth. "Well, I can assure you I was not! There's no way that renowned agency would even consider employing a bleeding-heart liberal like me."

Noticeably more laughter.

"However, I still wrote about the CIA in several of my novels," Brody continued. "To convey such an agency requires research, it's true, but it also meant I had to know what I was writing about. I'm not aware of any existing CIA program that invites fiction writers to spend a few weeks living the life of a field operative."

Still more laughter.

Then a single hand went up.

Brody pointed to the owner, who turned out to be the gorgeous woman he had made eye-contact with earlier. She was definitely worth looking at, again.

"Yes," he called on her.

"I've read all your books, Mr. Brody," she said.

"Well, thank you," he quickly interjected.

The chuckles continued.

The students were actually starting to loosen up and relax.

The woman's hair was long, settling well below her shoulders and was the most intense shade of black Garrett had ever seen. He wondered if she had Native American blood in her heritage. She had dark eyes too, which were big and penetrating. To say she was breathtaking would have been a gross understatement, but it was also too simplistic to describe her that way. Perhaps her true beauty resided in her dazzling smile, which was genuine, warm and quite engaging.

"You're welcome," she said. "But I've always wondered how you can write in such detail about things that seem outside your realm of experience. It's fiction, I know, but many chapters really swept me along on the words describing the action and emotions. Sometimes I wondered if certain events were even plausible, but then I did my own research and discovered a lot of truth behind your plots. How do you do it?"

Brody was not only impressed with her detailed analysis of his writing, but also what she was searching for with her question.

Of course, there was something else too.

For the first time since arriving at the University, Garrett found himself undeniably attracted to one of his students. While on the one hand, warning bells were going off in his head like air-raid sirens, on the other hand, he couldn't exactly ignore what was going on in his mind.

Or elsewhere.

For that matter, he was having difficulty fighting the urge to sweep her up into his arms and making mad, passionate love to her. She really was stunning and just plain delicious and he wanted to...

To break this increasingly distracting and unprofessional train of thought, before he made a complete idiot of himself, Brody picked up a black dry-erase marker and stepped back towards the whiteboard.

Garret started to write, but mis-spelled the first word, so he erased it.

"Nobody said a writer has to know how to spell," he said over his shoulder.

Amidst the laughter, some of the students clapped and Brody felt like he was doing stand-up comedy.

He wrote:

Research — immerse yourself!
Use real life experiences to create the sense of reality.
Develop the characters to reflect how you would behave.
Write first about emotion, then description of action.

Turning back to face both his students and the specific woman who asked the question, he said, "This sequence may not work for anyone but me, but consider the applications. Once I've decided on a topic or event I want to write about, I acquire everything I can get my hands on about the subject. I read and read and read some more, immersing myself in facts and details. Then, when I start getting a feeling for what I want to happen, I draw from my own life to add validity to the main character's reactions, both physical and emotional. Finally, while I may push the envelope of believability initially, I try to develop flaws in the characters and the action, thereby avoiding comic-book hero stories."

The good-looking student raised her hand again.

"Yes, go on," Garrett said supportively.

"It's the human flaws that make the characters not only come alive, but also seem vulnerable and realistic to the reader," she said. "But I think it's quite a challenge to write about your own shortcomings and put on paper what we don't like about ourselves."

Brody walked up the steps towards her. He couldn't help it. He was drawn to her like a magnet. Garrett worried the others would translate his body language and realize he wanted to jump in her lap, but it was too late. He was thoroughly committed.

"You are so right," Brody said. "Yet in looking in a mirror and writing what we know is true, we mature both as writers and as human beings. When you're pounding away on that keyboard, to describe some of your own personal faults can be quite startling to see come out as words. However, creating a bond between the reader and your characters is one of the primary goals of a good writer. If your audience finds something to identify with, you've won half the battle. Since we're all human and not perfect, we should be able to identify traits that will ring true on the written page."

He stopped.

She had been taking extensive notes on her laptop and looked up.

There was that incredibly inviting smile again.

Brody forced himself to turn and scan the faces of other students. "Anybody else?" He rested his hand on the top of her table, crossing two fingers.

The female coed saw this and smiled to herself.

This time at least ten hands went up.

"Okay, one at a time," Garrett chuckled. He pointed to a male student this time. "Go ahead."

"Most of your books are built around common basics, like action, adventure, and romance, of course," the student said. "Still, the stories are really about people trapped in huge events, sometimes historical turning points. How do you keep the perspective?"

Garrett smiled and slipped one hand into his pants pocket, while accentuating with the other. "Believe me, I'm tempted to solve those big historical events with my characters taking all the credit. But that's just not very realistic. However, history is full of people who took part in great events, but were never credited with anything. That's reality. So I just create someone like you or me, and throw them in the middle. Haven't you ever imagined you were part of some monumental moment in time?"

From then on, the discussion flowed with both enthusiasm and participation, until there was a noticeable air of barely-contained excitement. Brody's students went back and forth in a vibrant exchange of ideas and suggestions, with a flurry of solutions discovered for many writing challenges. It was obvious to see that they were not only involved with learning, but enjoying every minute of it.

To say the least, Garrett was extremely pleased.

"Well, I'm afraid we've run out of time," he announced after looking at his watch.

There was plenty of disappointment, as some students moaned and most of them hesitated interrupting the energy. In the end, they reluctantly started to pack up, but the conversations were definitely animated.

Brody cast a quick glance at the woman who had started the ball rolling and when he caught her eye, he said, "I want to thank everyone for such a wonderful opening discussion. This was a lot of fun."

There was no doubt his praise was directed at her and she just beamed at his words. Then Garrett faced them all again.

"Starting with the next class, I want you to bring in whatever project you're working on presently, whether it's a novel or short story," he said. "If it's on your laptop, just bring that. I want to start working with your individual styles and plotlines. Thanks. You're free to go."

The students exited the lecture hall, while sharing a steady stream of boisterous chatter. Garrett watched them leave with such a positive air of possibilities that he felt he had accomplished a lot on the first day. Turning to collect his briefcase, Brody suddenly realized someone was standing by the lectern.

Garrett couldn't help feeling delighted when he saw it was the woman who had asked the opening question.

Stepping forward quite confidently, she offered her hand.

They shook hands.

"It's an honor to actually meet you in person, Mr. Brody," she said.

"Well, thank you," Garrett said, but he didn't release her hand immediately.

Her fingers were long and warm, the skin incredibly smooth and soft, while her nails were healthy and perfect. There was great power residing in her hand, even if she didn't realize it. He finally let go.

Brody matched her smile. "You really started the whole thing going today. Thank you."

Her signature smile remained, with the same warm, dazzling impact as before. "I enjoyed your insights very much, Mr. Brody."

"Please, it's Garrett," Brody said. "Mr. Brody makes me sound like some stuffy old college professor."

They shared pleasant laughter.

"And you are?" he asked.

"Jessica Lawver," the woman replied.

"Aha," he said. "Now I know which name to make a little asterisk beside."

Jessica cocked her head and looked slightly concerned.

Brody almost panicked. He certainly didn't want her to think he was weird or psychotic or anything like that. "It's just my way of distinguishing students who actively participate in class, Ms. Lawver."

She smiled again. "Well, I plan on doing that every day, Mr. Brody."

He was pleased. "Great! I look forward to reading your writing."

That statement seemed to disarm her completely, as she frowned and backed up a little. "Oh, I don't think I'm a very good writer, really. I usually struggle and nothing comes even close to your books."

Garrett frowned, while shaking his head. "I don't want you to compare your writing with mine. While I'm flattered that you enjoy my books, there's no sense in judging your writing in that context. Each writer is unique. Your style and word choice express their own merit."

Jessica looked at him differently just then. Her mind was twirling with jumbled thoughts and emotions, but she didn't know quite how to express them. Brody stood a little over six feet tall and was broad shouldered. His curly brown hair was kept fashionably trimmed and his deep blue eyes were dangerously hypnotic. There was no doubt that Garrett was handsome, but not distracting like a male model. He had a rugged mannerism about him, without losing a bit of charm. In fact, she was drawn to him for reasons other than physical attraction. It was something more chemical and sensory than simply good looks.

Brody asked, "Do you have another class to get to right away?"

Jessica shook her head, but it wasn't really the truth. Something profound made her deny she had a class immediately following Brody's.

"Well, I'm heading across campus, so if you'd like to join me for lunch, we can talk about this in more depth."

"So what do you really care about, Mr. Brody?" she asked.

Her question was actually on everyone's mind in the classroom.

Garrett could tell that they all wanted to hear his answer.

"Well, just like Rick, I care about a lot of things," Brody replied. "But if you want to know what my true passion is, then I can sum it up in one word. Justice."

"Do you feel strongly enough about justice to die for it?" Jessica used Garrett's own line of questioning on him.

Brody didn't answer.

He didn't have to.

The look on his face and the way he slowly nodded his head was answer enough.

Everyone in that room believed him.

"One more thing, Mr. Brody," she said.

"Yes?" he replied.

Jessica slowly stood up.

Then, without any warning, she suddenly hurled a textbook right at him.

Without thinking and entirely as a trained response, Brody twisted around, vaulting into the air and deflecting the book away with a dramatic and perfectly executed roundhouse kick. The volume sailed away from hitting anyone and landed several rows behind Jessica. Garrett landed gracefully, assuming a defensive pose that presented him as someone who was not only skilled at martial arts, but most likely an expert.

Once again the students were completely speechless, awestruck by this unexpected event. However, Jessica remained standing, her arms folded across her chest, with the most mischievous smile on her face.

Garrett assumed a more relaxed stance, but there was no way he could pretend what just happened, hadn't happened. Still, he tried to act nonchalant, by slipping his hands into his pockets and facing Jessica.

"I hope I didn't damage that book," he quipped.

Everyone laughed, including Jessica.

"I imagine there was a reason for your actions, Ms. Lawver?" Brody asked.

A room full of heads turned in her direction.

Jessica nodded. "It was a test, Mr. Brody. In your book, *Afterburner*, your hero was very adept at a specific discipline of martial arts. I just wanted to see if the author was writing from experience or research, as well as his passion."

She abruptly sat down.

Brody couldn't help himself.

He smiled, and then laughed out loud, very amused and impressed by the woman's ability to challenge him in such a way. Without planning a thing, the other students were also visually and physically involved in the lesson. Jessica had applied his lecture into real terms, thereby evaluating the outcome and comparing it with her own theories. No matter what Brody might think, Jessica Lawver was far ahead of the typical student, because she practiced and tested her own assumptions.

The other students were entertained and realized that Jessica had engaged the instructor in a most unique style. There was a round of enthusiastic applause and Garrett insisted she take a little bow.

However, he immediately took back control of the class. "Now let's not let Ms. Lawver's unique example fade away simply as theatrics. Her point is very valid. If you're going to write about something, anything, you better be able to embrace it, live it, feel it, and defend it. Otherwise, it's just so many words on paper."

Once again, the hands went up in a flurry of excited waving.

"All right," Brody chuckled. "One at a time. Ms. Harrison, what's on your mind?"

"You can call me Sara, Mr. Brody," she said with a huge smile.

Everyone laughed at her teasing comment.

Garrett grinned. "All right, Sara, go ahead."

"Well, it seems to me that passion can come from so many sources and have various levels of intensity," she stated. "How does a writer focus on the right source and also maintain the necessary voltage?"

"Excellent question," Brody replied.

Then he exaggerated a shrug, which elicited more laughter.

Garrett put up his hand to silence the ruckus. "Seriously, Sara, your question is at the heart of every writer's soul. First, as you stated, the catalysts may vary. The secret is to harness the energy when it comes, no matter what induced it. Secondly, take the time to note what caused the passion and don't let it get away from you without directing it at writing. If you're especially angry, write about how it feels as soon as possible. Don't worry about spelling or grammar or punctuation. Just get the feelings down. If you're sad, happy, scared, lonely, horny, or even hungry, capture it."

"Also, don't forget to write for the *Blue Mesa Review*, which is the literary journal of the Creative Writing Program here at UNM," Sara

Lots of passing students smiled or laughed and Brody suddenly felt exposed and foolish. He smiled back, but hurried along to the University Library, where he wanted to look up some material on modern Native American relations with the federal government. He was onto another completely different plot and such research usually propelled his writing along, even if he didn't use but a small percentage of the facts he uncovered. It was just the germ of an idea, but Garrett was excited by the possibilities.

Jessica Lawver didn't try sneaking to her seat, but apologized for being tardy. Professor Strong didn't mind, for she had become a vital participant in his class too.

Jessica's mind was quickly focused elsewhere, however. Garrett Brody was dancing in and out of her brain, creating all sorts of pleasant thoughts and urges.

In fact, after her *American Modernism* class wrapped up, Jessica headed straight for her apartment, where she grabbed a quick bite to eat and changed into a skirt.

A short skirt, actually.

CHAPTER 4

PLEASANT
COMPLICATIONS

JESSICA SAT DOWN ACROSS from Garrett, crossing her smooth, shapely tanned legs.

Garrett wasn't blind. She had changed her clothes in between attending his class and coming to his office. Not only was her skirt a little bit too short, but she had the most fantastic legs he had ever seen. Brody wanted to touch. The collar of his polo shirt instantly felt constricting, even though the neck was unbuttoned.

Regardless of whether he was a gentleman or not, Garrett wished he had the nerve to peek. Instead of looking where he imagined he could catch a glimpse of her panties, Garrett never took his eyes from hers. His mind screamed with frustration, while his body felt like it was on fire.

Jessica pulled out a list of questions from her notebook, before removing a micro recorder from her computer bag. "I came prepared."

"So I see," Garrett said with a pleasant chuckle.

When she was all set up, Jessica spoke into the recorder microphone first. "I'm talking with Garrett Brody, the very successful author who has written seven New York Times best-sellers, as well as screenplays for three hit movies. Garrett is now working full-time at the University of New Mexico as a guest lecturer. Mr. Brody is an indefatigable researcher with a sharp eye, an inventive mind and a wide range of interests. His novels range from the Civil War, as you've never seen it, to current politics and all its strange bedfellows, from romance to thrills, from blackest evil to wriest comedy, and all with the balance and compassion that mark the true artist. In addition to the story line, Mr. Brody never fails to show his reader something new, be it in his characters, his attention to detail or his background, and to do it in a thoroughly enjoyable fashion. While his offerings may not be the typical fare found on the shelves of your local bookstore, they are every bit as satisfying, far more so to those who prefer their literature with a bit of a twist. While he is already considered a star, Mr. Brody continues to gain a discerning readership likely to make him, before all is said and done, a household name around the world.

"So that our readers may get in on the ground floor, so to speak, I have posed him a few questions, so you may get to know him, and perhaps be moved to give Garrett Brody a try, because you won't be disappointed."

Garrett was already impressed, as Jessica's introduction was polished, professional, and quite flattering.

Jessica posed her first question. "Mr. Brody, when did you first know you wanted to be a writer?"

"It was during Freshman College English," Garrett replied. "My professor suggested I had real talent as a writer and that I should pursue it seriously. She was instrumental in planting the seed, which I didn't seriously pursue until many years later, when I wrote my first novel."

Jessica said, "Not unlike Harlan Ellison, then, albeit in a much more positive sort of way. Do you, like he, send that professor copies of all your completed works?"

Brody replied, "Yes, because I owe her a great deal and sending her copies of my books is a great way to say thank you."

Jessica asked, "Did everybody you know think you were nuts? Did they support you anyway? Or did they figure you were always cut out to be a writer?"

Brody answered, "I come from a family of writers. My father majored in journalism, my mother feels very comfortable with pen and paper, while my sister is a published mystery author in her own right, so the support at home was always very natural. I think more people in my sphere of influence thought I would become a public speaker, minister or lawyer one day. However, over the years, there have been some people who have played critical roles in my development as an author, because they were convinced I had talent as a storyteller and some skills as a writer."

"Are you an outline-variety of author, or do you fly by the seat of your pants?"

"A combination of both, really," he replied. "I usually do start with an outline, but since I almost always see the ending of my books first, the outline seldom follows a true course. Sometimes the best writing comes when I'm letting the characters and storyline flow, as it will, tossing the outline out the window."

"How much research typically goes into one of your novels?"

"Before the Internet, research used to take considerably longer, because I spent lots of time at the library, writing letters and searching bookstores. Because of online auction sites alone, I am able to track down lots of material quickly, with minimal cost. Then add the ton of information available online and research time is cut in half. However, having said all that, it still usually takes at least six months to a year to collect all the material I think is necessary. I immerse myself in the details, but use perhaps less than fifty percent of the hard facts, because I don't want to weigh down the story with too much history."

"Are your characters spur of the moment, do you put a great deal of work into structuring them, or do you just begin with a name and let them grow to suit themselves?"

"Again, it's a combination of events. Names often change, so sometimes characters will have working numerical identifiers, to keep them apart. I usually write a thumbnail physical description of the main characters, but those details often change too. Support characters and sidekicks alter the most, because they usually define their own traits. Many of my readers have commented that they want more of the secondary characters, because I seem to do quite well with them."

Jessica nodded her agreement and off-the-cuff she asked, "Have you ever considered building a complete book around some particularly good secondary or sidekick character, just to see what they'd do if they had their own venue?"

"Well, not until this very minute actually," Garrett replied with a wink. "I have been approached to write sequels on several of my novels, but have declined. However, I might be tempted to write a novel on a sidekick. Hmmm, I shall ponder this for awhile."

Jessica couldn't help but laugh, so she paused the recorder temporarily. Garrett was so scintillating and entertaining, that she hoped there was a way to make this interview go on for hours.

What she didn't realize at the time, of course, was that Brody was thinking exactly the same thing. He waited patiently for Jessica to regain her poise.

The recorder clicked on again.

Jessica asked, "You've covered lots of historical periods, lots of different cultures, and taken a few really unusual looks at the world of the stories you have told. Have you ever considered taking a shot at alternative history?"

"Not really," Brody replied. "I am very open to most genres, so there isn't any reason I can't in the future. I am a history nut and there are a myriad of events, people and civilizations that fascinate me. Whether I actually write a true alternate history novel will have to be seen. Right now I like to dabble with history, giving a possible version to accepted historical conclusions."

Jessica continued, "Writing is mostly sweat, as most authors will attest, but my question is, do you work as hard to come up with the original notion, the core of a story, as you do creating it, or does an idea just leap into your head? What sorts of things prompt ideas for your stories?"

Brody liked the question and reflected on his answer for a few seconds. "Actually my book ideas come quite easily. I have several novels either in stages of rewrites or research, with more in outline or synopsis form. It is, without question, the writing of the novel that requires the sweat. I can dream a plot, read an article which generates an idea, or sometimes a friend will send me an article or book that sprouts into a story. I'm not sure how I would go about explaining how my mind works, believe me."

"What sorts of promotion do you typically use to forward the sales of your books, and which do you think have most fostered your increasing success?"

"Word-of-mouth is the best method to increase sales," he replied. "I have a very loyal readership and they tell their friends and associates, which leads to more sales. My publisher sends advance copies to a core group of national reviewers and anyone that I acknowledge in the book as well. Maintaining a premium location on bookshelves is an uphill battle all the way, which is why I do lots of book-signing appearances around the country."

"What a rush that would be for me," Jessica reacted honestly.

Garrett smiled and said, "I really enjoy meeting readers face-to-face. Some of them are serious fans and almost know more about my books than I do. I am thrilled to sign copies and have the opportunity to chat with people who like to read. It doesn't do my ego any harm either. Besides, the person who spends good money on one of my novels deserves acknowledgement for adding to my success, both financially and artistically."

"On the subject of success, do you think it will spoil you?" Jessica asked pointedly. "And, to continue that thought, what do you consider is your purest motivation, creation or fiscal advance? Well, obviously the two are not necessarily dichotomous, but do you feel that monetary goals may endanger the joy of writing for you? Though it is sad to say, some authors seem to fall from sweet inspiration to hacking, once money becomes a factor. Or do you disagree?"

Garrett was very impressed with Jessica's thought process. She was a skilled interviewer, but also had a talent for keeping the discussion both light and informative.

"First, I write for the love of writing," he answered. "Of course, there is tremendous financial reward. However, my satisfaction comes from finishing another book and reading or hearing how readers loved it. But let's be honest, I love the best-seller status too. I like seeing my books produced as movies. I don't know if success has spoiled me. Perhaps, but somehow I doubt it. Financial comfort has set me free to do more research, travel and writing. Since I have so many books waiting to be written, I think success has enhanced my process."

"Not to mention the whole prospect of becoming a household name," Jessica responded. "But which factor of fame and fortune do you find most alluring, or need we ask?"

"Actually, I'm not interested in fame at all," Garrett replied. "I don't think the loss of privacy is worth the recognition. Many authors who are successful don't worry as much about being spotted by hordes of adoring fans, as movie stars do. However, the fortune issue is very different. Eventually I would like to purchase a publishing house and employ all my friends, while operating a few select bookstores around the country. All of my aspirations require substantial funding. A few more best-sellers will make those dreams a reality."

"Theodore Sturgeon once said that writing is two percent inspiration and ninety-eight percent perspiration, which seems to be true, except in the rare occasion of obsessive inspiration," Jessica observed. "But, laying aside the importance of research in the good development of a storyline, do you find it enjoyable in and of itself, or more in the line of labor?"

"Writing is my true passion, so I really enjoy it," Brody replied. "Sure, it's hard work, but I love the headache I get from working out a plot problem. I am thrilled when one of my characters refuses to cooperate and I can't wait to get into the groove, when the words are flying across the page. I am never satisfied as a writer, but I do get to a point where the selected his favorite suede sport coat to compliment the look. A splash of cologne and he was off.

At 6:59 PM, exactly, Garrett buzzed Jessica's apartment. He had actually arrived fifteen minutes early, but didn't want to seem too eager, so he paced back-and-forth by his parked car. Then, gauging how long it would take him to walk from the parking lot to the secure entrance, he almost ran to get to the intercom at the right moment.

"Hello?" came Jessica's voice over the speaker.

"Hi, it's Garrett," he replied.

"I'll buzz you in," she said.

As soon as the irritating vibration began, Brody swung open the door and stepped inside. To his elated surprise, she was waiting for him in the hallway.

"Hi," she said.

Brody was very aware that she looked absolutely fabulous, so young and beautiful and obviously happy to see him. As he came closer, he admired her body too, which was highlighted by tight, tailored, faded-denim jeans, which not only complimented her heart-shaped bottom, but also exposed a peek of her sculptured tummy. To top it off, short shimmering silver chains hung provocatively from her pierced bellybutton. Her lime-green sleeveless top was quite snug, so that her nipples poked aggressively through the material.

"You look very handsome," Jessica said when he stood right before her.

"Thank you," Garrett replied, his eyes drinking in another thirsty scan, from her open-toed heels to her little silver-hooped earrings. "You look incredible."

"Do you really think so?" she asked.

His nod was quite emphatic.

They kissed.

It was warm and affectionate and entirely memorable, as they enjoyed this expression of mutual regard.

When they parted, Garrett asked, "Are you ready?"

Jessica reached into her apartment for her purse, pulled the door closed behind her, and said, "I am now."

She took his offered arm and they walked together to his car, where he held open the passenger door for her. Once she was comfortably situated, he practically skipped around to the driver's side. As Garrett drove, they chattered on about all sorts of topics, none of which were earth shattering, but all vitally important to the two of them.

The *High Noon Restaurant & Saloon* had a long-standing tradition of excellent food and great margaritas in historic Old Town Albuquerque. The couple was seated in a booth, but they instinctively sat next to each other.

Garrett quickly kissed her again, before ordering a pitcher of Sour Apple Margaritas. As soon as the waitress departed, the couple snuggled up against each other.

"I really missed you," he said.

"You did?" she seemed surprised.

"Very much."

"I missed you too."

The margaritas arrived and Garrett poured two glasses.

He lifted his and said, "Here's to a wonderful relationship."

Jessica tinked his glass and said, "I think there's no doubt of that!"

They both laughed and kissed again.

As easily as before, they settled into a comfortable conversation, moving from one subject to another, sharing ideas and viewpoints, but agreeing to disagree on some things. Jessica noticed almost immediately how comfortable she felt and how easily he made her laugh.

The waitress returned shortly after Garrett had reminded Jessica that they needed to look at the menu. A few minutes of silence were necessary to decide on final selections.

Jessica ordered boneless Idaho trout, pan-seared and finished with an orange brandy glaze and nestled on a bed of wild rice, accompanied with fresh steamed broccoli.

Garrett ordered a ribeye steak, grilled medium-rare and stuffed with jalapeno and garlic slices, with a *pasilla tequila coulis*.

"Now does this count as a date?" Garrett asked after the waitress departed.

Jessica nodded and entwined her fingers with his. "Yes, Mr. Brody, I consider this our first date."

"Then would it be too bold and rash to ask you out again tomorrow?" Garrett quickly followed up. "There's a lot going on this weekend and I'd like to spend it with you."

She smiled warmly and replied, "I'd love to."

They kissed again.

The church was first built in 1706. That structure disintegrated, and the present church was rebuilt in 1793 and had been in continuous use ever since. Confederate soldiers were buried in the center of the plaza, and several Civil War cannons guarded the east side of the Plaza. In front of *La Placita Restaurant*, sidewalk vendors spread blankets on the ground and sold silver jewelry.

Just south of the plaza was the *Rattlesnake Museum*, which boasted the largest display of rattlesnakes in the world, even more than the San Diego and Bronx Zoos combined. The couple lunched at *La Hacienda Restaurant*, eating *Carnita Asada* and grilled pork tenderloin. Like Garrett's typical breakfast eggs, the food was smothered in green chilies and served with fried potatoes. It was delicious. Since they were in no hurry, Jessica and Garrett lingered on the outdoor patio at the restaurant, sipping delicious margaritas and watching dark storm clouds drift towards the city from the mountains.

Shortly after leaving the restaurant, the couple was caught by a cloudburst and ducked into the *Albuquerque Museum*, situated a couple blocks east of Old Town. In addition to having a fine display of art and relics, the museum was hosting a rehearsal for Cinco de Mayo. They snuck into the auditorium and listened to *"Una Poloma Blanca,"* performed with strong voices and a dozen classical Spanish guitars. Before the next song was over, the rainstorm ended, and the pair headed back outdoors beneath sunny New Mexico skies.

Holding hands as they walked back to Garrett's car, Jessica was so happy she was practically skipping. Brody was not only fascinating and enthusiastic, he paid absolute attention to her alone. It was wonderful being with him, for everything seemed like an adventure, even something as mundane as grocery shopping. For Brody had asked permission to pick up a few necessities.

"I'm sorry this is so boring," Garrett explained while pushing the cart up and down the aisles. "But if I don't get some cat food, I'll never get in the door."

Jessica hugged him and said, "I'm just fine, Garrett. Get whatever you need, because I'm having a wonderful time with you."

They stopped to kiss, until Jessica figured out they were blocking the aisle. Pulling him aside, she apologized to the several people who had been waiting to get to one particular section of canned pet food.

"We're sorry," she apologized. "He's just a very wonderful kisser."

On their way across the grocery store parking lot, Brody pulled up and gently snagged Jessica by the elbow.

"I've really wanted to give you some feedback on your book manuscript," Garrett said unexpectedly.

"You have?" Jessica asked with surprise. "Was it that bad?"

Brody almost collided with one of the parked cars. "Not at all. In fact, I stayed up all night to finish it. You're a very powerful writer, Jessica. I was hooked and couldn't put it down."

She quietly, but intently, looked at him for a few minutes. "Well, I never expected that."

"Why not?" he wondered. "It's just my opinion, of course, but I'd like you to finish a draft of your manuscript before the semester is over. Your book is compelling and well-written, on several levels, which it why it should be published."

"You've got to be kidding," Jessica said, now very uncomfortable with what he was suggesting. "I never entertained that it was good enough for that."

Brody pulled her closer to him. "Perhaps someone will take an apposing view, but your novel is a reflection of true talent. It's not perfect, but that's okay. It needs editing and refinement, but we can work on that in class."

Jessica was stunned, to say the least. She never imagined Garrett Brody would give such a positive review of her writing, at least not at this stage. The manuscript needed so much work and there were passages not even written yet. The main character seemed too much like her and the supporting cast wasn't fleshed out enough. There were issues with tense, setting and mood, not to mention a few glaring continuity problems.

Yet even with all those criticisms racing around in her mind, Jessica realized that she was also thrilled beyond belief. Could it be true? A very successful published author was telling her that her first novel was also worthy of publication!

She jumped into his arms, almost bowling him over and planted an exuberant kiss on his mouth. Then she twirled around and cheered with sheer delight.

Of course, Garrett thoroughly enjoyed her excitement and applauded each new expression of her joy. Not only was Jessica entirely beautiful, her energy was a much needed shot of life for Brody. It had been several years since tragedy had stolen his true love and robbed him of such vitality. At that very moment he realized how much he had missed being happy.

After Garrett dropped her off and they had performed their ritual of extended kissing, Jessica entered her apartment building floating on a cushion of bliss. She was falling in love, her first novel might get published, and her moonlighting job was becoming more than just a flight of fantasy. She slipped the key in the lock and sighed.

"Where have you been?" came another woman's voice from across the hall.

"Hi, Mandy," Jessica said, turning around to lean against the door.

"Oh, my God, look at her," her friend named Amanda said to their other mutual friend, a tall and very attractive brunette named Stephanie.

Jessica sighed again and waved. "Hey, Steph."

"She's got it bad," Amanda said.

"Real bad," Stephanie agreed.

"He's a dream," Jessica whispered.

Her two friends ushered Jessica into their apartment instead, where they wanted to hear all about this new guy and what he was like and what was going on. This was no time for sleep. The girls all sat in a circle on the carpeted floor and Jessica held center stage as she told them all about Garrett Brody.

Even though it was well after midnight on the East coast, the best-selling author knew his literary agent would still be awake. James Tagget had the likewise bad habit of not sleeping. Garrett selected the memorized dialer on his cell phone keypad.

The line only rang once, before a voice answered, "What the hell do you want at this time in the morning?"

"Why hello, James," Brody said, trying to keep a straight face. "How are you?"

"Don't give me that crap," his agent snapped. "Every time you call, it means you're up to something."

"So suspicious, you are."

"With good reason."

"Is this any way to treat the author who made you rich?"

"Yes, because otherwise I might end up in jail."

"I'd post your bail."

"How sweet."

Garrett chuckled. "Well, I do need you to do me a favor."

"Oh, God, see," Tagget spouted. "I told you. I knew it."

"It's really not that complicated, James," Brody tried to sound reassuring.

"Uh, huh, that's what you said last time."

"*Afterburner's* a best-seller, isn't it?"

"Thank God, otherwise you'd owe my big time."

"I still owe you, my friend."

"That's right. So what's it going to be?"

"I need you to contact the proper authorities and request permission for me to visit the Los Alamos National Laboratory, here in New Mexico," Garrett stated quickly.

"You've got to be kidding?" Tagget asked incredulously.

"No, actually, I'm not."

"So, you're just going to waltz onto one of the most top-secret installations in the world and take a look-see?" his agent joked.

"I only want to tour the Lab's buildings from the outside," Garrett said. "I'm not asking for security clearances or anything like that. I just need approval to see the facility and get some color for my new book."

His agent replied, "Okay, Garrett, I'll see what I can do. I can't promise anything, you know, since you're probably not that popular with the government crowd."

"I know," Brody said. "Assure them I'll be on my best behavior and not go off snooping or anything like that."

Tagget laughed in his ear. "Oh, I'm sure that will make them feel better. I'll remind them that even with your propensity for trashing just about every government agency in existence, that you're really not much of a security risk, being a radical bleeding-heart liberal and all."

"Thanks, old buddy," Garrett said. "I knew I could count on you. Let me know as soon as you get the okay."

"Goodbye."

"Good night."

Click.

Brody went back to concentrating on reading and reviewing more manuscripts.

As a university lecturer, Garrett was aware that a sizable number of students lapsed into instant narcosis the moment their professors took the podium. There were usually two reasons for this, combining poor lecturing and poor listening.

Brody believed that poor lecturing resulted from unskilled delivery or from material that failed to engage the students, such as rehashing what was already in the textbooks.

clubs and organizations, and classes were offered in many general-interest and academic subjects.

Life in Los Alamos, as in most of the American West, was quite informal. The citizens had a reputation for being friendly. Most people entertained on a casual level and men rarely wore ties, even to work.

Admission to the Lab's secure areas was expressly prohibited. Visitors were allowed to access only the non-secure locations that had been specifically approved on the individual 982 form filed by their Laboratory host. All visitors were required to wear a visitor badge, and uncleared visitors were escorted while in security areas. Citizens of foreign countries received special approval before visiting the Laboratory and also wore a badge while on Laboratory property.

Brody presented his valid passport and driver's license at the admittance gate. He was directed to the visitor's parking area, where he was met by another security agent, who escorted Garrett to the Visitor's Center, where he would be processed. After a security analysis was completed, his temporary visitor badge was issued.

"This security badge is an indication of authorized presence in approved areas only," the armed guard informed him. "Security badges are the property of the US Government and must be returned before you depart the Laboratory. You must wear your badge above the waist, front side of body, photo side out, at all times while on Laboratory property. Please remove your badge only after leaving Laboratory property, and keep your badge safe from damage or theft. Do you understand these instructions as I have explained them?"

Garrett nodded. "Yes, thank you."

"Your guide will be with you momentarily," the guard went on. "Please make yourself comfortable until then."

"Thank you," Brody said as he picked an empty chair and sat down. He was a bit nervous, because he really didn't know what he was expecting to find from this visit. Of course, as far as his publisher, agent, and the Federal Government were concerned, he was merely conducting research for a new book. In fact, Garrett was actually quite surprised his request had been authorized in the first place, since his typical plots revolved around spies, secrets, and conspiracies.

"Mr. Garrett Brody?" a pleasant female voice inquired from the open doorway to his left.

Garrett quickly stood up and was surprised to discover a very attractive woman standing before him. "Yes I am."

They shook hands.

The woman was professionally dressed, but a white lab coat also gave her the appearance of authority. She was, without a doubt, a redhead. Add to that her captivating green eyes, and she would be considered quite striking.

The woman smiled warmly. "I'm Carla Denato, Director of Public Relations. It's a pleasure to meet you."

For various reasons, some of them obvious, Brody immediately noted the significance of her first name. He returned the pleasant smile with one of his own. "Well, thank you, Ms. Denato. I feel very fortunate to be allowed a tour, especially since I'm a novelist and have been known for spinning more than my fair share of lurid tall tales."

Ms. Denato's laugh was genuine. She pointed towards a secure door. "If you'll follow me, we'll get started."

At the keypad, Carla punched in a series of numbers and letters with blinding speed, far too quickly for Brody to keep track of the sequence. The electronic bolt opened and she held the door open for him. "After you, please."

Garrett stepped through and waited for her to join him. They walked side-by-side down a long corridor, with many solid doors to either side.

"Is there any specific area or project at the Lab that you're interested in seeing, Mr. Brody?" Carla asked. "I can't show you certain top-secret operations, but if you..."

"Just a general tour would be fine, Ms. Denato," Brody interrupted. "I merely want to get a feel for the place, for color and atmosphere. The Lab is background for my latest novel, not a central theme."

She almost looked disappointed. "I see. Well, much of the Lab is organized like any college campus, sprawling and somewhat disjointed. Each of the secure buildings house specific departments and teams focus on funded research projects, maintaining their own level of whatever security is deemed necessary by the contracting organization."

"I'm in your hands, Ms. Denato," Brody said. "I will happily go anywhere you wish to take me."

The woman looked at him with slightly wider eyes, perhaps because of the inflection in his voice. While Garrett hadn't meant anything provocative or suggestive, it certainly sounded like an intimate invitation. The woman cocked her head a little and said, "Well, it's been a long time since anyone turned themselves over to me so easily."

He blushed.

Carla giggled and tried to save him from further embarrassment. "Let's be on our way, Mr. Brody, before either of us says something inappropriate."

Suddenly Garret asked, "Did you know Dr. Flavius Newman?"

Carla's smile vanished completely and she didn't answer.

Brody waited patiently.

Still, Carla Denato said nothing.

Garrett sighed and took a step back before he said, "I'm sorry, Ms. Denato. I didn't mean to pry into things that are really none of my business. It was just that I was the one who found Dr. Newman, before he died. I was wondering if you knew him, because I would like to find someone who did. His death had a profound affect on me."

His honesty completely disarmed her. Carla started walking again and Garrett naturally hurried to catch up to her. For a few uncomfortable minutes they walked side-by-side in silence.

Then Carla abruptly stopped. "I'm sorry if I seem rude, Mr. Brody. I just haven't been able to come to terms with Dr. Newman's death."

"I understand," Garrett said. "I've been having my own challenges too."

She nodded understandingly. "I imagine you have."

"Did the police tell you what he said to me before he died?" Brody asked.

"Yes," was all she said.

"Are you the key?"

She shrugged. "I don't know. I don't know how I could be, because we didn't work together directly and while we socialized, it was the typical after-work thing with tons of people. You know, a few beers and pizza, bitch about work, then head our separate ways?"

Brody smiled.

However, there was something about the way Carla Denato had answered his question that indicated she was not telling him everything. It was in her eyes, as she looked up and to the right, as if she was making it up as she went along.

"Well, let's not dwell on such unpleasant subjects," he said. "I'm here for a tour, after all."

Ms. Denato recovered her public relations smile and began telling him the history of the Lab and what was housed in each of the buildings on campus. It was a sprawling facility, which would take several hours to cover, even superficially. She specifically pointed out the World War II structures and their importance for the Trinity Project's development of the first atomic bomb.

Garrett listened to her presentation about the national labs' research in reservoir fracture mapping, microborehole drilling, reservoir management and fluid identification. He also gained insights about companies throughout the world working within the Technology Partnership program.

One of the most exciting exhibits Ms. Denato showed Garrett was a huge walk-in safe, to which she had the combination. This was important because he saw materials in size and form entirely new to him.

The safe contained spheres of precious metals in extremely pure form available for neutron cross-section work. Brody held in his gloved hand a sphere of solid gold and a similar one of platinum, a small one of iridium, one of silver and one of U238.

Most impressive by far, he held a hemisphere of Plutonium, worth at least 1 billion dollars. The plutonium was silver plated for handling, since it was a strong poison as well as being appreciably radioactive. In fact, while the other spheres had the usual cold feel of room temperature metals, the plutonium was evolving enough energy from continued radioactive decay, to feel quite warm to the touch, a considerable contrast to the other spheres.

This was a breathtaking experience for Brody and one he would never forget.

"That was incredible," Garrett said as they exited the metals research building. "I never expected to be allowed to do that!"

Carla Denato smiled. "I thought you'd enjoy that, Mr. Brody. It's a highlight of our VIP tour."

"I did indeed. Thank you very much."

"Let's head over to the Bradbury Science Museum," Carla suggested.

The Bradbury Science Museum displayed exhibits about the history of Los Alamos National Laboratory and its research. Many of the displays were interactive and featured videos, computers, and science demonstrations. Garrett thoroughly enjoyed himself there too and took copious notes.

Garrett found it all very interesting and tried to keep his questions general in nature, focusing on gathering information that wouldn't be considered classified or sensitive in any way.

As they were leaving the museum to return to the visitor's center, a Lab senior technician approached them. His white coat, disorderly hair and wire-rimmed glasses all added to the stereotypical picture of a mad scientist. However, he was reasonably young, perhaps in his mid-30's,

CHAPTER 7

GETTING TO KNOW YOU

IT WAS ANOTHER DAY and Garrett knew that effective lecturing was not simply a matter of standing in front of his class and reciting what he knew. As speaker, he exercised a special form of communication, in which voice, gesture, movement, facial expression, and eye contact either complemented or detracted from the content. Brody was well aware that his delivery and manner of speaking immeasurably influenced his students' attentiveness and learning.

In fact, by now the participation was enthusiastic and regular, though there were a few students who were basically quiet by nature. Rather than make them uncomfortable by trying to solicit verbal feedback, Brody broke the class up into impromptu groups of four in hopes the smaller discussions would elicit involvement. Garret just walked around and eavesdropped on their conversations, only offering input when somebody asked for it.

Then, after about thirty minutes, he asked for their solutions to the plot problems he had given them. Much to his delight, the students offered a number of viable alternatives, thereby giving Brody food-for-thought on his own writing projects.

"It isn't a committee deciding for you, but different viewpoints and life experiences offering a unique perspective," he summarized the exercise. "Now I don't advise this for everything you write, or you might get bogged down with nitpicking. Find somebody you trust, someone who won't threaten you with their criticism."

A hand shot up.

"Yes?" Garrett said to Mary, a gifted poet who had several of her poems published in national publications. In fact, Brody was very impressed with her poetic skills overall.

"What if you don't have somebody you trust, like the person you described?" she asked. "Since poetry is such a personal thing to me, I don't usually share it with anyone, until I'm satisfied it's finished. I'm not receptive at that point for input, since it might change the entire meaning of the poem."

"The main benefit an artist gets from criticism is increased ability to view her own work from the viewpoint of the poem's audience," Garrett replied. "There is often confusion about critiquing poetry. I know talented poets who consider critiquing a bad, useless, and dangerous thing, because poets critiqued too soon may stop writing altogether. Or they may revise a single work endlessly, trying to achieve an absolute, thereby finishing nothing. One revises to improve. When your poem gets the message across, then it's good enough. It can always be improved, but there's no end to it. If you revise endlessly, waiting for perfection, then you haven't learned how to decide that something is done. Relying on someone to read your work can give you that thermometer to gauge whether your poem is completed."

Another question.

"Okay, Bob, shoot."

"I struggle when I'm working with female characters, because I'm a guy and I don't know what they're thinking or how they're feeling."

Garrett grinned and chuckled. "Well, taking into consideration that I might get in trouble with all the women in this room, join the club."

Everyone laughed good-naturedly, especially the female students.

"I've found the best way to overcome this handicap is to ask women open-ended questions," Brody continued. "This class is the perfect opportunity to expand your experience. Give one of your fellow female classmates a description of the event you're writing about and ask them how they would feel, what they might think, and especially how they would handle the situation. Take notes and use those specifics. The responses won't ring true for every woman, of course, but it can give you some understanding of your characters."

Unfortunately, time had run out again. Glancing at his watch, Garrett said, "Well, that's it for today. Great questions. Don't forget to have your revisions to me over the next several days and remember the writing assignment on mood. I want ten opening sentences that set the mood of a story. Thanks everybody."

The students all applauded. They had thoroughly enjoyed the session as well.

After class, Garrett and Jessica strolled leisurely back to the faculty parking lot. They held hands and talked about all sorts of topics, but the conversation inevitably cycled back to writing.

"I wish my inspiration came from more convenient sources," Jessica said. "It's difficult to find the time to drive up into those hills for the solitude I seek."

Garrett was sensitive to her dilemma. "I understand your quandary. I guess that's why I listen to movie soundtracks while writing. It helps create certain moods."

"I could try that," she said. "I'm sure there's something on CD that might duplicate the same atmosphere."

"Well, I wouldn't go so far as to say that," Garrett said. "It's pretty much impossible to copy New Mexico's environment with music alone. It's one of the reasons I moved here. There's nothing quite like a sunset in the Land of Enchantment."

Jessica snuggled against his arm, which made Brody chuckle with delight. Before he realized it, they were pulling up outside his condominium.

"Would you like to come in for a minute?" Garrett asked. "I have to feed my cat, before he trashes the place."

"Of course," Jessica replied happily. "Besides, I'd like to see your place."

Brody was elated and as he unlocked the door, he hoped she might spend the night. However, there was no way he was going to rush things. While this relationship seemed to be developing very fast, he was deathly afraid of sabotaging it.

Once inside, they were greeted by a very loud and demanding meow.

"I'm sorry, big guy," Garrett spoke to the cat.

The tomcat rubbed and bumped up against Jessica, purring incessantly. She scratched and pet the cat, suddenly surrounded by swirling hair.

"I'm sorry about his shedding," Garrett said as he closed the door behind her.

"Don't be," she said. "I love cats."

"Well, he's obviously figured that out."

"What's his name?"

"General Sherman."

"After the Civil War general?"

"Yup. That cat knows how to lay waste to anything and everything."

Garrett went directly into the kitchen, where he grabbed a can of cat food from inside the pantry. Then he rummaged about looking for the can opener.

"I know it's here somewhere," he mumbled to himself. "I just used it yesterday."

Jessica looked around. "You have a very nice place, Garrett. It's very comfortable, cozy, and inviting."

"Thank you," he called from the kitchen. "Make yourself at home."

General Sherman suddenly jumped off the sofa and scrambled into the kitchen as soon as he heard a can opening. The cat's nails click-clicked noisily on the tiled floor, which made Jessica chuckle. Then she just naturally wandered around. Stopping at the first bookcase of many, she perused the selection of titles. On the top shelf, all in a neat row, were first edition hardback copies of Brody's twelve published novels. On the other shelves, title after title of history books and reference guides were arranged alphabetically by author.

"Would you care for something to drink?" Garrett asked as he joined her.

"No thank you, I'm just fine," she replied, taking his hand.

"Find anything interesting?" he asked.

"You can tell a lot about a person by what they read, of course," Jessica stated. "In this case, however, since you're an author, it's more important to look at what reference materials you keep close at hand."

"Is that so?" he wondered. "What have you uncovered in your analysis?"

She giggled. "There is a very diverse selection here. It would take me years to read through all this fascinating stuff."

Garrett suddenly pulled out a small gift-wrapped box from behind his back.

Jessica took it, but asked, "What's this?"

"A little something for you," he replied.

"For me?" she replied, obviously intrigued and excited.

Jessica carefully unwrapped the present, slowly lifting up the lid of a black velvet jewelry box. "Oh, Garrett."

He held the box as she lifted out an 18K gold necklace, with a multi-gem Kokopelli-shaped pendant attached. Draping it over her hand, she marveled at the workmanship.

Then Jessica simply felt foolish.

Garrett served up breakfast, which consisted of crispy bacon and blueberry sourdough pancakes with melted butter and maple syrup. The freshly brewed coffee topped off a splendid start to the day.

"You can cook too," Jessica remarked after smacking her lips. "You are indeed a very nice catch, Mr. Brody."

He leaned across the table to share a very nice kiss. "I think I'm the one that's coming out way ahead." Then he stared into his coffee cup.

Jessica sensed there was something profound on his mind. "What's bothering you?"

"Oh, it's just an ongoing self-criticism I battle every semester," he replied. "I wonder if I'm any good at teaching?"

Jessica was very surprised by his self-doubt. "Of course you are."

"Some students seem naturally enthusiastic about learning, but many need or expect their instructors to inspire, challenge, and stimulate them," Garrett said.

"Which you do naturally, Garrett," Jessica said.

"Now you're being biased," he said.

"I am not," she countered. "I've had plenty of traditional lecture courses, believe me. In your class we're learning by doing, writing, designing, creating, and solving. You don't allow passivity to dampen our motivation and curiosity. You pose thought-provoking questions. You never tell us something, when you can ask a question that leads to understanding. In fact, when I'm meeting with my team, we all agree that you've encouraged us to experiment and reach out. That's why you're an incredible teacher."

"Well, thank you, Jessica," he said. "I need positive reinforcement, like anyone else, but you have really made me feel pretty competent after all."

As agreed earlier, Jessica went into Garrett's library to write, while Brody remained in the dining room, where he worked on his laptop. It was understood that neither would succumb to their lustful desires for each other, until they had dedicated at least five hours to serious writing.

Garrett actually used most of the time to read his students' work. Some of the writing reflected talent, while other pieces were too wordy or just plain boring. To be fair, however, Garrett realized that he had only started working with these authors and with positive criticism the writing would improve. He also had to guard against projecting his genre and style on other authors, because the effects could be detrimental, to say the least.

Brody was after improvement and growth, not manipulating the students to fall into some controlled mold.

Jessica came out from the library, stretched, and gave Garrett a kiss on the cheek. "I've got to go home," she said. "Otherwise I'll never get anything done, like laundry, dishes, and stuff like that."

"I could hire a housekeeper for you," Brody suggested with a smile.

"So you can keep me hypnotized as your love slave?" she quipped.

He nodded.

"Not likely," Jessica said.

He followed her to the door, grabbing his car keys.

She gently placed her hands on his chest. "You don't have to drive me home all the time. I'll be just fine."

"Not likely," he mimicked her.

When they reached Jessica's apartment, rather than just sit around watching TV or some other lazy pastime, Garrett chipped in and helped with the chores. It did no good for her to protest, because Brody ignored her. He cleaned the toilet bowl, sink and shower, before vacuuming. While she did several loads of laundry, Garrett switched out the towels, changed the sheets on the bed and dusted too. So, what might have taken Jessica all day, actually took only a few hours to complete.

"There, now your place is as clean as a whistle," he said, admiring his handiwork.

Jessica gave him a big hug and a kiss. "You are an angel, Mr. Brody."

He smiled and pointed her to the door. "Let's go see a movie."

They sat in the very back row of the dollar movie theater, off in one far corner. This wasn't just so they could make out during the film, but also so they could be by themselves, to whisper comments without bothering anyone else. Jessica picked the movie, which she had seen several time before, but wanted to see with Garrett, because the film was an adaptation of his book *Covert*. They whispered back-and-forth about the changes made in the storyline and how the screenplay was different from the novel. The theater was almost entirely empty, so their chatting didn't interrupt anyone's enjoyment of the movie.

"Was it difficult for you to change your book for a movie?" she whispered.

"The first time was very difficult," he replied quietly. "Now it depends. For the most part I understand what is necessary to make a story work on the big screen. I focus on the action scenes first and blend in the sexual tension and adventure themes. The most challenging part for me was cutting for time. It was hard to know what to delete."

Jessica shook her head. "I wouldn't be able to cut out anything. I have a hard enough time as it is with editing."

They both quietly laughed.

"I'd be quite willing to assist you when the time comes," he offered.

"I'll take you up on your offer," she said.

When the movie was over, the couple went to grab a late-night cup of coffee. They sat outside under the stars and sipped at mugs of the daily special brew, while enjoying each other's company. Strawberry cheesecake was the unanimous choice for dessert and sounds of immense satisfaction escaped from both of them.

It was Jessica who looked at her watch and sighed.

"Time to go?" Garrett asked.

"Yes," she said. "Time always just zips along when I'm with you!"

He held her close to him as they walked to the car.

"Do you want to spend the night?" Garrett asked as he climbed in behind the wheel.

Jessica seemed very disappointed as she sat beside him in the passenger's seat. "I want to, but I just can't. I've got so much to do and you're really distracting, in a good way, of course. Will you forgive me?"

He hadn't started the engine yet. Leaning over, Garrett kissed her. "Of course, silly. I just like being with you."

"Believe me, I want to be with you too," Jessica said. "That's the problem. You're like a drug. The more I'm with you, the more I need to be with you."

"You don't have to explain," he said. "I don't want anything to endanger this relationship. I'll drive you home and we'll see each other tomorrow. Okay?"

"Thank you," she said. "I can't wait until tomorrow!"

They kissed goodnight outside her apartment door and once Garrett heard the deadbolt slip into place, he returned to his car. The drive home was lonely, but it also gave him time to think. As he pulled into the garage, Brody had made up his mind about something important.

It was late again when Garrett called his literary agent.

His greeting this time was much friendlier. "Hello, Garrett, how did it go?"

"Just fine, James," Brody replied. "The tour was conducted by a very attractive female public relations manager and I got all the background color I needed."

"Great," Tagget said. "Is there something else you needed?"

"Well, yes, I have another favor to ask," Garrett replied hesitantly.

Brody's request was not, however, greeted with the typical negative response.

"Sure, what's on your mind?" Tagget asked nicely.

"I know you're not taking on any new clients, but I want you to read a manuscript from a local talent here at the University."

"Well, I can't exactly claim it's unsolicited, if the work is recommended by you, now can I?" Tagget asked.

"Consider it a personal favor," Garrett said.

"I can tell by the sound in your voice that it means a lot to you, Garret, so I'd be happy to read it."

"Thanks, I'll send it as an attachment via email," Brody said. "It's in draft form and needs editing and refinement, but I think it's really quite good."

"Well, then, I'm looking forward to reading it," Tagget said.

"It's not anything like what I write, James," Garrett continued.

"That should be refreshing."

"The main character is…"

"Stop overselling," Tagget interrupted him. "The less I know the better, so I don't have any preconceived biases, okay?"

Garrett acquiesced. "You're right. Thanks."

"No problem, Garrett," Tagget said.

"Goodnight."

"Before you hang up, check your calendar for an available day sometime in the next two weeks."

"Okay. What's up?"

"One of the big Hollywood studios is interested in producing your title *Brazen Chariots*," Tagget informed him.

"Do they want a pitch?"

"The usual. You'll have twenty minutes to sell them on it."

This time, it was Brody who sighed. "What morons. Do they honestly believe I can sum up a book like *Brazen Chariots* in twenty minutes?"

Tagget chuckled. "Yes, they do and yes, you can. I'll let you know when I have a firm date. Goodnight."

Click.

Garrett stared at his cell phone for a moment, before tossing it on the bed. He went to take a nice long hot shower, where he reveled in the feeling of steaming water beating down on his aching shoulders.

The night was like all others, as Brody managed to get about four hours sleep, before he sat upright in bed, jolted awake by the same nightmare. The images were so hauntingly real and horrific. Garrett had trouble breathing as he battled a sense of panic and despair. Finally, he calmed down and made his way to the shower, where he once again stood under the hot water for a long time.

As he toweled dry his hair, he couldn't stop longing for Jessica, so once he was dressed, he drove straight to her apartment. The sun was barely peeking over the foothills as Brody drove into the parking lot. He hesitated getting out, because he worried that calling on her so early in the morning was exceedingly rude.

In the end, however, he couldn't overcome his need for her.

At the outside entrance, Garrett buzzed her apartment.

There was no answer, so he turned to leave.

"Who is it?" Jessica's sleepy voice came over the intercom.

"It's Garrett," he replied.

"I'll buzz you in."

He pulled on the door and walked down the hallway. Jessica's apartment door opened and she stepped out, dressed only in an oversized T-shirt.

"This is a very pleasant surprise," she said.

"I know it's very early, but I just wanted to be with you," he replied.

"Would you like to come in?" Jessica asked.

Before he could respond, the apartment door across the hall opened and a blonde-haired, blue-eyed woman stepped out. "Hi, Jessica," she said, before stopping to check out Brody.

"Hey, Mandy," Jessica said warmly. "I'd like you to meet Garrett Brody. Garrett, this is my best friend, Amanda Deere."

Amanda just bubbled with enthusiasm. Jutting out her hand, she said, "Oh, my, it's so nice to meet you. Jessica has told me so much about you. She loaned me her copy of *Afterburner* and I just started reading it last night. I couldn't go to sleep without finishing it. You really are a great writer. I was so wrapped up in the story and the characters, especially Kathleen. She was so brave."

Brody thought Amanda was as cute as a button, amused that the cliché popped into his head. Not his type at all, but that didn't mean he wasn't still drawn to all her energy.

Garrett shook her hand and said, "It's nice to meet you Amanda, and thank you for the compliments. I think *Afterburner* is my best book and based on feedback like yours, I might be right. And you're so right, because Kathleen's character was fun to write."

Amanda just beamed as she looked over his shoulder at Jessica. "He's even better looking than you described!" Then she giggled as Brody blushed. "It's been so nice to finally get to meet you, Garrett. I've got to get going, because I've got tennis lessons and the instructor is cute, not a hunk like you, but he'll do. Bye."

Then Amanda was off down the hall, out the door, and gone like a puff of smoke.

Garrett turned around and said, "Wow, she's exhausting and I only talked to her for a few minutes."

Jessica pulled him inside her apartment, then jumped into his arms and gave him the most passionate kiss. After a number of minutes they stepped apart and she said, "You are just the sexiest man alive and even my best friend adores you."

He was still savoring her kiss.

"Come on in," she said while yanking his hand. "We can chat, while the coffee-maker brews a pot."

Even though Garrett had helped her with the chores, he hadn't really looked around her place. Jessica's apartment wasn't very big, but it was extremely neat, comfortable, and warm. The colors were all Southwestern and Native American, with an enormous oil painting of a herd of stampeding bison over the corner kiva fireplace.

"That's incredible," he commented while admiring the work.

Jessica stood next to him and said, "I picked it up at an art fair, years ago, just before graduating from high school. It's so powerful and the colors intensify the motion. I just love it."

"I can see why."

She moved along the hallway.

"Your place is fantastic, Jessica," Brody said. "Let's come here more often."

"I like your place better."

"How come?"

"Because your condo is spacious, intellectually stimulating, and your refrigerator is always full of goodies," she replied with a straight face.

"Aha, I knew it," he exclaimed good-naturedly. "You love me for my food."

She laughed and they kissed again.

"Do you want to see the rest of the rooms, or not?" Jessica asked.

"Yes, sweetie, lead the way," he replied.

He checked out the kitchen and then the guest bedroom, which was really Jessica's office. Garrett also enjoyed looking at the books on the shelves and listening to her explain what her routine consisted of and how her writing progressed.

"What's this?" Garrett asked as he picked up a magazine about professional wrestling. "I didn't know you were really into this stuff."

She nervously laughed and took it from him. "It's just research material, that's all. My central character is a female wrestler, remember?"

"That's right," he said. "I think you've done an excellent job relating a profession that's quite unique. I especially was impressed with how well you described her feelings and the injustices inherent in the world of professional wrestling. It goes to show what you can produce with extensive research."

She nodded. Then, with something akin to desperation, she pushed him towards the master bedroom. "Let's make love. I'm so hot for you I can't stand it."

Garrett insisted that Jessica perform a simple striptease, before undressing him as well. He was very playful and made their lovemaking into an extended series of role-playing vignettes, which only made her even more amorous than usual. They slept for the rest of the morning and well into the afternoon, making love every-so-often.

It was dusk when the two of them finally emerged from the bedroom. While Garrett took a shower, Jessica ordered pizza delivered, since neither of them felt like going out for dinner. It had certainly been a lazy day.

Over ice-cold beer, pepperoni and green olive thin-crust pizza, and classical jazz playing way down low, the two of them sat together on the couch, while snuggling and smooching the night away. They ended up back in bed, of course, where their lovemaking was very relaxed and gentle.

The next morning Jessica woke up to the sound of water running in the shower and she joined Garrett under the steaming spray. They washed each other and dried each other, but were unsuccessful in avoiding a heightened desire from all the contact. This led to lovemaking and more snoozing, before the aroma from an automatically brewed pot of coffee made them both wake up.

"What are we going to do today?" Jessica asked. "After all, it's Memorial Day weekend."

"Well, you're coming with me on a little road trip," Garrett announced.

"Yippee," she reacted. "Where are we going?"

"Southern New Mexico," he replied. "I have to do some research and you can be my assistant, if that sounds okay to you?"

It was the respectful and courteous tone in his voice that made Jessica cuddle up to him and eventually sit in his lap. "I'd love to help you. It sounds so fascinating."

"We'll probably spend the night in Roswell or somewhere nearby," he told her.

"I'll go pack," she volunteered.

"Make sure you bring comfortable clothes you can hike around in," he called after her. "I make a habit of getting out of the car and traipsing all over the place."

Right after a light breakfast, the two of them set off on this adventure. Jessica had difficulty sitting still she was so excited, so she chattered constantly, which greatly amused Garrett. The drive went by quickly and the conversation never faltered.

Southern New Mexico was mainly flat and empty. Occasional mountain ranges rose above the endless acres of prairie, but those were widely spaced, often visible for hours across the flatness, and were only seen towards the west. Driving across this barren expanse was still a worthwhile and rewarding experience for Jessica, as Garrett was so adventurous. He had selected state routes along forgotten side roads with virtually no traffic. The two-lane road was unexpectedly narrow and winding, following the Pecos River valley through sleepy farming villages with small fields and patches of woodland.

Then the road climbed up and across a low plateau, the trees faded away and quite suddenly the land opened out, with rolling grass and scrub-covered hills extending to the far horizon. Interstate 40 interrupted the unchanging scenery, but then there was nothing of note until Encino, a tiny windswept town built as a halt along a branch line of the Atchison, Topeka and Santa Fe railway. They stopped in a little café for lunch and took a walk around town to stretch their legs.

"I love this," Jessica told Garrett as the strolled along. "Not many people get to see the heart of the Southwest, much less any rural part of America."

Kildare built just a small claim shack, before work began on the house. First the kitchen was built, with attic bedroom above, then later the front part of the house which comprised the main living room, with two bedrooms and a hallway above. Other outbuildings were added at intervals, although the large barn was not added until after the Kildare family had departed. Apparently, they left in September 1953, after Kip became tired with the hardships of life on the prairie. By this time, his father had also left his nearby ranch and returned to Texas, so both properties were put up for sale at the same time. The rest of the family was not keen about having to leave. There was a photograph and what looked like a page from a diary taped to the back. It was faded with time and water stained, but with some help from Jessica, they were able to decipher the handwriting.

September 11, 1953: The family will soon be driving away, leaving our home behind. It is a beautiful, clear morning and as we topped the hill and could see the mountains, it was as if nature had willed that it be a breathtaking last look. Every pine tree on the distant peaks stands out clearly. The hustle and bustle of packing for the move has occupied us for a long time, but now it's for real. Never again will we come home here again. If I did venture back, which I certainly hope to, it will never again be home.

Jessica stared at the photograph, not even trying to hold back the tears trickling down her face. Garrett took her into his arms and gave her a big hug. He was very drawn to her compassion and the ability to project her emotional attachment to life around her.

The house remained uninhabited, though it passed via a realtor from the Kildare to the Reynolds family, who lived for a time in a ranch a few miles away and used this dwelling as temporary accommodation for farm hands and later for storage of documents. Ownership passed from the elder Mr. Reynolds to his son, then his son's wife. Now the property apparently belonged to a group of ranchers.

"This site should be restored and presented as a well-preserved example of an early Dustbowl or Depression-era homestead," Jessica suggested.

"You're right, of course, but I doubt anyone would be willing to finance such a project these days," Garrett observed. "It's pretty difficult to promote history to a generation of video game enthusiasts."

"I bet you could do it," she stated.

"You have a lot of faith in me, don't you?" he asked.

"Yes, I do," she replied.

"Why?"

"Because I've seen you in action and I know the man."

"Thank you."

"There's nothing to thank me for. I'm convinced you can do anything you set your mind to."

He took her hand and they exited through the open front door and down the steps. "Perhaps you sense that in me, because I feel like I can do anything with you."

Jessica stopped him and they kissed again.

Garrett took a few more pictures and jotted down some details he might use in some future book. Then they headed for the car.

Garrett found his way back to NM 246, which was bendy, quite hilly and still without any villages, with only a few well-separated ranches interrupting the scrub-covered plains. They reached Roswell in time for dinner and checked into a hotel for the night. Even though they were exhausted, they still made love before going to sleep.

Garrett slept through the night and only the sunlight peeking into the room through the curtains awakened him. Sitting up, Brody was quick to realize that the usual nightmare had not visited him. Looking over at Jessica, he silently thanked her for her love, which was making a profound positive impact on his life and mental well-being. He slid over closer and kissed her.

She stretched and yawned, before taking him into her arms. "Good morning."

"Hello, gorgeous," he said. "How did you sleep?"

"I always sleep like a baby with you," she answered.

They snuggled and smooched for awhile, before taking showers. Then, while Garrett was packing the car, Jessica arrived, dressed for another day's adventures. She had picked out tan hiking shorts with large cargo pockets, a bright-red polo shirt, and hiking boots. As she came out to the parking lot, Garrett ran his hands up along her tan thighs. She really liked his touch.

"You have the smoothest legs," he said as his fingers danced along the skin.

"You better stop that," she warned with a smile. "Or we'll never get anywhere."

He pouted a little, but said, "I guess you're right. I just can't believe such a drop-dead gorgeous woman is interested in me. I must have done something good in my previous life."

"You're sweet," she purred. "I think I'm pretty lucky too."

In spite of their mutual desires, after checking out, they climbed into the car and drove away. A few hours later, the windows were down and with the CD player blasting away, the two of them were singing Frank Sinatra hits at the top of their lungs. They could smell the piñon and sage while winding their way through rugged canyons. Vibrant colors radiated all around them, with pink, orange, red and purple hues. Snow melting off the highest peaks kept the canyon streams full, so wildflowers were blooming everywhere, adding to the rainbow effect of light blues, royal blues, yellows, oranges, heather, jade, periwinkle, reds, forest greens, tobacco brown, and a painter's easel full of shades of purple.

"What's our first stop?" Jessica asked.

"Rockhound State Park," he replied. "We're going to be prospectors for awhile."

"This is so much fun," she squealed with delight. "I can't wait."

The main mineral deposit in the park was chalcedony or jasper, a hard material that occurred in various colors including red, white, pink and an attractive whitish-banded agate form. The jasper was found as small outcrops in solid rock and required chiseling for them to extract. Geodes and a similar nodular variety of jasper, known as thunder eggs, occurred in bands of softer rock, but obvious veins had been excavated to a depth of several feet, but again some time and effort was necessary. One material Jessica had an eye for was perlite, a shiny black glassy rock was exposed at various locations in prominent deposits several feet thick, from which it was simple to break off smaller pieces. Garret had come equipped with a hammer and several chisels, so their excavation was quite successful.

"I'm going to take some of these and have jewelry made," Jessica commented after taking a huge swallow of water.

"I thought you might," Garrett said. He wiped away the sweat from the back of his neck with a towel. "I know the perfect jeweler back in Albuquerque for just such a project."

"Now what?" she asked, suspecting the trip was coming to a close.

"We'll start the loop back to Albuquerque," he announced. "I need to get back in plenty of time to prepare for class this week."

Jessica was a little disappointed, but knew she had homework as well. "Can we do this again soon?"

"Absolutely," he replied. "I have several more things on my list I want to see or experience first-hand, so don't be surprised if we take off somewhere again next weekend or the one after that."

"Oh, goody," she chirped.

They got back into his car, but this time cooled off in air conditioning for awhile, as Garrett headed north. The scenery was still captivating at times, with dramatic canyons and gullies rising up out of nowhere, before the landscape would once again revert back to prairie and desert, interspersed with yet more abandoned and dilapidated ranches. It was obvious that making a go of it in the New Mexico range was tough in the best of times.

Jessica fell asleep and Garrett sat back and enjoyed the drive. However, he was never able to stop thinking about Dr. Newman's bullet-riddled body for very long. The murder intrigued him, for many reasons, but mostly because he had discovered the body himself and that made the crime personal. In spite of a vow he had once made, Brody decided then-and-there that he had to investigate the murder on his own.

CHAPTER 9

STICKS AND STONES

"I WANT YOU TO research anything using the letters C, A, R, L, and A, in that order," Brody instructed. "Acronyms, synonyms, anything you can think of."

"They spell Carla," Jessica said after writing down the letters.

"That's right." Garrett said.

"Can I ask why?" she wondered.

"Several days before this semester started, I was out backpacking with two fellow professors from the University," Brody began his explanation. "We were traipsing around Bandelier National Monument and on our third day out, we stumbled upon a dying man."

"Oh dear," Jessica reacted, her fingers covering her mouth. "How terrible."

Brody nodded and continued with, "He was stark naked and had been shot four times. Whoever attacked him left him for dead. Based on what I deduced on my own, Dr. Newman actually crawled to that hiking trail, before collapsing from loss of blood."

Jessica was understandably horrified by his tale, but she was fascinated too. "So what does the name Carla have to do with his murder?"

"Carla is the key," Garrett recited Newman's last words. "That's what the man said before he died."

"That's all he said?" Jessica asked with surprise.

Brody nodded.

"So, I'm assuming the police questioned anyone named Carla that had anything to do with this Dr. Newman," Jessica stated the obvious.

"As far as I know, with a C or a K," Garrett replied.

"I never thought of that," Jessica said. "It can be spelled with a K too. Then why are you assuming it's with a C?"

"The laws of probability," he replied. "But I don't think Carla refers to a woman's name anyway."

"You don't?"

"Nope. I think it's more complicated than that."

"Which is why you want me to conduct research into anything that uses those letters in that exact order," Jessica arrived at her own conclusion.

"Yup."

"Are you sure you don't want me to look into Karla with a K?"

"If you want to," Garrett replied. "But I don't think you'll turn up much."

She shrugged. "Okay, you're the expert. I'll focus on C."

Jessica gathered her things and gave Garrett a suggestive kiss. "I'll be back later."

"Would you like to spend the night?" he asked.

She nodded. "I would love to sleep with you. It's wonderful waking up next to you in the morning."

"Even with my stubble, bad breath, and bloodshot eyes?"

Jessica retraced her steps and gently scratched him under the chin. Garrett responded just like a big cat, blinking his eyes and sticking his chin out further. This action made her giggle with delight and she kissed him again. "You know, you're just a big old baby yourself."

"I know," he replied.

"Well, for your information, what I really notice in the morning is how warm you are, how attentive you are, and how well your circulation works," Jessica stated.

He put his arms around her and hugged her close. "I really do wonder what I've done to deserve such a wonderful woman in my life."

"I think the same thing about you, you know," she commented. "I think we're deserving of happiness and love, Garrett. Every living person has the right to seek those things in life."

He kissed her with as much feeling and compassion as he was capable of delivering. Jessica felt it and responded in kind. Finally, she broke away.

"I've got to attend the Works-in-Progress session tonight," she said backing away. "My *Professional Writing* professor is reading several chapters from his non-fiction book on webpage design. It's an excellent opportunity to hear, over a *cafe au lait*, what the UNM creative writing community is working on."

"I know, sweetheart," he said. "I'm sorry I detained you."

"You could come with me?" she suggested.

He shook his head. "For a number of reasons I must decline. One, you would be distracted by my presence. Two, I don't want to steal anyone's thunder, in case somebody recognizes me, and three, I must work on my book outline, or my agent will kill me."

Jessica was a little disappointed, but also accepted his reasons were valid, especially the one about him being a distraction.

"I'll still be up when you get back," he said, tossing her the car keys. "It's parked in the driveway."

Jessica waved and hurried from his place, driving straight to the local coffee shop that hosted the monthly event.

Garrett fired up his desktop computer and sat down for a few hours of serious writing, even if it was only creating a plot outline and a few character descriptions. This time his fingers danced across the keyboard, as he could barely keep up with his mind churning out ideas. It didn't take very long for him to realize he was in the "groove," a place he loved to be, when the story seemed to write itself.

It was several hours later when the front door opened and Jessica called from the foyer, "I'm back."

Then she came into the study and gave Garrett an exuberant kiss.

"Yum, that was nice," he said.

"I'm going to bed," she announced. "I'm so tired I can barely keep my eyes open."

"Do you want me to come with you?" he asked.

Jessica could tell he had been productive writing and she really was exhausted, so she replied, "You just keep at it, Garret Brody. You can always wake me up later, when you come to bed."

He shook his head. "I shouldn't do that. Get a good night's sleep."

They kissed again and she skipped off to the bedroom.

After another three hours of explosive creative energy, Brody took a break and poured himself a neat whiskey. He allowed General Sherman to crawl up into his lap and pet the cat while editing what he had written so far. He suddenly paused.

For some unexplained reason, the vision of Dr. Newman's perforated back loomed once again into Garrett's mind. With such startling clarity that it was unnerving, his memory zoomed in on the bullet holes. Brody sat up straight, General Sherman spilling off. The cat meowed with surprise.

"I'm sorry," Garrett said as he pet the cat.

However, the image just wouldn't go away. There was something uniquely perplexing about the wounds, as if some clue to the murderer existed in the arrangement. This fact troubled Brody even more, for he couldn't recall anything from his previous experiences that would initiate his reaction. Perhaps it stemmed from something he had read once? The dark bullet holes formed a perfect diamond pattern, almost like a chessboard. Was there really significance?

It was after three in the morning when Garrett finally crawled into bed. Jessica rolled over and snuggled up against him. She was soft, smooth and warm, which made his blood stir with desire. Gently he kissed her and she mumbled affectionate nonsense. He scooted down under the covers and kissed her again. This time her eyes opened and she whispered, "I missed you."

He put his arms around her and they kissed more passionately.

"Would you like to make love?" she asked sleepily.

He kissed her again.

"Me too," she said after he lifted his lips from hers.

"I love you," he whispered in her ear.

Jessica rolled on top of him and hugged him hard. "I love you too."

After a spirited lovemaking session, the man and woman fell asleep right where they were, too exhausted to separate. Garrett's sleep was no longer invaded by nightmares and he slept through the night, holding Jessica very close.

Dawn arrived with the chirping birds and sunlight filtering in through a gap in the curtains. Eventually the sunshine crept its way across the bedroom, until it settled on Jessica's sleeping face.

Rolling over, one eye opened as Jessica looked at the clock. Suddenly, she leapt from the bed. "Oh, my God, I'm going to be late for class."

Her exclamation startled Garrett awake too. He sat up in bed and watched her scramble into the bathroom, where she planned on taking a quick shower.

"May I join you?" Garrett called out after her.

"Oh, yes, I'd like that," she replied, coming back to the door. "You can scrub my back."

"Among other things," he said.

It was Jessica.

"My challenge is deciding which voice will work better," she said. "Do you have some kind of test you use to help you decide which viewpoint is right?"

"New writers are often baffled when trying to choose a point of view for their stories and novels," Garrett replied. "But, actually, the choice is easy. Over ninety percent of all modern speculative fiction is written using the same limited third person point of view. This means that although the narration refers to all the characters by third-person pronouns, such as he, she, or it, each self-contained scene follows the viewpoint of one specific character. There's a reason for this. It's easier to write. Remember, though, that first person can really be intriguing.

"As to a test, it's really a matter of reading some of what you've written aloud. I prefer to not know everything that's going on in everyone's minds. So, for the most part, I'm going to keep a limited view when writing. First person is even more limiting, because the reader only knows what the main character is thinking, but that can build more mystery into the story. In the case of your manuscript, Jessica, I think first person is perfect, because the story revolves around your central character and her insights are really what makes the story come alive."

"Thank you, Garrett," Jessica said. "I thought so too, but it's comforting to have a second opinion from you."

He smiled and pointed to another raised hand. "Yes, Peter."

In this manner, the class went by quickly, with lots of questions to field and answer, while Brody fired off some of his own. The students were growing as writers and it showed in their questions, which had also matured and developed over the life of the course.

"That's it for today," Garrett announced. "Thanks for participating. Please make sure, if you haven't done so already, to arrange a meeting with me. The semester is rapidly drawing to a close and I still have a number of you to talk to."

Right after class Brody scheduled three afternoon student meetings, but he planned on spending his free time with Jessica. They walked together to his car, but she seemed very distracted.

"Is everything okay?" he asked as he held the car door open for her.

"I won't be available this weekend," she announced hesitantly.

"You won't?" Garrett reacted with disappointment. "How come?"

"I'm spending it with my girlfriends," she explained. "We planned this trip a long time ago, before I met you."

"Where are you gals going?" he asked.

"Las Vegas, actually," she replied.

His eyebrows went up. "I see. Would you like some company?"

"That would be nice, Garrett, but not this time," she answered. "This is just a girl thing, a little getaway and if you came along, I'd want to make love all the time and that wouldn't be fair to my friends."

"I understand," Brody said, pouting a little.

She kissed him. "I'm sorry, honey. I'll make it up to you."

"It's okay, Jessica," he said honestly. "It will give me some quality time to do some writing. I've been a little remiss in that regard."

"Would you like to go see the Lobos play baseball against the University of Utah, when I get back?" she suggested.

"Sure, that would be fun," he replied with a big smile. "Now you be good."

Jessica suddenly didn't want to go to Las Vegas. She wanted to be with him.

He put his arms around her and kissed her on the nose. "Now don't go getting cold feet. Your friends are counting on you. I'll miss you, but that's a good thing, because think how much I'll want you when you get back. Go have a good time."

"I'll call you," she said. "I promise."

He chuckled. "You don't have to check in, sweetheart. I trust you implicitly. Just be careful, that's all."

She climbed into the passenger seat and Garrett went around to the driver's side. As he sat behind the wheel, he was given the most incredibly wonderful kiss. After Jessica leaned back, he licked his lips and sighed.

"That was very nice, I do say," he said.

"I love you, you know," she said.

"Yes, I do know," Garrett said. "Let's go back to my place for awhile and fool around. Then I'll drop you off at your apartment so you can pack, while I have my student meetings."

The couple made love and took a nap, before Jessica went back to her apartment. She insisted it would be better if Garrett didn't drive her and her friends to the airport, so he reluctantly kissed her goodbye. Brody returned to the University, where he met with several students from his class.

Jessica's friends, Amanda and Stephanie, always accompanied Jessica to her wrestling matches. Not only did she have reliable female moral support, but her friends provided lots of morale-building input as well. Besides, in some ways, Jessica felt her friends offered better advice than even her manager, who had once been a professional wrestler too. They also helped her pack, making sure Jessica didn't forget any of her various costumes, since she might make several changes during a match.

On the way to the airport, Jessica was strangely subdued, for she missed Garrett already. Amanda wanted to comment on her uncharacteristic silence, but decided it could wait until they were airborne.

The girls boarded the plane and sat together in the coach section, three across. Jessica always took the seat on the aisle. Once the flight had taken off, the three women started talking about all sorts of subjects, laughing and having a marvelous time together.

"Look at me," Amanda said, looking down at her chest.

"What are we supposed to look at?" Stephanie wondered.

"My breasts," Amanda replied.

"What about them?" Jessica wondered.

"I'm just worried I'll lose my boobs altogether," Amanda said. "Every time I get back in really good shape, I get smaller and I like my boobs."

Jessica said, "I'll lend you some of mine."

They all burst into laughter.

"So, when are you going to tell Garrett about your wrestling career?" Amanda asked suddenly. "Right now he thinks it's only part of your research, right?"

Jessica shrugged. "I don't know, but pretty soon. Otherwise, he'll figure it out on his own. He's not stupid."

"You're not ashamed of it, are you?" Stephanie asked pointedly.

"You know I'm not," Jessica said vehemently.

"Then what's the problem?" Amanda asked.

"It isn't a problem exactly," Jessica said. "I just don't want anything to get in the way of this relationship, that's all."

"If Garrett truly loves you, then he'll love you for who you are," Amanda stated. "Wrestling is an integral part of your life right now, so he'll just have to accept it."

"I know that," Jessica said.

"The sooner you tell him, the less chance there is he'll discover it on his own," Stephanie added. "He might think you lied to him or that you have other things to hide as well. Something like this could really damage your relationship."

"You're right, of course," Jessica said. "As soon as we return from this trip, I'll tell him."

"That's good," her friends said in unison.

Then the conversation turned to the upcoming match, her competition, and how the typical male wrestlers were threatened by Jessica's capabilities.

"They're egos are very fragile," Stephanie commented. "They only fuss, because women aren't supposed to be tough enough to beat up men."

Jessica was well aware that strong mental toughness led to good technique, tactics, strength, conditioning, flexibility, recovery, and nutrition. She quietly went over her five daily drills that conditioned her. There was a warm-up, then standing offense and defense, bottom position, top position, and recovery/conditioning. The repetitive drills gave Jessica an attitude of success and the confidence to deliver victory after victory.

"I can take anyone down at anytime," Jessica said to herself. "They can't take me down. No one can ride or turn me. I can control anyone."

Goal setting and self-confidence played a critical role on the wrestling mat. Jessica paid closed attention to her diet, year round training, and religiously performing seven different stretches to help avoid injuries. She also practiced her stance, motion, level change, penetration and drive to the finish. Every workout focused on three different categories, which were offensive skills and drills from the feet, counter offense skills, and drills from the down position.

The *Las Vegas Orleans Arena* was packed with screaming, cheering, and enthusiastic wrestling fans. Jessica was nervous with excitement, but more than that, she was planning on finally making her mark on the world of professional wrestling. Tonight her nasty bad-girl image converted into the vamp with honor, so she was switching sides. After appearing in her trademark all-black getup, Jessica would later change to red, white and blue spandex, with a long ponytail. She hoped it would stir up a positive reaction from the crowd.

Jessica was one of the few female wrestlers in the business who paired off against male wrestlers, because she could hold her own and still look convincing. The problem, of course, was finding men willing to face off against her, knowing that the script usually called for the man to lose. Losing to a woman in this business was hard on the ego.

"Now remember, make the most of your opportunities," Stephanie coached Jessica as they waited for the main event. "Don't leave that mat feeling you held anything back. If you give it your all, you will have no regrets, regardless of the outcome. Seize the moment! Rise to the occasion!"

Jessica was pumped up.

The loudspeaker squawked for an instant, before the announcer's voice echoed throughout the arena. "Ladies and gentlemen, may I have your attention. Tonight we have gathered the best women in wrestling, to face off against a pack of vicious men, bent on tearing off the girl's clothes and humiliating them. What do you think of that?"

The audience went insane.

Jessica rolled her eyes and shouted over the din, "Sometime these idiots make me sick."

Amanda laughed and patted her best friend on the arm. "Just go out there and rip off a few heads. That will make everyone take notice."

"Remember," Stephanie shouted. "Be intense, yet relaxed, when you step on the mat to do battle! Get totally psyched up and attacked your opponent relentlessly."

"I will," Jessica said.

"Control the tempo," Stephanie went on. "Use your motion and body fakes to control the tempo or close the gap. Never stand around. Use body fakes to put your opponent on the defensive, so you can get a hold of him."

"Ladies and gentlemen," the announcer's voice boomed everywhere. "Leading the women on this one-sided battle is none other than the wicked *Temptation*!"

"That's your cue," Amanda said, while pushing Jessica out from behind the curtains. "Go kick some male ass!"

The spotlight was almost blinding, but Jessica knew to look out in the crowd. She was entirely dressed in black leather. Her one-piece bustier had plunging cleavage, no back and thong bottoms, with knee-high black boots.

The applause was deafening and everyone was on their feet. The arena was rocking with motion and noise. A heavy-metal rock soundtrack echoed all round her and she was swept up in the pandemonium and adoration. Jessica strolled along confidently, vamping and cavorting her way to the ring. Temptation was definitely the favorite and her fans were rabidly loyal and fiercely protective of their heroine.

The match faced off five women wrestlers against four male wrestlers. It was supposed to be a lopsided contest, as the main attraction was for the decidedly male audience to witness the thrashing a beautiful women. The titillation of ripped costumes and mild sadomasochism whipped the crowd into a frenzy. Chanting for domination and humiliation, the arena rumbled like some primordial gathering of gladiators fighting to the death.

Jessica grinned to herself. The entire thing was a hoax, as these wrestlers had been practicing the intricately choreographed story for months. In fact, her outfit had already been pre-ripped in spots, so the cloth would tear easily. It was just a matter of looking convincing, right down to the fake blood and screams of terror.

Still, Jessica had no intention of being on the losing side. It had been agreed that the women would suffer horribly for most of the match, with only Jessica's character *Temptation* lasting out the vile male assault. Then, at just the right moment, she would change both her outfit and her character's alignment, from evil to good and therefore would prevail against the onslaught from these depraved men.

Back in Albuquerque, Garrett was once again reading Jessica's book manuscript. He was starting to wonder how she was able to write so convincingly about the world of professional wrestling. It was as if she had lived the part, for her description of each event was too meticulous and too full of emotional integrity to just be artistic skill.

He took off his reading glasses and lay back against the big pillow on the sofa. Closing his eyes for a moment, Garrett pondered what was going on in his mind. Could it be possible that Jessica had once been a professional wrestler? She seemed too cultured and refined to have ever been involved in anything so seedy and contrived. Besides, she was young to be experienced enough to compete on that level, or so he assumed.

Yet he was also painfully aware that he knew nothing tangible about professional wrestling, only relying on his preconceived notions. After reading Jessica's book, Garrett was faced with a newfound admiration for the central character's challenges and triumphs. If Jessica had actually experienced only half of the incidents she wrote about, then Brody was the first to admit that she was worthy of even more respect and compassion, not his pity or suspicions. There was a tremendous amount of inner strength radiating from Jessica, so perhaps such physical prowess made her more complicated and diverse. This line of reasoning merely made him want her more.

The next day, as soon as Jessica got back into town, she immediately called Garrett. He was thrilled she was back and invited her to spend the afternoon and evening with him. She agreed, of course, promising to make dinner as well. Since he knew she was such a fabulous cook, Brody was delighted.

CHAPTER 11

KISSED BY THE SUN

NESTLED IN THE VALLEY of the majestic Estrella and South mountains, the five-diamond *Wild Horse Pass Resort and Spa* featured a meandering river throughout the resort, an equestrian center, jogging trails, tennis courts, two 18-hole golf courses, the Wild Horse Pass Casino, a 17,000-square-foot spa and more. The resort was conveniently located just 11.5 miles from the Phoenix Sky Harbor International Airport on the Gila River Indian Community.

After checking in, the couple went to their suite to unpack and relax for a few minutes. Garrett was pooped from the drive and suggested taking a nap.

"It's so gorgeous outside," Jessica whined a little. "Let's not stay inside."

"Okay, then let's lounge by the pool," he suggested.

"That sounds wonderful," she said happily. "I want to get one of those silly fruit drinks with the tiny umbrella."

Garrett quickly changed into his swimming trunks, but Jessica seemed to be moving very slowly. He waited impatiently by the door.

"Go ahead to the pool, honey," she said finally, noting his pacing. "I'll be down in just a minute."

"Okay, but don't be too long," he jokingly scolded. "I get lonely really fast."

It was only about ten minutes later, when Jessica joined Garrett by the swimming pool, which was surrounded by guests sunbathing. Brody had sought shelter from the blazing sun under a huge umbrella.

"This is fantastic," she said after kissing him. "I could stay here forever."

He gently patted her butt as she went by, although her bathing suit was hidden by her knee-length cover-up. Jessica sat down on the lounge chair beside him, crossing her legs. Garrett handed her a fruity drink with the required pink paper umbrella.

She took a long cool sip and sighed, "This is delicious! Thank you."

"It's very nice here, isn't it?" he said.

"How did you know about this place?" she asked.

"There was a writing conference here just last year," he replied.

Jessica was glad she brought her sunglasses. She started to fan herself with her hand.

"It's quite hot," she commented.

"Would you like to take a dip?" he suggested.

"That sounds marvelous," Jessica said.

She stood up and slipped out of her cover-up.

However, Garrett almost stopped breathing.

For Jessica was wearing a black Brazilian thong bikini, which more than aptly complimented her tight body. In fact, just about everyone poolside was now staring at her, unless they were asleep or dead. Brody watched Jessica slide into the crystal-clear pool and tread water, waiting for him. With a very pronounced index finger motioning for him to join her, Garrett made his way to the edge, his knees quivering like jelly.

He dove in.

The water was cool and so refreshing.

Jessica swam up to him and greeted her lover with a very suggestive kiss.

"You are a very naughty girl, do you know that?" Garrett stated.

Jessica nodded. "Yes, I know."

"You really enjoy making me hot for you, don't you?" he asked.

"Yes, I do," she purred.

"So what if I made love to you right here?"

"I'd like that very much, but we'd get arrested."

He frowned. "Yes, I guess that would be considered lewd and socially unacceptable behavior."

Jessica giggled. "Can you wait until we go back to the room?"

"I don't have any choice, do I?"

She shook her head.

He pouted.

"Let's swim and play for awhile," she suggested. "I promise to make the wait worthwhile."

The couple had a marvelous time, splashing about and playing tag, while smooching and laughing. There was no one at that pool that couldn't see how much in love they were. Later they returned to the room, made love and slept. Jessica opted for room service and the couple ate outside on their private balcony, watching the fantastic reddish-orange sunset. They went to bed early, but didn't go to sleep right away.

The next day started with a hot air balloon ride. While the balloon inflated, Jessica and Garrett received a preflight briefing. The balloon soared to 400 feet to give spectacular 360-degree views of the mountains and valleys surrounding Phoenix. After gently floating with the wind, the balloon landed on the desert floor, where tables were set for a wonderful lunch. A famous local chef prepared delicious hors d'oeuvres in his unique hybrid of classic French cuisine and southwestern fare.

They took off again, floating silently over the Sonora desert, sipping champagne and watching coyote, javelina and other desert critters. Jessica thoroughly enjoyed the solitude and beautiful scenery below them. A certified pilot skillfully brought the balloon's basket to within inches of treetop level, giving the couple incomparable views of the desert landscape.

After landing, next came a carriage ride. With a choice of broughams or Cinderella carriages, Jessica felt more than pampered. The ride was just the thing for them to chitchat, uninterrupted by telephones or noisy people. Later Garrett was feeling more adventurous, so they climbed aboard an authentic stagecoach, pulled by a team of four horses, to tour Arizona's beautiful Sonora desert again, from the ground this time.

The clip-clop of horses' hooves echoed off the historic storefronts of Old Town Scottsdale as they enjoyed their romantic carriage ride past the fascinating shops and galleries of "the West's most Western town."

For dinner Brody selected *T. Cook's at the Royal Palms*, which was located within an intimately scaled resort of flowers and fountains, citrus trees and stately old palms. The restaurant itself was decorated in a style that reflected Spanish, Moorish and Mediterranean sensibilities. A giant hearth dominated the room, and windows let in sunshine and views of greenery. Tiled floors, heavy furniture and terra cotta-colored brick walls gave the place warmth and elegance.

Like the decor, the food had a Mediterranean flair. For dinner, the couple both ordered grilled beef tenderloin in a red wine reduction over gorgonzola-spiked Israeli couscous. The signature mussels appetizer, sautéed in Chardonnay-thyme broth, was excellent, as was the antipasto platter, with medallions of roasted duck breast and grilled loin of lamb. The desserts were ornate constructions they hated to ruin.

After dinner they went dancing at the *Kyote Ballroom* in Tempe. Jessica was thrilled to discover that Garrett had paid in advance for tickets to attend a Milonga Dance, which consisted of a variety of Argentine Tango, Vals, and Milonga music. Light refreshments were served and there was an enthusiastic crowd of people dancing. The spacious wood floor was delightful for dancing all styles of social dance with adequate seating for all. The central ballroom was decorated in a simple and modern style, but with a decidedly Latin flair. Giant floor-to-ceiling mirrors lined one wall, while a row of barstools were strategically placed behind a low bar-like counter on the opposite side. People were either dancing or gathered in groups sipping soft drinks and chattering.

Garrett pulled Jessica straight out onto the floor.

"I don't know how to tango very well," she protested.

"Neither do I," he replied. "Who cares? I just want to dance with you."

No other dance connected two people more closely than the Argentine tango, emotionally as well as physically. Part of this was because of the dance position. Garrett and Jessica faced in the same direction and danced cheek to cheek. She loved every minute of it, because they kept their arms around each other for every number.

Brody was aware that creativity and improvisation were valued more than correctness by the best tango dancers, so he experimented with his own style. Garrett focused on Jessica and his connection with her. In turn, she listened to his body language and imagined what Garrett was thinking and feeling. She enjoyed the sensations of her arms around him and his around her.

Suddenly Garrett paused. He gazed at her and let his face express intense passion and desire, which made Jessica almost melt in his arms. What was truly amazing was how he was always aware of his partner. Brody knew exactly where Jessica was, before he could get her to where he wanted her. He was quick to notice where she deviated from the path he was shaping for her, so he was able to get her back into the flow, while still presenting her in the best possible light. She knew she wasn't that skilled a dancer, but with Garrett's care and attention, Jessica felt like she was.

Brody contemplated her words and nodded. "I'll try that. Thanks."

The taxi came to a stop outside a small office building and the passengers got out after Tagget paid the fare. They stood together looking at the front entrance.

"Don't expect much when you step inside," Brody warned. "These places are usually really scary or very boring."

He held open the door for Jessica and Tagget.

A series of framed movie posters lined all the walls, but the atmosphere in the office was like that of stockbroker. Several people were coaxing investors over the phone. The famous executive producer was always hustling, forever short of funding. However, he was dressed in an expensive tailored suit and looked the part of a bank president, which was not too far removed from his real purpose. The man waved and snapped his fingers for an assistant to look after his guests.

The three of them were ushered into a conference room, where the producer's representative showed them where to sit.

"Would you like bottled water?" the young man asked.

"Yes, please," Jessica spoke up. "Three bottles."

The assistant hurried off.

Tagget tapped Brody on the arm. "Jessica will make sure you don't die of thirst."

Garrett didn't see the humor in his agent's comment, but the other two smiled at each other. Jessica rested her hand on Garrett's arm then and gave him a dazzling and supportive smile.

"You'll do just fine, honey," she whispered.

Six people filed into the room. Introductions were made, handshakes exchanged, and everyone was seated. On one side of the room was nervous expectation, while on the other side the mood was of bored resignation.

Garrett stood up and said, "Frankly, the commercial movie is anything aimed at the box office. *Brazen Chariots* was a blockbuster best-seller in print and would easily translate into that same category on film."

Brody then handed out his treatment to demonstrate his abilities to weave a good tale, while still making it an enjoyable read. The treatment told a story, that hopefully everyone around the table would like seeing as a movie. The basic ingredients were there, including the central and important secondary characters, the major events of the story with obstacles, reversals, and barriers that affected the action. The climax and ending were included. This document wasn't a tease for the producer, but was a full account of what was involved in the story.

It was up to Garrett to create the selling energy for the benefit of the producer and his investors. "The next global conflict won't be about oil. In but a few years, the last reserves will have been exhausted. No, the upcoming wars will be fought over the most basic resource we have. Imagine the world fighting over water?"

Brody waited for just a split second, before he slammed his hand on the table. Everyone at the table jumped, including Jessica and Tagget. Garrett leaned towards them with incredible intensity and very quietly said, "*Brazen Chariots* isn't another story about armed conflict. It's about the very basic human struggle of survival, when those elements of life we take for granted are consumed. Think what your lives would be like if you knew that bottle of water before you was the last one you would ever drink?"

Then he stood straight and sat down.

The producer picked up the treatment and read it, which was a profound implication that he was interested in the project. Lifting his reading glasses, he stood up and everyone else did too.

"Thank you for your time, Mr. Brody," the man said. "I'm intrigued. Is there a screenplay?"

"Yes, I have it with me," Garrett replied.

"Leave it with us, please," the producer said.

"Of course," Brody said.

"We'll get back to you," was the proclamation.

Everyone shook hands and the meeting was concluded. In all, it took less than twenty minutes, from start to finish.

Once outside, Jessica waited for Garrett's reaction, but even Tagget was quiet until they climbed into a new taxi.

"What did you think?" she asked, not able to contain her curiosity.

"Better than I expected," Tagget said.

Brody shrugged. "They always seem interested at the time. The screenplay might swing them either way. It's all about money and investors and star power. If they have someone big in mind to play the central character, then it might already be decided."

"Let's get lunch and we can talk about Jessica's book," the agent suggested.

They went to the *Cafe Rodeo* at the *Luxe Hotel*, which was Rodeo Drive's signature restaurant. Jessica was hoping to spot a movie star, as they were seated al fresco along Rodeo Drive. The sumptuous menu offered a wide selection of inspired California cuisine, which tantalized her palate.

CHAPTER 13

UNSOLICITED REMINDER

THE DOOR CHIMES JINGLED melodiously as another customer entered *Weck's*.

Garrett looked up, but the sip of coffee never made it past his lips. In fact, as soon as Brody recognized the man entering the restaurant, his stomach turned. He set the cup down, crossed his arms across his chest and waited.

This unwelcome person immediately spotted Garrett and approached Brody's table, neither smiling nor frowning. It might be said he was expressionless, if such a thing was possible.

"It's been a long time, Garrett," the man spoke as he grew nearer.

Brody was glad his back was against the wall. "What do you want?"

"Well, now that's not a very nice way to greet an old friend," the new arrival said as he pulled out a chair and sat down.

"We were once business associates, Lucas," Brody said coldly. "That never meant we were friends."

Garrett's favorite waitress Maria approached the table. "Would you like to see a menu, sir?"

The man shook his head. "No, that won't be necessary. Just a cup of coffee, please."

Maria smiled and said, "I'll be right back with your coffee."

When she was gone, the man leaned forward and offered his hand.

Brody didn't budge. His eyes narrowed.

If this old acquaintance was bothered by the lack of a friendly reception, he didn't show it. Leaning back, the man clasped his hands in his lap and waited patiently.

The cup of hot coffee arrived a few seconds later.

"Thank you very much," Brody's uninvited guest said politely.

Maria smiled again and went to serve a different table.

Brody studied the man as he took another sip of his coffee. Lucas Perret was well-dressed, his clothes both comfortable and flattering, without being an overt fashion statement. The man was good-looking as well, but that came from being distinguished and wise, rather than magazine-cover features. Even with a touch of gray hair at the temples, Lucas was undeniably handsome and didn't look his age.

"I expected a certain hesitation to give me a bear hug as a greeting, Garrett, but I never would have guessed that I deserved such a chilly reception," Perret said after tasting his coffee.

Brody forced a smile. "I just never expected to see you again, Lucas, that's all. I thought we had an agreement?"

Perret nodded and added some sugar. "Which I'm still honoring, Garrett. I just came here to advise you on a certain sensitive matter."

Brody picked up his cup of coffee. "I don't need your advice."

Perret frowned. "Stop being so belligerent."

"Ha, that's pretty funny, coming from you," Brody replied.

Perret sighed and ran his fingers through his stylishly cut hair. "Why are you so damn obstinate with me? There is no reason for such behavior."

This time Brody leaned forward, his third finger jutting out with a pronounced and very vulgar gesture. "See this? That's what I think of you and your business partners."

Perret shook his head with disappointment. "I never expected you to stoop so low, Garrett. Did I treat you so poorly that I deserve such disrespect?"

That question actually hit a soft spot with Brody. He stopped for a moment to reflect on his emotions, realizing that he was acting very strangely indeed. Then, with something akin to a revelation, he stuck out his hand in a much more friendly motion.

"I'm sorry, Lucas," Garrett said quietly. "I apologize. Seeing you again really caught me off-guard and I'm afraid I've acted most rudely."

Perret's face lit up with a warm and genuine smile. The two men shook hands and the negative air seemed to vanish in an instant. At least that's what one of them believed.

Brody made a little wave to the waitress and when Maria came up to the table, Garrett said, "I'm ready to order breakfast now, Maria, if that's okay?"

"Of course, *Señor* Brody," she said sweetly. "What can I get you?"

After placing his order, Garrett looked at Perret.

The man shook his head. "No thank you. Coffee is just fine for me."

"I'll be back shortly with your meal, *Señor* Brody," Maria said with a flirtatious smile.

When she was out of earshot, Perret commented. "I see you still have your winning ways with the ladies?"

"So, you said you came here to give me some advice?" Brody asked, ignoring Perret's comment.

"Not exactly advice, Garrett. More like filling in the blanks, so that you can make an informed decision."

"Decision regarding what?" Brody asked.

"I have it on good authority that someone fired shots at you while you were vacationing in Phoenix," Perret stated.

"So it seems," Brody replied, only mildly concerned that the man knew of the incident. For Lucas Perret had access to just about every source of information known to man. In fact, accurate and timely information was what Perret thrived on.

"You don't seem too concerned."

"I'm not."

"You might consider your companion's safety next time."

Instantly Brody's mood grew very dark. So much so, in fact, that Perret set his cup down and pushed his chair back.

"Is that some kind of thinly veiled threat?"

"No, not in any way," Perret said defensively. "I just don't think you always consider how your methods might affect other people."

"I've never forgotten what happened to the last woman I fell in love with," Garrett said, his voice as cold as ice. "Be forewarned. If any of your hooligans comes anywhere near Jessica, I'll kill them all, plain and simple."

"Did you kill the shooter in Phoenix?"

"I sure as hell wouldn't tell you if I did."

Perret crossed his arms. "My organization can't protect you."

"I know that."

"So this gunman doesn't concern you?"

"No."

"Why not?"

"Because, whoever it was, wasn't trying to kill us. Those shots were just meant to frighten me away."

"How do you know that?"

Brody looked at Perret with something akin to pity. "Lucas, come on. I used to get paid for knowing things like that. If the shooter had intended to kill us, it would have been quite easy. I was unarmed and the two of us were entirely naked, so even a rank amateur would have had the drop on us."

Perret's eyebrows went up, but he decided not to say what was on his mind.

Garrett smiled thinly. "Jessica is not only my lover, Lucas. I hope to be her husband one day, if she'll have me."

Perret hadn't expected that. He drummed his fingers on the tabletop for a minute, before he said, "So you're already aware of what Jessica Lawver does on the side?"

Brody felt very strange all of a sudden. The tone of Perret's voice created a definite level of uneasiness. "What do you mean?"

"That in addition to being the typical college coed, she's also **Temptation**, a female professional wrestler," Perret stated.

Garrett took another sip of coffee to cover his initial reaction. Then, as he put the cup down, he chuckled. "Oh, that. Well, I'm hardly the one to make judgments on what people do moonlighting, now am I? Besides, she's pretty talented."

Perret looked at Brody with narrowed eyes, but then nodded. "Yes, she is. I would say gifted, in her case."

The meal arrived and Garrett dug into the hot breakfast with relish. After a few bites, he looked up at Perret and asked, "Are you sure you don't want something to eat? The food is really quite delicious here."

Perret chuckled. "Apparently. No, I'll pass. I don't do breakfast."

Garrett's eyebrows went up. "Well, that explains a lot. Didn't your mother tell you that breakfast was the most important meal of the day?"

Perret smiled in spite of himself. "Yes, she did, as a matter-of-fact."

"I thought so," Garrett said. "Your mother, unlike you, was a wise person."

"Leave my mother out of it." Perret said. "We were talking about you."

"No, actually we were talking about Jessica," Brody corrected him.

"So this wrestling thing doesn't bother you at all?" Perret asked.

While Perret apparently knew more about Jessica than he did, this fact was only mildly disturbing to Brody. He shook his head. "Why should it bother me? Jessica's life is her own and she doesn't need my approval to pursue anything."

"All that stuff is rather sordid and contrived," Perret pointed out.

Garrett sat up straighter, his face full of barely-controlled contempt. "Who are you to point fingers? Your entire existence is based on sordid behavior. Besides, what Jessica does in the ring is none of those things. She displays physical prowess far beyond my capabilities, while still being a woman of incredible depth, beauty, and intelligence."

Perret folded his arms across his chest again, but said nothing.

"So why are you here again?" Brody asked after taking another bite of his eggs.

"I recently received an inquiry from the Los Alamos Lab regarding a certain college lecturer who seemed to be making a nuisance of himself," Perret replied.

"I wonder who that could be?" Brody mused.

Perret frowned. "What are you up to, Garrett?"

"None of your business."

"I can make it my business."

"You can try."

"Oh, let me assure you, if I decide to get involved, I can shut you down."

Garrett seemed unimpressed. He exaggerated a yawn and said, "Lucas, your imitation of a peacock ruffling his feathers is quite impressive, by an entire waste of time with me. There's no way you can outmaneuver me."

Perret stood up and folded his napkin to lie across his coffee cup. "I must be on my way, Garrett. It was good to see you again."

Brody waited to comment until Perret was long gone. He took a long sip of coffee and under his breath said, "Bastard."

After paying for the meal, Garrett drove to Jessica's apartment and invited her to join him on another excursion. This time the adventure was in Albuquerque itself, as Brody wanted to explore Petroglyph National Monument.

As they walked among the petroglyphs, Jessica was acutely attuned to the sights and sounds of the high desert. A hawk spiraled down from the mesa top, while a roadrunner scurried into fragrant sage, and a desert millipede traced distinct patterns in the sand. There were other spirits present beyond what she could see with her eyes or hear with her ears.

Jessica sensed the history of a people who lived along the Rio Grande for many centuries. Through images they carved on the shiny black rocks, she had a glimpse into the past.

Petroglyph National Monument stretched 17 miles along Albuquerque's West Mesa, a volcanic basalt escarpment that dominated the city's western horizon. The monument protected a variety of cultural and natural resources, including five volcanic cones, hundreds of archeological sites and an estimated 25,000 images carved by native peoples and early Spanish settlers. Many of the images were recognizable as animals, people, brands and crosses, while others were much more complex. The carver possibly only understood their meaning. Those images were inseparable from the greater cultural landscape, from the spirits of the people who created them and all who appreciated them. For Jessica, it was a place of tremendous respect, awe and wonderment.

"Thank you for bringing me here," she whispered, afraid to disturb the spirits.

Garrett took her hand and gently squeezed. "It's really quite magnificent, isn't it?"

"Yes, indeed," she said. "There is so much solitude here, even this close to the city and so much history. It's impossible to deny how closely these people were attached to the earth around them."

Brody pointed out some of the more artistic and intriguing examples of carvings, while carrying on a lively discussion of identifying what they represented. Often it was a case of point-of-view, much like making shapes from passing clouds. It all depended on your point-of-view. Still, even when Jessica and Garrett couldn't agree on a specific shape, they so enjoyed the exchange of their analysis.

Later the went out for dinner, but it had been a long and mentally exhausting day, so they called it an early evening and went to Brody's condo to turn in. Jessica was spending most of her free time at Garrett's place and just about every other evening. She would never dare suggesting it become a more permanent arrangement, mostly because of her fear that moving in might disrupt Brody's writing schedule. It was apparent enough that their relationship had adversely affected the progress on his latest novel. Besides that, she had become pretty lax with her workout schedule too and Stephanie had commented about this lack of focus on her physical conditioning.

Still, even with these thoughts preying on her mind, Jessica couldn't wait to make love and fell asleep in Garrett's arms. Brody was quite content and quickly fell asleep as well.

It was after midnight when Garrett's cell phone rang. He reached for it as quickly as possible, so the harmonic tones wouldn't wake up Jessica. Brody slipped away to the den and answered it.

"Sorry to be calling so late, Garrett," said James Tagget.

"It's okay," Brody said, stifling a yawn. "What's up?"

"*Brazen Chariots* is a go," his agent said. "They've offered one million dollars for the book rights and your screenplay, with one percent of the gate."

"Not acceptable," Garrett replied. "Four percent of the gate. It's going to be a box office hit and they know it."

Tagget sighed. "They may walk."

"Let 'em."

"Are you sure?"

"Never more sure in my life."

"You're the boss. I'll get back to you."

"No matter what the answer is, can't it wait until a more decent hour?"

Tagget chuckled. "No problem. Go back to sleep."

"Not likely. Now my brain's awake and you know what that means?"

"Well try something different for a change, my friend," Tagget suggested. "Climb back into bed, cuddle up to her and see if you can't get your mind to relax."

Garret smiled. "You're right. I'll try your suggestion."

"Perhaps there's hope for you after all, Garrett," Tagget chuckled. "Jessica is the best thing to happen to you in a long time."

"You're right," Brody said. "I'm very much in love with her."

"I could tell. Now go back to sleep."

"Goodnight, James and thanks."

"Don't mention it. Goodnight, my friend."

Click.

Garrett did go back to bed, slipping under the covers and scooting closer to Jessica. She rolled over into his embrace and he kissed her very gently on the lips. They snuggled for awhile, sleepily enjoying each other's affection, until both once again drifted off to sleep.

CHAPTER 14

ACRONYMS, SYNONYMS AND ANTONYMS

"HAPPY AND SAD ARE antonyms," Brody repeated as he wrote them on the board.

"Stones and rocks are synonyms," he said after writing them next.

"However, an acronym is an abbreviation coined from the initial letter of each successive word in a term or phrase," Garrett continued. "In general, an acronym is made up solely from the first letter of the major words, rendered in all capital letters."

Every student was taking notes, while most of them had no idea exactly why.

"Now before you start thinking this is a remedial English class, I'm pointing out these differences for a reason," Brody stated as he walked up close to the front table. "It's okay to break some rules, in fact I promote rule-breaking, but grammar has some pretty strict rules and it's dangerous, from a literary sense, to dispense with things your readers are comfortable with. Remember your audience.

"Poorly chosen words can kill enthusiasm, impact self-esteem, lower expectations and hold people back. Well chosen words can motivate, offer hope, create vision, impact thinking and alter results. I have learned over the years that words have as much power as thoughts and actions.

"If you want your writing to impact people and influence thought, learn to select words that create a visual of the desired outcome and choose each word as if it mattered."

Up went the hands.

"Yours went up first, Samantha," Garrett recognized her.

"How do you know if the words you've selected are effective?" she asked.

"By using arguments that make sense, you can convince the reader to see your point of view," Garrett replied. "This isn't about vocabulary, because if the words don't have meaning, they lose their power. It's all about context, pacing, and actual word selection. There must be an emotional attachment to your words, so that in a specific order they evoke feelings."

"How does the power of the written word differ from that of the spoken?" Rick asked when he was selected.

"Ultimately, whether written or spoken, what controls the meaning of a particular word?" Garrett answered with a different question. "Is oral speech superior to the written word? The speaker can be judged by the inflection in her voice, the volume used to deliver her message, hand motions, body language and all sorts of visual and verbal tools to enhance delivery. Is that possible with the written word?"

Most of the students shook their heads, but Jessica's hand went up.

Garrett couldn't help but smile. "Yes, Jessica?"

"All those visual and audio elements are crutches the speaker relies on, Garrett," she said. "In this modern era, we have become so accustomed to noise and flashing lights, that we expect to be entertained. The written word, however, is much more subtle. The message sticks in the brain, where it germinates and grows. Thoughts, especially those generated by what we read, a far more powerful, in the end, because they sneak into our minds and stick inside. Every great revolutionary was a reader or writer and understood the power of words to captive or ensnare the masses. Without words, we would have no language and no spoken message."

"But aren't I more powerful, more able to influence others, with what I say?" Rick countered. "Not everyone reads, but everyone can hear."

Garrett grinned to himself and backed up slowly, letting the dialogue develop and grow at its own pace. He wanted to see what a room full of writers would do with this topic.

"The spoken word always has more power than the written word," Karen stated emphatically. "Hitler's *Mein Kampf* is a complete bore to read, but his speeches of hate galvanized a nation to go to war and try to enslave all of Europe."

"Yet all of Hitler's ideas and even his plan for world domination were clearly outlined in his book," Gary interjected. "He wrote down his doctrine of hate first, as written words, to expound his rhetoric."

"Aren't speeches written first?" wondered Tom, one of the quiet ones. "When we speak, we're still using words. What Mr. Brody is trying to convey to us is the inherent power that lies within every word, depending on the order we put them in. This is true for speech writing, screenplay writing, or the great American novel. They all use words, which are the very building blocks of language and thought. The power resides in the word itself, regardless of the media used to present it."

So on went the discussion, back-and-forth, generating a lively, but civil discourse on word usage, sentence structure, vocabulary, technological advances in communication, and even the future of language itself.

Brody monitored the session and made sure everyone had a chance to voice their opinion, before time ran out. As he looked at his watch, he waved his hands over his head. "Okay, let's settle down and wrap this up. That was a great discussion. There were many ideas bounced all over the room and some of them were incredibly valid. However, how many of you wrote it all down?"

No hands went up.

"No one?" Garrett asked, amused.

The students all shook their heads.

"So unless we recorded today's class, all of that energy, creativity, and deep intellectual thought was lost," Garrett said. "What a shame. Perhaps the simple act of transcribing what was said would have captured it for posterity. Consider, if you will, how many words we shared today in communication. Some were powerful and some were not. What made the difference? Think about what transpired between all of us here in this room."

He paused for at least twenty seconds to give them time to reflect.

"Class dismissed," he said then. "Thank you and don't forget to wrap up your editing on your major projects. Manuscripts need to be in their final form soon."

As Jessica and Garret made their way to the parking lot, she was still fired up from the class discussion. "That was fantastic. I never have argued so much over words before. It seems so simple to expound on the powers of speech, but where would we be without words? The challenge is to write what we say with the same influence."

"I am very entertained by such animation," Garrett said. "Your enthusiasm is just bubbling over and is contagious."

She twirled around and squealed with delight. "It's an incredibly beautiful day, I'm in love with an incredibly wonderful man, and I just used my brain so much I have an incredible headache. What more could I ask for?"

Brody shrugged. "An incredible lunch?"

They laughed together and shared an affectionate kiss. Then Garrett drove to his place. Jessica volunteered to feed General Sherman, while he felt motivated to do some editing of the writing he had done earlier in the week.

Then Jessica made a pitcher of iced tea. She carried two glasses into the den, where Garrett was sitting at his computer and gently messaged his shoulders.

"That feels very good," he commented, groaning from the release of muscle tension. "Please don't stop."

She kissed him on the cheek and read some of his work over his shoulder. He didn't seem to mind, but just kept his fingers dancing across the keys.

"How does it come so easily for you?" she asked.

"Grab a chair," he suggested.

Jessica went to the dining room and came back with a straight-back folding chair. She set it to his left and sat down.

"It used to be a real challenge to write," Garrett began. "I had to edit, rewrite, re-edit, over and over. The struggle was irritating at times, but I stuck at it. The only reason it looks effortless now is because I've been doing it for a number of years. I have a basic formula and I just write what comes to me, not worrying about where it goes. Eventually it all comes together and I clean it up."

She took his left hand and played with his fingers. "I sometimes think you came into my life to make sure I finished my book."

He nodded. "Oh, I don't think there's any doubt of that."

Jessica looked at him with wonder in her eyes. "Do you really think so?"

"Yes, I do. Motivation can come from anywhere, but I think our destiny lies together. I have discovered a whole new reason to write and it's because of you."

She rested her chin on his shoulder and kissed his earlobe. "I feel the same way about you. I love you very much and the energy reflects itself in my writing."

Garrett turned around in his chair and pulled Jessica to him, so she could sit on his lap. It was awkward, but the two managed to sip iced tea, smooching every-so-often.

Jessica suddenly jumped up and fetched her briefcase.

"What's up?" Brody asked, surprised by her actions.

"I just remembered I have some research to share with you," she reported.

Garrett immediately spun his chair around and said, "You do? That's awesome. What did you find?"

"Your assignment was to locate all the acronyms that used the letters C A R L and A, in that exact order, right?"

"That's right."

"Well, here they are," Jessica said, handing Brody a sheet of paper. "It's everything I could find, using all the search engines and resources I know of."

"Thank you, Jessica," Garrett said.

With genuine interest, he read the list she had compiled.

The acronyms included:

Center for Advanced Research on Language Acquisition
Combined Altitude Radar Laser Altimeter
Conservation Assets Recreation Lands Assistance
Center for Astrophysical Research in Latin America
Continental Advanced Rapid LADAR Atmospheric
Computer Amplification Repetitive Liquid Access
Corrective Action Reactor Leak Assistance
Chemical Absorbed Remedy Lethal Assessment
Central Atlantic Regional Land Acquisition
&
Computer Assisted Retrieval Los Alamos

The final entry snagged Brody's attention.

"Los Alamos," Garrett said aloud. "It can't be a coincidence, can it?"

"Do you believe in coincidences?" Jessica asked.

He shook his head.

"Me neither."

He put his arms around her and they kissed.

"I sure do like you, Ms. Lawver," he said.

She enjoyed hearing that. "I like you too, Mr. Brody."

"So the plot thickens," he quoted.

Jessica hugged him even tighter. "This is so much fun."

"Even if it entails getting shot at?" he asked pointedly.

She had to think about that. "Well, I guess so. I mean, that's why I have you along, to protect me, isn't it?"

He nodded slowly, but her words once again painted painful reminders of his failure to do that very thing in the past. Perhaps he should drop the whole thing right then and there?

Jessica ran her finger along his furled brow. "Why the scowl?"

"I was just wondering if I should just forget this silly notion that I'm a detective and turn whatever we have over to the authorities?" he answered her.

She looked into his eyes and he didn't look away. When she found what she had been looking for, she smiled. "No, I don't think that would be the right thing to do."

"Why not?"

"Because it wouldn't be right for you. Justice is at stake here and it's your passion."

"Well, one of them."

Then he squeezed her tight butt with both hands.

She squealed with delight and plopped herself in his lap again. "I want to make love on your desk."

"You do?" Garrett was amazed.

"From this moment on, every time you sit here to write, you'll remember a glorious sexual experience on this very spot." She folded her arms, pleased at how undeniably accurate her statement was.

However, as Garrett began to unbutton her blouse, he said, "So, instead of being a very prolific and successful author, I'll be lost in pornographic daydreams."

She giggled and nodded. "I've always wanted to entirely distract a man."

Brody pulled her hair back and licked her neck. "Oh, I can assure you, Ms. Lawver, you're entirely too distracting."

Just as Jessica wished, they started making love right there on his desk. With barely a thought to the mess they were making, Garrett pushed aside all the books and papers he had gathered for his new novel, making space for their shenanigans. Hoisting her up, he plopped her down on her bottom and they kissed in earnest. Everything ended up on the floor, including the laptop, which fortunately managed to land in the wastebasket first, thereby cushioning the fall.

Once again, like a man possessed by some wild animal, Garrett attacked her with sheer abandon. They tore off each other's clothes, while taking time to wrestle and kiss, before Jessica succumbed with a shiver of surrender. Their lovemaking was intense, indeed, but there was no doubt these lovers were sharing deeper emotions than superficial lust or sex could ever express. Each union was another level of commitment, almost religious in nature and binding in intent. So much so, in fact, that Brody made up his mind that their relationship had to grow into a permanent arrangement, whatever definition that entailed.

After regaining their wits about them, they both dressed and adjourned to the kitchen, where Garrett constructed two multilayered Dagwood sandwiches. Jessica looked at hers with amazement.

"How am I supposed to eat this?" she asked, sizing up the mouthwatering target.

"Like this," Garrett replied, lifting his and angling it, opening his mouth wider. Then, quite disgustingly, he took a huge bite.

Jessica started to laugh and just couldn't stop. Pointing at him, she was hysterical with delight. "You look like a hippopotamus."

He couldn't say anything in his defense, of course, for his mouth was too full.

Jessica grabbed a knife from the drawer and cut her sandwich in half.

"That's sacrilege," Garrett protested after swallowing.

"No, it's good manners," she countered. "Besides, I don't want to make a mess."

Brody looked down, saw all sorts of condiments and portions of his sandwich had oozed out, and dropped onto the plate. He grinned. "That's half the fun, picking up the stuff that gets away."

She just shook her head. "I never imagined I could fall in love with such a slob."

After lunch, they cleaned up the kitchen and went out on the back deck for awhile, to soak up the sun and relax, while the meal digested.

"Don't get too comfortable," Garrett warned her.

"Now where are we going?" Jessica asked, fully prepared for another exciting day with Garrett Brody. He never seemed to run out of things to do that were both educational and a lot of fun!

"You'll see," he replied.

True to his word, after about an hour, Garrett opened the door for Jessica and she climbed into his less-flashy four-door sedan. As he backed out of the garage, she was trying to guess where they were going.

"To a museum?" she asked.

"Nope," he replied.

"To a movie?"

"Nope."

"To a restaurant?"

"We just ate, silly."

"To a hotel?"

He shook his head, laughing.

"To the Mall?"

"Nothing that boring."

"Shopping is not boring."

"If you say so."

"Where then?"

"You'll see."

Jessica sat back in her seat with a huff and played idly with her purse strap. "Can't you at least give me a hint?"

"Sure," Garrett replied. "It has to do with book research and weapons."

"Weapons?" she reacted with surprise.

"That's what I said," he replied as he looked over at her and smiled.

Jessica sat quietly, wondering what could possibly be his final destination.

About ten minutes later Brody turned off the main road onto a side street. The drive quickly came to a dead end, but Garrett pulled into a parking lot and turned off the engine.

They were parked outside a gun shop, with an attached indoor/outdoor firing range.

Jessica was not prepared for that. "Here?"

"That's right, because I'm going to teach you how to shoot a gun," he replied.

"You are?" Jessica reacted as they climbed out of the car.

"I might not always be around to protect you, Jessica," Garrett said firmly, while taking her hand. "I want you to be comfortable using a firearm, just in case. Besides, think of what useful knowledge this will be for your future writing endeavors."

She giggled nervously. "Okay, so now I'm supposed to write action, adventure and romance too?"

He shook his head. "No, you leave that genre to me, please. I don't like competition."

Jessica kissed him on the cheek. "Oh, honey, don't worry. I won't endanger your standing with the reading public. I could never associate myself with such edge-of-your-seat suspense, x-rated depravity, and mindless blood and guts."

Then she skirted out of his reach, as he tried to tickle her. Jessica did, however, wait for him at the front door of the gun shop, because she had no intention of entering the store without him. As it was, she was the only female in the place and many heads turned to check her out. The many gawking stares were only confirmation for Garrett as to just how breathtaking she truly was.

Jessica tightly held onto Garrett's arm.

"May I help you, sir?" the store clerk asked.

Brody managed to pull out his wallet, even with Jessica so close, and removed his state firearms registration card, recently renewed in New Mexico. He also had a federal firearms license and permit to carry a concealed weapon. Since Jessica didn't realize the significance of such legal documentation, Garrett decided to skip the explanation until later.

"What are the fees for membership?" Brody asked as he slid the ID's across the counter.

"The initiation fee is one hundred dollars," the clerk replied. "Part of the fee will cover new member orientation and a photo ID badge. The yearly dues are one hundred and fifty dollars. The first year you join, the dues will be prorated for the number of months available for you to shoot that year."

"I want to join as a Full Member and sign this young lady up as an Associate Member," Garrett told the clerk.

"Great!" the man said. "Here are the forms and I'll run your licenses."

"What are the training requirements and benefits for an Associate Member?" Brody asked as he started to fill out the application.

"All new associate members, whether sponsored by a charter member or new member, must attend the new member orientation course and pay seven dollars for the NRA First Steps manual," the man replied. "The associate gets her own photo ID badge and two guest badges, and keys to the gate and clubhouse. The associate can visit the range alone, which means it isn't necessary that she be accompanied by the sponsoring full member."

Garrett passed over his credit card and completed filling out the forms. Jessica quietly stood by, watching, remembering, and learning. She was well aware that many male eyes were sizing her up or undressing her completely. Such scrutiny didn't make her uncomfortable, because she was used to it, but Jessica was still glad Garrett was so obviously capable of handling himself.

The clerk returned with the cards and handed them back. "We're still running the federal ID, since it's pretty important."

"No problem," Brody replied. "I would also like to use the range today, once everything has cleared."

"Of course," the man said.

"I brought my own automatics, but would like to purchase 9mm ammunition for use on your range, if that's okay?"

"You can purchase 9mm reloaded ammo for as low as $7.99 a box."

"Great, I'll take two boxes," Garrett replied. "I have plenty of clips."

Later, as Jessica made sure her ear protectors and goggles were in place, Garrett gently slid a clip into place, chambering a round. He carefully handed the 9mm to her, and then stood directly behind her, lifting Jessica's arms to help her assume the proper firing stance.

"Now sight along here," he spoke loudly so she could hear him. "Aim and when you feel comfortable, just squeeze the trigger."

"Should I close one eye?" she asked.

"Only if it makes it easier for you to line up the target," he replied.

Jessica was very nervous, but also felt Garrett's wonderful body pressed up against her and his strong arms were comforting. Concentrating, she aimed, took a breath and fired.

Blam!

It had a kick, but much less than she expected.

Blam!

Jessica fired again.

Her fear subsided and a bit of confidence developed quickly.

Blam, blam, blam, blam, the shots went off until the clip was expended.

This time Garrett showed her how to eject the empty clip and load in a fresh one. "Only in the movies does someone slam a clip into place, to add that extra sense of drama. It's much safer and easier on the gun to slowly slide it in and out."

She licked her lips and said, "Just like you do."

Her suggestive words made him take a deep breath. "Okay, you temptress, get your mind out of the gutter and back onto shooting."

"Yes, sir," she replied, once again assuming a proper stance.

Blam!

After three full clips, Jessica had the hang of it and Garrett stepped away, so she could do it on her own. The handling of a firearm seemed to come naturally to her, which didn't really surprise Brody. It did, however, come as an eye-opening experience for her. After awhile, she set the 9mm down and flexed her fingers.

"Had enough?" he asked.

Jessica nodded, but carefully passed the automatic over to him and said, "I want to see you shoot."

He hesitated.

"Please?"

"Okay."

Brody slipped in a new clip, chambered a round and took his preferred combat stance. Instead of a stationary target, he flicked the power switch on the shooting station wall. The classic FBI silhouette started coming closer on the pulley. Garrett concentrated for a moment, and then popped off the entire clip in a matter of seconds. He ejected it and slid in another, emptying it as well before the target came to a stop.

Jessica was speechless.

The pattern of bullet holes formed a perforated heart shape in the middle of the target's kill zone. To say the least, Brody's aim was near perfection.

"Let's call it a day, honey," Garrett suggested. "Your hand must be sore."

She merely nodded. There was a quivering sensation of vibrations going up and down her arm, much like after being slammed hard to the mat. While she removed the ear protectors, Garrett gathered up the unused bullets, spare clips and the automatic, making sure the chamber was empty and the safety on. He repacked the 9mm in its padded case, and then offered Jessica his hand.

"Come on, sweetheart," he said. "You've earned an ice cream treat, don't you think?"

"Strawberry," she chirped.

He chuckled and pulled her along.

After stopping for ice cream cones, they headed back to Garrett's place, to relax and discuss her reactions to firing a gun for the first time. While accepting the numbness in her fingers and lingering ache in her elbow would eventually go away, the experience was one she would never forget.

"Well, now you know what it's like to shoot," Garrett stated. "If you ever decide such information belongs in something you write, you won't have to make it up."

Jessica leaned back on the sofa and reflected on her emotional reaction to handling a gun. It was nothing like she had imagined, but neither was it something she couldn't handle. It was just different.

"Thank you for taking me there," she said finally. "I'm not much of a fan of guns, but it was still something quite profound. There was a strange sense of power and the inherent responsibility that goes along with it."

Garrett never ceased to be impressed by where Jessica's mind took her. She was far more astute and mature than her age might suggest, yet so very young in body and spirit. There was no denying that his attraction to her verged on addiction, because she always made him want more and more. Leaning over to her, he kissed the softest and moistest lips he had ever known.

When they parted she said, "I think someone likes me."

"Oh, yes," was all he said.

"So, Mr. Garrett Brody, best-selling author and college lecturer, how did you learn to shoot like that?" Jessica asked. His impressive display had been on her mind ever since leaving the range.

"Lots of practice," he replied.

"Uh, huh," she said.

"You don't believe me?" he asked with faked surprise.

"No, I believe you."

"Then why the look?"

"Because practice isn't explanation enough. There's more to it than that."

Garrett shrugged. "Some practical experience too, of course."

"What's that doubletalk supposed to mean?"

"I've had occasion to use the skills I possess."

Jessica lowered her chin, narrowed her eyes, and raised her eyebrows, just like a school teacher does when they know a pupil is sidestepping the question. "And?"

"And what?" he tried to act innocent. Yet inside he was starting to worry about where this conversation might lead. He wasn't ready to talk to Jessica about certain incidents from his past.

"It's not as simple as that, Garrett," she said. "People don't just learn everything you know from research and you know that."

He nodded.

"You once asked me if you could trust me," Jessica said. "I want you to trust me completely, so here's a perfect opportunity to test me."

"I don't have to test you," he said.

"Well, I think you do," she said.

Garrett was a little taken aback by her defiant attitude, but neither did he think it was wise to argue with her. He could clearly see how important this was to her. "Okay, since you feel so strongly about it, I once had a job that required carrying a gun."

"Is that when you got shot?" Jessica asked, leaning forward with interest and compassion at the same time.

"Yes, in the line of duty."

"Were you in the military?"

"Yes, but that was in my youth. I didn't get shot while in uniform."

"Law enforcement?"

"Sort of."

Jessica sighed. "My, my, we are being evasive."

Garrett sighed too. "I don't mean to be."

"Of course you do," she came back.

He was actually trying to remain cooperative, because there was a part of him that knew Jessica wasn't a threat. Besides, a large part of love was safeguarded with trust. Perhaps he should tell her everything.

"Were you a cop?" she asked.

"No, something a little more covert than that."

"A secret agent?" Jessica asked incredulously.

Garrett laughed. "Goodness no, nothing as glamorous as that!"

"Then what exactly did you do?"

"It's rather complicated to explain."

"Try me."

"It was more along the lines of government research," he said. "I delved into people's lives, or countries, or corporations. It depended on the nature of the mission."

Jessica was taking in every word. She once had been convinced that divulging her secret life as a professional wrestler would cause a stir. In this case, she wasn't sure anything would surprise Garrett Brody.

"So investigating things comes naturally to you?" she surmised.

He smiled. "Yes, it does indeed. I seem to know where to look and instinctively know who to talk to."

"So who did you work for?"

Garrett got up and retrieved the whiskey decanter. "Would you like some?"

Jessica shook her head and waited patiently as he poured himself a healthy measure into his favorite heavy cut-glass tumbler.

Garrett sat down and swirled the brown liquid around, as if he was trying to organize his thoughts for the closing statement at a sensational murder trial.

"What was the question again?" he asked.

Jessica leaned forward and gently pet his forearm. "If this is too difficult for you, we can…"

"No, it's okay, I think," he interrupted. "I just have to get used to talking about something I've spent years trying to forget, that's all."

For the first time since meeting Garrett, Jessica saw vulnerability in him. This revelation came as something of a shock, for while he was a very loving and affectionate man, he had always been very confident and self-assured too, which is why he was so sexy. In this light, he looked more like a little boy, faced with the uncertainties of growing into manhood. Garrett's face was etched with contemplation and doubt. He took another swig of whiskey, set the tumbler down and cleared his throat.

CHAPTER 15

TOO CLOSE FOR COMFORT

"I USED TO WORK for a small government agency nobody has ever heard of," he said finally. "It was housed in a nondescript office building, on a dead-end back street on the North side of Chicago. There weren't very many of us and our work, for the most part, was really nothing more than research."

Jessica held his hand. "But when you think of it, it causes you a great deal of pain, Garrett. I can see it in your eyes and hear it in your voice."

He looked at her and knew exactly why he had fallen in love with her. "Only you would be able to perceive those things. You've gotten very close to me and that gives you insights other people don't have."

"It's also because you wanted me to get close to you," she said. "Otherwise, you could have prevented me from seeing this part of you."

He nodded. "That's true, of course. I love you very much, so I want to share the real me with you."

"Thank you," she said. "I feel very special and needed."

He put his arms around her and they hugged.

When they separated, Jessica felt compelled to ask more questions. "Did Dr. Newman's murder stir up some of these old memories?"

"I think so," Garrett replied. "There's more to his murder than meets the eye."

"But you're not sure why?"

"Not yet."

"But you're going to find out, aren't you?"

"Yes."

"Because it's in your nature."

He nodded.

Jessica smiled suddenly. "This is all going to end up in a book one day, isn't it?"

Brody smiled back. "Of course."

"You will be flattering, won't you?" she asked.

That comment made him laugh. "Even with a thesaurus, there are only so many words I can use to describe how really beautiful you are, Jessica. But I promise to try using them all."

"I didn't mean that," she protested.

"Would you prefer I write about your favorite sexual position and how vocal you are when you have an orgasm?" he asked.

Jessica turned several shades of red. "You wouldn't?"

"Why not? Nobody but you would know it was you."

"But I would know!" Jessica exclaimed.

He put his arms around her and squeezed. "With such passion radiating from you, I think we should make love right now. Otherwise all that spontaneous energy might go to waste."

"You're a wicked, wicked man."

"I suppose you're right."

"The passion I'm feeling is hot, I agree, but it's not exactly sexual at the moment," Jessica stated firmly. "I'm not through with you yet."

Garrett heard the warning bells go off in his mind. There was something about her mannerisms that made him wonder if they were about to talk about things he didn't feel comfortable sharing with her yet. It wasn't a good time to face the darkness. Not enough time had passed since Carla had been...

However, Jessica couldn't resist asking anyway, "So, exactly what kind of research gets you shot?"

He smiled awkwardly. "The dangerous kind."

"You're avoiding my questions again."

"Perhaps."

"Why?"

He shrugged. "I internalize everything."

That statement made her laugh out loud. "Did some shrink tell you that?"

Garrett shook his head. "No, a woman."

He abruptly stood up and just walked away.

Jessica chased after him. "I'm sorry, Garrett. I didn't mean to upset you."

"It's okay," he replied.

"Then may I ask you another personal question?"

"I guess so."

"Why weren't you seeing someone when I met you?" Jessica asked. "I mean, you're a very good-looking man, with money and confidence and a wonderful personality. I'm just amazed that there wasn't some woman already in your life."

Just like before, Garrett rudely moved away from her again, crossing over to the patio doors, which he opened and stepped outside. Jessica, of course, was very surprised by this repeat behavior and didn't know quite what to do. Eventually she followed him outside to stand beside him, but she remained quiet for awhile.

"I keep saying things that hurt your feelings, Garrett," Jessica finally said. "I don't mean to cause you such pain."

He looked over at her and tried to smile. "It's okay, honey. No harm done."

"Did you think my question was unreasonable?"

"No, not at all."

"Well?"

"There was someone before I met you, Jessica," Garrett said slowly, hoping his reply would satisfy her curiosity.

"Oh," she said. "So, what happened?"

Garrett suddenly stood very erect, a serious blackness distorting his face. His dark expression frightened Jessica and she backed away. He came straight at her, however, tight-lipped and furious.

"Do you really want to know what happened?" he demanded, his voice almost vicious.

Barely able to respond, she managed to say, "Not if it makes you so angry."

"Ha!" he snapped. "What do you know about real anger?"

She started to cry. "I'm sorry, Garrett. I didn't mean to pry."

Brody came even closer, his face just inches from hers.

Jessica cringed, now very much afraid of him.

"She's dead!" he shouted. "Murdered before my very eyes."

"Oh, Garrett," Jessica sobbed. "I'm sorry. I didn't know."

Then, in an instant, his rage vanished. Garrett's features softened immediately, his eyes filled with sorrow and compassion. Slowly, he put his arms around Jessica and hugged her. "Shh, it's okay. I'm sorry."

Jessica cried hysterically, holding onto him very tightly. She was so in love with him and his terrible revelation somehow made her feel very inadequate.

And something else.

She was afraid.

Not of what Garrett might be capable of, but what had happened to him in the past. Such a horrible event might have changed him deep down inside.

"I had no right to lose my temper with you over my past," Garrett said. "Please forgive me?"

She just nodded, too emotional to say anything right then. Even with this dark side suddenly exposed, Jessica still felt safe in his arms. There was no rational explanation for her feelings, but she somehow knew his hostility was directed at ghosts, rather than at her.

After awhile they sat together on the sofa. There was an uncomfortable moment of silence, before Garrett spoke. "I haven't made peace with my loss yet, I guess."

"Such a terrible event would be very difficult for me to come to terms with at all, Garrett," Jessica said. "Time is the only thing that will heal such pain. That, and love."

He looked up at her and smiled. "Your love."

She smiled in return. "That's right. I love you very much."

"I know you do," he said.

She wanted to say more, but thought better of it.

However, Brody had sensed her need to talk, so he asked, "Is there something else you'd like to know?"

"I'm almost afraid to ask you anything else," she said.

"I don't blame you," he said. "There's no excuse for acting the way I did. Especially since I'm so in love with you too."

Jessica scooted closer and they kissed. "I've already forgiven you, Garrett. Don't let it dig at you."

"Okay, honey, I won't," Garrett said. "Go ahead and ask. I promise I won't overreact."

"What was her name, if you don't mind me asking?"

"Carla."

"Oh, my God," Jessica reacted.

Garrett nodded. "Yes, it seems the name follows me around."

Jessica took his hands in hers and said, "I know I can't exactly understand your pain, because I've never experienced anything so horrible, thank God. But I can offer you my love, because I can't imagine being more in love with anyone in the world."

He smiled and said, "Thank you. Your loves means everything to me, so I'll gladly accept it and cherish it."

"I'm sorry I was so invasive," she said.

"Curious is a better word," he said. "I once warned you about what happened to the cat."

"Yes, you did."

He pulled her to him and they gently kissed.

Then, quite unexpectedly, Garrett turned the tables on her. "So, **Temptation**, how did you get involved in the world of professional wrestling in the first place?"

"What?" Jessica asked, almost choking on the question.

Garrett looked her straight in the eye and asked, "How does an incredibly gorgeous woman like you, end up in a ring wrestling men twice your size?"

She blushed with embarrassment and asked, "You know?"

He nodded.

"Are you mad at me?" Jessica asked.

He shook his head.

She sighed with relief. "I'm sorry I didn't tell you earlier. I was afraid of how you might react."

"So we both were keeping secrets from each other," he observed.

"But we feel better now that they're out in the open," she said.

They lay back on the couch and Jessica played absentmindedly with his shirt buttons. Garrett savored being with her, quietly and patiently waiting for her to open up her heart and soul.

"I want to know how you got into wrestling?" Garrett asked.

"I watched wrestling on TV and when I read about tryouts for women's wrestling, I showed up," she replied. "At first I was a little skeptical, but then I went for it and I am so happy I did. It has been the most amazing experience of my life. Such a rush and I love the adrenaline I feel in the ring."

"What are your impressions of professional wrestling thus far?" he probed.

"I love it. The training is very grueling, but there is still a lot for me to learn. The fans have been incredible and very supportive. Most people really do not understand the work, both mental and physical that goes into being a wrestler."

"So how do you rise to the occasion for your biggest matches?" he asked.

"Few athletes perform at the same level in major competition as they do during the season. Unfortunately, many athletes tighten up and hold back. Great champions are able to get the most out of themselves when it counts! Champions perform at their optimal level of emotional arousal and do the little things necessary to win the close matches.

"Intense drilling helps me perform instinctively in the heat of battle. I fight for every point in the practice room. This scrambling instinct helps me in matches. I always try to think positively, particularly during the weeks and days leading up to major competition. I visualize myself executing my game plan, winning against my toughest competition and having my hand raised in the Championship Venue as my cheering section cheers. I study videotape of some of my best matches. This helps me visualize and think positively. I also study video of my toughest potential opponents and picture myself implementing the game plan I need to defeat those adversaries."

"Are there any other things you do to prepare for victory?"

"I must get proper rest and nutrition," Jessica replied. I control my weight so I can focus on my performance. I make certain to warm-up properly before matches. This helps prepare my body for battle, while helping reduce anxiety."

"So just how do you propose I should deal with the stereotypes still racing around my head?" Garrett asked.

"I will educate you," Jessica offered.

"Oh, I should like that."

"Do you think you'd enjoy some of my wrestling moves as a prelude to great sex?" she asked coyly.

"Yes, indeed."

"Think again," she said. "I wrestle to win, not to tease. When I throw a man out of the ring, he doesn't come back to me looking for affection."

Garrett grinned. "You could be a little gentler with me, couldn't you?"

"Not likely."

"Then maybe we should square-off sometime and see who comes out on top?" Garrett suggested as he sat up straight.

Jessica knew he was provoking a reaction from her, so she faked a yawn and said, "I will consider your challenge sometime in the future, but until then, you still have a lot to learn about me."

"Then how about this time I interview you?" Garrett requested.

Jessica grinned and kissed him. "I would like that."

"Okay, here we go," he said. "Did you complete any formal professional wrestling training?"

"I train every day with my personal trainer," she replied. "Stephanie is a wonderful instructor and I'm learning more and more every day. I also study a lot of videotapes and ask a lot of questions."

"Do you have any creative control over your character?"
"What character? I am *Temptation*!"

Garrett chuckled, but loved the gleam in her eyes.

"How are women wrestlers perceived in the United States?" he continued.

"I think that more and more people are tuning in to watch women's wrestling," Jessica replied. "Now that we're offering such entertainment, I can't imagine the United States not wanting to watch! The men I compete with and against are incredible, every one of them have great individual abilities, talent and skill. Everyone is so different and offer different things. I really think people would enjoy watching wrestling!"

"How would you describe your wrestling style?"
"I'm fast, high-flying, action-packed and passionate!"

"Should professional wrestlers be viewed as role models?"

"Yes, all athletes should be viewed as role models. Wrestlers go into the ring to compete and win, using their physical and mental strengths. I believe in my abilities, inside and outside of the ring. I try to show that in my wrestling style. I feel that all athletes encompass drive, dedication, and determination."

"What are your career goals?"

"My goals are to continue wrestling for as long as it remains fun, to keep training hard mentally and physically for whatever life brings me. Nevertheless, I also want to explore new things. I have recently fallen in love with a wonderful man and I want to share life with him too."

Garrett smiled. "Thank you."

"You're welcome," Jessica said.

"Should women wrestlers wrestle men?"

"It's obvious that most men have a huge weight and strength advantage over most women, but there are plenty of women who can take on the men!"

"Describe a typical day in your life."

"I used to wake up at around 4:30 am and go straight to the gym by 5:00 and workout until 8:00. I'm usually starving by then, so I eat my first of five meals throughout the day. It might be oatmeal or cream of rice, with six egg whites and all my vitamins. Then I attend my college classes during the day, but head straight for the gym again around 5:00 pm. I try to train until 8:00 pm, but lately I've been distracted and addicted to a man I've fallen in love with, so my regimen is out-of-kilter!"

"Do you have any special words or a message for your fans?"

"Please believe in yourself, anything and everything is possible. Be yourself and don't try to be anyone else, because you're perfect just the way you are. Train hard both mentally and physically and listen to your body!"

Brody scooted closer to her. "I want to make love."

She giggled and said, "Me too."

When they started undressing each other, it was immediately different, for both of them went at each other with needy desperation. It was a form of wrestling, but Jessica wanted Garrett to assume the dominate role and she surrendered to him without much of a struggle.

CHAPTER 16

FACT OR FICTION?

WHAT ROLE DID BRODY's students play when they entered his classroom? How many of them would play the passive learner, expecting the information to flow from his lecture into their notebooks and then their minds? These questions and more were at the forefront every time Garrett began each session.

The primary purpose of Brody's lectures was to transfer information from him to his students, of course. Yet before developing the content of the lecture, he always opened by clearly stating the purpose of each lecture. Garrett described in general terms what he was attempting to teach. It wasn't necessarily in measurable terms, because Brody was looking for creativity, which was different in each application. By contrast, if he had a specific objective, then he was looking for a precise outcome. Depending on what he was trying to accomplish, Brody would assign an objective that demonstrated if the students had learned the content of a lecture.

The classroom was arranged in a U-shape, with tables and chairs for 30 students. This was an ideal format for Brody's group lectures. It allowed him the ability to interact extensively with the students and use a variety of smaller group discussions and various media as well. Best of all, he could easily maneuver throughout the room to engage each student in productive question and answer dialogue.

Garrett commonly asked the students for questions. This gave them an opportunity to clarify their understanding of the content. Then he would ask questions of the students, which were often answered by the same participants, especially Jessica, Rick, and Samantha. Brody made sure that several questions focused on the main points of the lecture. Before ending the session, he used an overhead transparency, computer-generated slide or flipchart to review the key elements discussed.

Brody was convinced the most effective technique he could use to help ensure interaction was to ask and encourage questions. His questions were used to introduce material, stimulate interaction throughout the lecture, and summarize content. Involving students through questioning helped maintain their attention, which was critical when topics were complex.

Garrett usually asked questions of the entire group. He had to guard against some students dominating the discussion, but that hadn't proved to be necessary. Brody always used students' names when asking and answering questions, because this recognition was a powerful motivator. Since the beginning of the semester, most of the class members had actively participated in the discussions and Garrett carefully avoided putting anyone in an embarrassing situation.

However, Garrett also had another intellectual concern.

They were known as perpetual writing students.

Many creative writing courses at universities around the country were known as parties. The problem sets in when the party never ends. Some students went from three years of undergraduate workshops, onto a two-year Masters course, followed by a year hopping around the country, capping it all with a tenured position teaching creative writing, without publishing anything at all.

In Brody's opinion, that was taking a good thing too far.

"Endurance is the key thing," Garrett informed them. "You have to write badly, before you can write well. It's usually impossible to know who will win through in the end, but that shouldn't keep you from trying."

One solitary hand went up.

It belonged to Rick.

"So why do some books get published at all, Mr. Brody?" he asked. "I mean really, some of it is pure shit!"

Garrett couldn't help but laugh. Most of the other students were laughing too.

"It's a business I don't pretend to understand, Rick," Garrett replied finally. "Some of it has to do with the celebrity novel, which has ruined publishing forever. Some famous person decides to write a piece of fiction, and I use that term loosely, which is published, because there's a brand recognition name associated with it. It's just a money-making venture, rather than literature."

"Then why do we struggle to learn how to write, creatively or otherwise?" asked Samantha. "We should go out and become a movie star first, then write our novels."

Laughter.

"No argument with that," Garrett replied.

"All this creative writing stuff," interjected Gary. "It's really not about being creative at all, is it? It's about being marketable."

Brody became very serious and said, "Creative writing gets a bad name, Gary, because some students think they're being experimental, when their fiction is invariably quite conventional. They demonstrate weaknesses with craft, structure, and character. More than once, I've read narratives that profess creativity and are nothing but junk. If I criticize the work, I'm accused of being a stuffed shirt. The industry may churn out hundreds of titles that couldn't pass for toilet paper, but there are still quality writers out there learning the trade and producing art."

Gary wasn't finished. "But Mr. Brody, you can say that, because you've become very wealthy from your writing. I've read your books too and they're very entertaining, but they'd hardly pass as literary masterpieces."

Everyone in the class looked shocked and silence pervaded.

However, Garrett wasn't even fazed. "You're right, Gary. I will never stand with the likes of Hemingway, Twain, Hawthorne, Melville, or Steinbeck. Then I'm not trying to, either. I write what I like to read. Apparently, I write books that many other people like to read as well. Being a best-seller doesn't mean I'm some literary giant, believe me. It means, as you so aptly pointed out, that I'm marketable. However, after awhile, if my books were crap, as Rick suggested, the market would vanish. Readers, for the most part, demand a certain level of quality. I have to keep getting better, or my fans will fade like the wind."

Gary then asked, "So if we want to make a living at this writing game, we should write what we like to read? Is that the bottom line?"

Garrett replied, "Making a living and getting rich are two different things, Gary. You can make a comfortable living doing many things, but the percentages are against writing providing much more than spending money. Very few authors end up making the royalties I've enjoyed and thank God, I've been so blessed. However, I love to write and would continue doing so, if I made only chump change. It's got to be in your heart, Gary, down where it's safe from the naysayer critics of the world."

No other hands went up.

"I must apologize for getting up on my soapbox just now," Brody said. "But Gary and I just had a very important discourse that all of you need to pay attention to. You're young and full of possibilities. That's how it should be. If you think, for one moment, that you're going to make as much money writing, as you would being an accountant, think again! Out of this entire class, one of you, and I mean only one, will probably have a shot at making a living doing this. The rest of you will struggle and most of you will give it up in the end. However, a few of you won't care if you never make a dime from your efforts, because it's part of your soul and has to be expressed. I salute you, for that perseverance will pay off in other ways, even if it's only intrinsic."

"Where do your ideas come from?" asked Gary.

"That's probably the question most commonly asked of authors," Garrett replied. "The answers vary widely."

Samantha asked, "How do your books take shape? Where do you find the plots? Do the characters come to you full blown or do they develop along with the storylines?"

Garrett replied, "They almost always begin with a blip of an idea. Very quickly, I'm thinking about characters. The plotting usually comes to me from my research. Wherever it comes from, it has to grab me, shake me down deep. After all, that energy has to sustain me throughout the arduous process of writing."

"What is the first step you take when you're about to start a new novel?" wondered Sara.

"I ask myself who are these characters?" answered Brody. "Who's the hero, who's the antagonist, and who's the hero interacting with? I try to get a sense of the biography of the people involved. In addition, I generally like to get a strong sense of story before I start, because I like to know where it ends and how it ends before I start to write it. Once I have a basic plot, I start to do research, which could be a little or it could be a lot. *Afterburner* was almost two years of traveling around the world doing research."

"Do you always know how the story is going to end before you start? Does it ever change?" Gary asked.

"I do know how it's going to end, but I often change it before I actually get there," replied Garrett. "When I say that I change it, it's not that something is radically different, but I might arrive at the same feeling in a different way. In *Brazen Chariots*, for example, I didn't know how I was going to end it, but I knew what I wanted to have happen for Katherine and Richard. I knew emotionally and psychologically what sort of feelings they should have, what kind of closure there would be, but I didn't know how I'd get there exactly, until I was almost a third of the way into the story."

"What does researching a novel really entail?" Jessica asked, more for the benefit of her fellow students, because she was intimately aware of how Garrett went about this task.

Brody smiled and said, "Sometimes it's traveling, going to different places, taking a camera, taking pictures of different sites and locations, bringing a video camera, and interviewing people. I often talk to experts or role models for characters I plan to write. I spent a lot of time interviewing US Army Rangers to get a sense of the hero of *Brazen Chariots*."

"How do you get your inspiration for the villain, say for instance, Peter King of *Cross Hairs*?" asked Kim.

"In the case of King, I spent time visualizing someone I truly detested from my past," Garrett replied with an exaggerated scowl. "So in his case, Peter was based on a real person."

"In terms of characters, some authors say that as they're writing the characters, they become real people, and start talking for themselves or speaking for themselves. Is that true for you?"

Garrett nodded emphatically. "I just create the characters and they take over. However, I'm still the boss and they do what I tell them to do, but only to a point. As I write, the characters do become more and more real to me, so the book only works if that happens. I really get into them, think like them, talk like them, play music like them. When I'm writing each person's scene, I create my own little world in which that person exists, so the character comes to life more and more as I'm writing a book, they become more real, but they don't really take over."

"Are your characters generally based on someone specific?" It was Jessica.

"Absolutely," Garrett replied. "In *Time Clock*, every single character was based on people I have known over the years."

"How do you pick the people's names and appearances?" she added.

"I can't write my characters unless I know what they look like," Garrett said. "I often clip out a picture from the newspaper or a magazine of someone who I think is my character. I pin the pictures up behind my desk and stare at the photos until I get a sense of how he or she might act."

"Do you ever go back to a finished book and wish you had changed something?" Rick asked.

"When it's done, it's never truly finished, but only abandoned," Brody replied. "I always feel that I can improve a book."

"What is the most difficult part of the writing process for you?" asked Karen.

Brody contemplated his answer for a moment. "Getting started, I guess. Once I begin writing a book, it accelerates and I become immersed in it, taken over by it. I get up earlier and earlier, often three or four in the morning, and get in two long writing sessions a day. That's the part I love the most, the writing. I also love the research, talking to people, traveling around, finding out how things work, how people do their jobs. I could do that forever. That's a problem, because I get intoxicated by the research. I often have to force myself to stop and get to work."

"What authors and books inspired your writing?" Rick asked.

"The writer who most made me want to write was Alistair MacLean," Garrett replied. "I read MacLean's *Ice Station Zebra* and *Where Eagles Dare* and wanted to write stories like that. Also, Jack Higgins, Hammond Innes, Douglas Reeman, and Clive Cussler are all favorites of mine."

"What is your day-to-day schedule like?" asked Gary.

Now this time Brody had to stretch the truth, for lately, considering his relationship with Jessica, his writing discipline had really suffered a setback. "When a novel is starting to move, I get up earlier and earlier to try to grab several morning hours before the workday starts, or before coming to class. Later I go to my private office and write for another four or five hours. I get up earlier and earlier, until the time I go to bed and the time I wake up almost meet."

"How often do you write with movies in mind?" Sara asked.

"Good question, but a complicated one," Garrett said. "I always write my novels with the thought that they could be made into movies, but Hollywood is so capricious that I don't count on anything. If I wrote a novel that was really just a thicker screenplay, then I'd be creating a deficient book, and there's no guarantee Hollywood would ever buy it or make it."

Jessica signaled Garrett he had run out of time, in fact, he had gone a few minutes past. Looking at his watch, Brody sighed.

"Okay, that's it for today," he announced. "That was certainly a very spirited question-and-answer session. I hope it helped. I'll see you all next time."

As Jessica and Garrett made their way to the faculty parking lot, Brody said, "I've been thinking about something ever since last weekend."

"What is that?" she wondered

"I want to see you in a professional match," he stated.

Jessica squirmed a little. "Are you sure?"

"I'm very sure," he replied. "I want to witness you living your passion. It means a lot to me."

"I'm in a world federation sponsored event being held in the *Salt Palace Convention Center* this Saturday," she announced.

Brody cocked his head and asked, "So exactly when were you going to tell me about this?"

She shrugged. "I don't know."

He tickled her until she scooted away.

"Pack your bags and we'll drive up to Salt Lake this afternoon," Garrett informed her. "It will give you plenty of time to rest before the match."

"Okay, I'd like that," Jessica said, before returning to kiss him. She felt relieved that Garrett had so willingly accepted her passion, while also enjoying his enthusiastic support.

Before packing, Jessica knocked on Amanda's door.

The perky blonde-haired woman opened it wide. "Hey, where have you been? You've got to get ready for Saturday night's match."

"That's why I'm here," Jessica said. "I'm driving up with Garrett."

Amanda didn't say anything for a moment. "So you finally told him?"

"Yes," Jessica replied. "He wants to see a match for himself."

"Good for him," Amanda said.

Amanda's roommate Stephanie came up to the door and said, "Hey, Jess, how are you?"

"She's heading up to Salt Lake with Garrett," Amanda announced.

"Oh," was all Stephanie said.

"I still want you to be there for me," Jessica said, her voice quivering with emotion. "I can't do this without you guys."

Stephanie gave Jessica a big hug. "Don't worry, we'll be there."

Jessica started to cry anyway. "I know I've been a lousy friend since meeting Garrett. I'm sorry. I'm just so in love with him and I'll probably mess it up anyway, besides losing my best friends in the entire world."

"Oh, don't be ridiculous," Amanda protested. "You won't lose us, girl. Besides, we're just jealous, that's all. Garrett is a fabulous guy, so you'd be a fool not to want to be with him all the time. Based on how he treats you, I think you've found the perfect one."

"I sure hope so," Jessica said.

"We'll meet you outside your dressing room." Stephanie stated reassuringly.

Jessica kissed and hugged them both. "Thanks."

Garrett drove from Albuquerque to Flagstaff, Arizona, where they stopped for dinner and then from there on to Salt Lake City, another 500+ miles. Jessica fell asleep and Garrett settled back and enjoyed the drive. There was something about the road and passing headlights that made thinking about his book plot seem natural. When he exited for gas, Jessica stretched and yawned, before giving him a sleepy kiss.

"Are we there yet?" she asked like a child.

He laughed and answered, "No, not yet."

"Would you like me to drive for awhile?" she offered.

"No, that's not necessary," he replied. "I'm enjoying the drive. It gives me lots of time to write in my head, work through plot problems and flesh out characters."

Jessica got out of the car and went to the restroom, while Garrett paid for gas, soft drinks, and munchies. When she returned to the car, Brody was leaning against the Jaguar, waiting for her.

"Did I take too long?" she asked sheepishly.

He shook his head. "No. I just like watching you walk. You move like a cat."

Jessica quietly growled and purred, which solicited a very passionate kiss.

After they were both comfortably seated in the Jaguar, Garrett started the engine again. He pulled out of the gas station, merging with the traffic pattern onto the interstate once again. After a few minutes, when Brody had settled into the rhythm of the highway, Jessica scooted a little closer and rested her head on his shoulder.

"Thank you for doing this," she said quietly. "I can't begin to tell you how much your support means to me."

Her words meant a lot to him too. "I want to see you living your passion."

"Now don't get upset if it looks like I'm getting a thrashing," she warned. "Almost everything in the ring is staged, so if I cry out in horrible pain, I'm just acting."

"Okay, I'll try to remember that," he said.

"Let's talk about something other than wrestling," Jessica said suddenly. "If I spend too much time focusing on it, I might psyche myself out."

Garrett nodded his understanding and changed lanes to pass a slower vehicle. "So how is the rewrite progressing on *Voices in the Wind*?"

She sat up and replied, "I'm almost finished with my final draft."

He could hear the excitement in her voice. "Awesome."

So the couple engaged in a lively conversation about writing and Brody took every opportunity to coach Jessica on how to improve her book. They went back and forth discussing plot, characterization, mood and setting, while hammering out solutions to every question she had regarding her novel. The time just flew by.

The following day, after spending the night in an inexpensive hotel, they reached Salt Lake City. Garrett went straight to the *Salt Palace Convention Center*, but they had arrived ahead of schedule, so Brody paid for admission and found an open parking slot near the main entrance.

"What can I expect when I watch my first professional wrestling match?" Brody asked. "I don't want to act like a fool, or worry needlessly when you get tossed around."

Jessica kissed him very lovingly and whispered, "I love you very much."

He grinned and ran his fingers up and down her long neck.

"Right now I'm a *heel*, which means a bad guy, but tonight I'll officially become a *tweener*, which is wrestling slang for someone in between good and evil," Jessica explained. "Sometime later I'll be forced to choose sides and be labeled a *baby-face*, or good guy."

"Will you change costumes with each personality change?" Garrett asked.

She nodded. "I'm not too thrilled about the baby-face look yet, so I'll make some more changes. I want to still look sexy, so the fans won't be convinced I've become a good guy. They need to doubt my sincerity for awhile."

"I think I know where your naughty streak comes from after all," he observed.

"When I turn up the heat, to pump up the crowd reaction, I give them whatever gets the best response," she went on. "I'm a diva, it's true, but I'm not just eye candy. My fans know I'm a wrestler and I can entertain them with some pretty awesome moves."

"So what do they like best?" Garrett asked.

She wiggled her butt in the car seat. "My tight ass, of course. I just climb up on the ropes, bend over so they can all get an eye full and shake it. It's usually enough."

"Will I get to see that tonight?" he asked with barely controlled anticipation.

Jessica grinned. "Of course."

He looked at his watch. "You better get going, honey. You said you wanted plenty of time to prepare."

She kissed him again. "Make sure you go to the Special Events window and ask for your ringside seat. It will be under your name. I love you."

She opened the door and climbed out, skipping off towards the security entrance, where she showed her identification for admittance. Garrett waved. He was nervous, more about what his reaction would be to Jessica's wrestling, than anything else. Brody just didn't want to act like an idiot. He would be jealous enough just imagining what all those fans were thinking, so he had every intention of concentrating on the show and ignoring the rest.

At least that's what he kept telling himself.

In truth, he was also worried about how he would react if it even appeared she was hurt. Sure, the entire match was scripted and her falls were choreographed in advance, but much of it was impromptu as well. Garrett just didn't know what to expect and that lack of knowledge made him uncomfortable, because in the past he would never have gone into any situation without as much information as possible.

About an hour later, Brody went to the ticket booth and received his ringside seat assignment. He made his way along with throngs of fans, slightly dazed and amazed. He had never experienced professional wrestling before and the sights and sounds were as alien to him as the backside of the moon. Jessica's match was the main event, so Garret had to sit through several secondary or minor contests before he would see *Temptation*.

Jessica had a new costume to show off for this event and she couldn't wait to appear before the crowd sporting yet another provocative look. Besides, she wanted *Temptation* to dazzle Garrett Brody.

Just before the start of the main event, *Temptation* was waiting in the gorilla position, the staging area just backstage of the entrance curtain. Jessica was more nervous than usual, but she was well aware of the cause. The man she loved and adored would be in the audience tonight.

"There you are," Amanda called out from behind her.

Jessica spun around and ran to her two friends, hugging them both. "Oh, I'm so glad you're here. I was beginning to fret."

"Is he here?" Stephanie asked expectantly.

"Ringside," Jessica replied. "I already peeked to make sure."

Her friends seemed pleased. They each kissed Jessica and started the usual motivational pep talk. Amanda made certain *Temptation* was suitably attired, while Stephanie went over the game plan once again.

"They're gunning for you tonight," her trainer said. "Stay clear of *Ajax* and don't get boxed in. He's a cheap-shot artist and isn't too thrilled about losing to you, so he's going to make you work for it. Just don't let up. Keep your eye on his bimbo partner too, because *Nails* will try to sneak up on you and score a few nasty hits of her own."

"I know," Jessica said.

"We brought you something to really put you over the edge," Amanda announced, lifting up a big box with lots of air holes punched in the lid.

"What's inside?" Jessica wondered a little squeamishly, realizing it must contain something living.

"A prop that will really enhance your image," Stephanie said. "Open it."

Garrett was uncomfortable in his seat and was aware of how out-of-touch he was in certain regards. The fans all around him were from every walk-of-life he could imagine. There were little old ladies screaming and huge truck drivers who perhaps should have been in the ring. There were clean-cut professional types, minus their briefcases, along with entire families, and trashy females with surgically enhanced bodies and multiple body piercings, who were known as Ring Rats, female fans who frequented wrestling events to flirt or pursue sexual liaisons with wrestlers. Then there were scores of adolescent teenage boys holding placards and chanting.

In that very awkward moment, Brody realized he was acutely jealous, for most of them were clamoring for the woman he knew as Jessica Lawver. Except her wrestling persona was simply *Temptation*.

The lights dimmed and spotlights floated all throughout the arena. Camera light bulbs began flashing as soon as the far curtain parted. Out stepped one woman and the reaction was spontaneous and loud.

Jessica's latest outfit was a shimmering green, snakeskin patterned bustier and thong, with matching boots that went up past her knees. Slithering over her shoulders was a real snake, which wrapped itself around her left arm, head bobbing up and down, tongue whisking out in reptilian defiance.

Suddenly the snake reared back its head and hissed.

The crowd went wild.

There was no need for canned heat, when cheers or boos were pumped into the arena via the sound system, because the woman's seductive and suggestive entrance caused plenty of reaction as it was.

Imitating her snake companion, Jessica hissed too.

"*Temptation's* a heel now, but she wants to be a baby-face, just another evil woman torn by her inner self," the man next to Garrett shouted over the din. "You can just feel the good in her trying to get out."

Garrett looked over at the middle-aged, balding gentleman with utter amazement, for there were tears in his eyes and he was seriously involved in the action unfolding. According to Jessica, this person was a mark, or a fan who believed wrestling matches were real.

Perhaps if Jessica hadn't told Garrett that her entire match was a worked shoot, which meant most of the action was part of a scripted segment that took place in the show, with elements of reality thrown in, he would have fallen for it too. On top of that, the smart fans were meant to believe that everything was contrived, but many of Jessica's moves were unrehearsed to deliver an added element of surprise.

She continued up to the center ring, where she handed the snake over to her trainer. *Temptation* held the python up over her head, encouraging the crowd to express their delight even more.

Jessica went to the center of the ring and waited for her opponents.

The speakers rumbled and suddenly the arena vibrated with the throbbing rhythm of drums and bass guitars. Her challengers were about to arrive.

Their entrance was just as flashy, but since they were supposedly the good guys, *Nails* and *Ajax* wore red, white and blue and looked squeaky clean, with their matching platinum-blonde hair. *Temptation's* rivals entered the ring and acknowledged the crowd's cheering and applause. They were the obvious favorites.

Then *Ajax* and *Nails* began circling around their quarry, hoping to catch *Temptation* off guard. Jessica passed her snake over the ropes to Stephanie.

Temptation was ready for the opening siren, coiled and ready.

The deafening wailing cry of the starting signal made Garrett jump in his seat.

Jessica didn't let her opponents hang out with their backs to the line very long. Nothing good would develop if *Temptation* was forced to chase them, so she acted bored and bent over to tie the laces on her hip-hugger black-leather boots. Right on cue, she wiggled her very shapely bottom at the crowd in Garrett's section.

The thong cut to her outfit left very little to the imagination and the audience, even the women, cheered, whistled, and showed their appreciation for *Temptation's* physical endowments. For while ½ of the arena was marveling her heart-shaped tight ass, the other half was getting an eyeful of ample cleavage.

Nails acted horrified and tried to appeal to the crowd's more puritanical nature.

If there was any.

Which apparently there was not.

A tremendous series of boos echoed throughout the stands and suddenly loud chanting reverberated everywhere. "*Temptation, Temptation, Temptation!*"

Ajax, who had been slowly working his way closer and closer to *Temptation*, had abruptly cut the angle and then charged. The maneuver completely caught Jessica off guard.

At least that was supposed to be the way it looked.

Ajax hoisted *Temptation* off the mat, so she was laying stomach first across his shoulders, known as the Standing Fireman's Carry. *Ajax* then released Jessica's head and pushed her body out so she was 90 degrees to where she was previously. Then *Ajax* fell backwards so Jessica landed on her face and chest.

A thunderous roar of shock filled the center, as most of the fans were entirely unprepared for this disastrous turn of events.

Temptation regained her feet, but *Ajax* then ran and slid feet first at Jessica. He popped up and locked his ankles around *Temptation's* neck. *Ajax* pushed his body off the apron and fell forward, somersaulting onto his back and throwing Jessica clear over the ropes. She took a very hard bump, going right through one of the ringside announcer's tables!

Garrett came to his feet and started to move in that direction.

Both Amanda and Stephanie saw him coming.

Yet suddenly Brody halted.

Fighting every internal voice screaming for him to make sure Jessica was okay, he eventually retreated to his chair.

Stephanie looked at Amanda. "Wow, that sure took a lot of willpower."

Mandy nodded and smiled. "I don't think he's the typical guy, Steph."

Jessica managed to escape from the shattered pieces of the long table and scooted back onto the mat, while *Ajax* was marching around cajoling a reaction from the crowd. *Nails* was all over him in a display of barely-acceptable sexual innuendo.

Like a bolt of lighting *Temptation* counterattacked, lifting *Ajax* up so he was laying stomach first across her shoulders. Jessica pushed her victim up and over her head and dropped him stomach first across her knee.

As *Ajax* grunted and rolled onto his back, *Temptation* grabbed both his ankles and started to spin. The momentum lifted him off the mat as he was spun around by his legs. Jessica suddenly launched him out of the ring.

Then *Nails* set upon *Temptation*, jumping on Jessica's back and pulling her hair.

Jessica yanked *Nails* over her shoulder and as the other woman wrestler landed badly, *Temptation* applied a standing head scissors on *Nails*. *Temptation* jumped up in the air and landed on her feet with her victim's head still in the scissor lock.

Through all of this, Garrett could barely watch the action, much less enjoy what tremendous choreography was taking place. To appreciate the physical conditioning and sense of timing required executing some of these flawless moves, Brody needed to become emotionally unattached, and that was never going to happen. Swept up in the acting, he cringed with each blow and grimaced with every counter-move.

Add to that, *Temptation* was the recipient of some questionable referee interference, which distracted Garrett completely. Still, logic dictated that these bad calls were all part of the story as well.

The battle went back and forth, neither side gaining a clear advantage, but with every stunning feat of derring-do, the crowd was obviously growing more partial to Jessica.

Suddenly, the conflict turned on a single move, as *Temptation* clapped her hands around *Ajax's* head to break away from the dreaded Chin-lock and Arm-lock holds he had meant to disable her for a pin. Spinning away from his powerful grip, Jessica scratched down his back with their long fingernails.

Ajax cried out like a whipped animal.

"Something I learned from your ho," Jessica cried out, pointing at *Nails*.

The crowd went wild, screaming and applauding, mixed with general pandemonium. It was professional wrestling at its most contrived and most dramatic.

Ajax staggered and propped himself up in the corner, trying to catch his breath and regain some strength. *Temptation* was not about the wait for this to happen. She charged and ran up the outside ropes, but as she reached the top, kicked *Ajax* in the chest, while performing a back flip to land on her feet. She quickly delivered a series of body blows that staggered Ajax and he fell to his knees.

While her male opponent was down, Jessica performed a cartwheel towards *Nails*, hitting the woman in the head with the side of her foot as it came up in the air. *Temptation* cried out in victory, as the blow apparently knocked *Nails* unconscious.

Jessica slid to land on top of the sprawled form of *Nails* and pinned her easily, waiting the mandatory count of three. Suddenly vaulting to her feet, *Temptation* barely avoided a vicious counterattack by *Ajax*.

Yet one opponent was out of the way!

Garrett just shook his head in wonder, never imagining the woman he loved could put on such a display, much less so convincingly. It was violent theatre, staged to be convincing, while entirely impossible.

Jessica warily eyed *Ajax*, spitting and hissing like a corned snake.

It was obvious that the climax had arrived. It was time for one of them to lose. The man and woman circled like two predators waiting for the perfect opportunity to pounce. When it came, the final combat was bound to be spectacular. In fact, wrestling fans demanded it.

Temptation ran, vaulted, somersaulted and jumped high to land so her legs were over *Ajax's* shoulders. He fell backwards and Jessica ended up sitting down on his chest, where she grabbed his hair and twisted, hissing loudly.

To avoid the incredible pain Jessica was pretending to inflict, *Ajax* flopped over on his stomach on the mat. *Temptation* grabbed him under the chin and performed a forward flip, wrenching the neck back. The audio special-effects people behind stage added the horrible cracking sound.

Temptation stood up and raised her hands in triumph.

Then Jessica dropped her body across the supposedly unconscious *Ajax*. She wiggled her butt up in the air for the crowd.

Then *Temptation* pinned *Ajax* with ease.

The match was over!

As ***Temptation*** exited the ring victoriously, two famous professional wrestling TV and radio announcers, Devin Knight and Eric Gold, who were looking for an impromptu interview, immediately approached her.

"What a match!" Devin shouted over the crowd noise as he moved to block Jessica's path. "You were incredible."

"Thank you," ***Temptation*** spoke into the handheld microphone, while still trying to catch her breath after all the physical exertion.

"That was a brutal contest," Eric observed.

"It was becoming very intense, which has been showing up in our matches lately," she agreed. "We really were trying to beat each other silly."

"It was as nasty a fight as I've ever seen," Devin commented.

"No cat-fighting, that's for sure," Jessica said. "It was just a solid wrestling match with great intensity."

"You are right about the intensity going through the roof," Eric observed. "You are becoming a wicked woman out there."

"That's why they call me ***Temptation***, Eric," Jessica purred. "I'm so hot men are willing to go to their own destruction just to touch me."

The crowd roared their approval.

Devin winced when he recalled how the match had started, because of the opening slam Jessica took was that stiff. "I thought you were dead after ***Ajax*** caught you early."

"It hurt, believe me," Jessica said, turning to show them the nasty bruise that was already purple along her left hip. "He meant to put me out right away."

"But ***Temptation*** bounced back and punished ***Ajax*** for the rest of the match," Eric observed.

"I knew I had to keep him occupied," Jessica said.

"What about ***Nails***?" Devin asked, inching the microphone closer to Jessica's mouth. "She wanted to kill you."

"I think I'm too trusting sometimes," Jessica said. "I earned my card, and that was that. ***Nails*** deserved a gentle reminder that good girls finish last."

"We've heard a lot lately about some of your fellow female wrestlers being jealous that you're one hot babe who can beat up the men?" the interviewer pressed this line of questioning.

"You're really looking to get my butt kicked the next time I walk into that locker room, aren't you Devin?" laughed Jessica. "Look, at first, the respect factor I got from the other babes wasn't very high. However, after

I went through the developmental program, and started honing my skills and building a style, then I started getting the respect I deserved. The locker room has changed from what it was just six months ago. It's just awesome now. It's like a slumber party with friends who..."

"What?" interrupted the interviewer. "Tell us more!"

"Let's leave that thought work on your imaginations, okay?" Jessica laughed.

The two men also laughed, right along with the audience, none of which had left the arena yet. There were other matches yet to come.

"Saying all that, being both strong and feminine, *Temptation* is the one who will make more women fans tune in to watch pro wrestling," Devin said. "Do you agree?"

"That's right," Jessica agreed.

"Have you ever considered doing a men's magazine shoot?" Eric asked. "You've got a fantastic body."

"You never know," replied Jessica. "If my manager thinks it's a good idea, well, I'm very open-minded, and proud of my physique."

"It's getting hot in here!" Devin shouted over all the background noise.

"Hey, it's tough trying not to sweat and keep your makeup from running," Jessica laughed.

"You heard it here first, fans," Eric announced over the mike. "*Temptation* has just agreed to pose. Let's let her know how many of us would buy that issue."

A thunderous roar rose up from the center's stands.

Devin grinned. "There you have it, *Temptation*. Your fans have spoken."

Jessica couldn't help but blush, while wondering what Garrett was thinking just then. She waved to the crowd, but didn't say anything. It would be up to her man to decide if it was okay to pose in anything less than a bikini.

"So where do you think women are headed in wrestling?" Eric continued the impromptu live interview.

"The level of intensity is climbing and it's going to get a lot more physical, and not just in the hair-pulling, rolling around on the mat kind of physical," she replied. "I want the bouts to look more like the men's bouts, with that level of physicality and intensity. I'm not just some babe in high heels, because I can kick most men's asses!"

"That's obvious," Devin said. "Thanks for stopping to talk and good luck on your next match in Rosemont, Illinois."

"I'll see you there," Jessica replied, heading toward the locker rooms, waving to the enthusiastic crowd.

Two hours later, Jessica Lawver emerged, no longer playing the part of *Temptation*, but escorted by her two friends, Amanda and Stephanie. As the three women crossed the parking lot, only one car yet remained, a green Jaguar XJS. Garrett was leaning against the automobile, but stood up straight as soon as he spotted them coming. Suddenly Jessica broke away from the other two and scampered across the blacktop, to throw herself into Brody's open arms. They kissed for a long time.

Finally, she stepped back, panting from the passionate exchange. On the one hand, she was blushing from embarrassment, while still very turned on by how much she wanted to make love. Instead, Jessica grabbed Stephanie's hand and pulled her closer.

"Garrett, you've already met Amanda, but this is my other good friend and personal fitness trainer, Stephanie Patterson," Jessica introduced them.

After a little wave to Mandy, Brody shook the other woman's hand. "It's a pleasure to meet you."

Stephanie said, "I couldn't help but notice your reactions during Jessica's match, Mr. Brody. I was not only impressed that you could handle what was going on in the ring, but you also seemed capable of handling all the banter outside the ring as well."

Garrett shrugged. "I'm not sure how I managed to do it, really. I have very strong feelings for Jessica and it was a struggle not to get involved. In the end, however, I didn't want to do anything that might reflect negatively on her chosen passion. I just had to accept that this is what she wants to do and embrace it. She's obviously capable enough to look out for herself and doesn't need some overly-macho boyfriend trying to rescue her from the nasty bad guys."

Everyone laughed together.

"Would everyone like to go somewhere and have a drink to celebrate Jessica's very impressive victory?" Garrett then asked.

His offer was enthusiastically accepted and the women all climbed into Brody's car, Jessica sitting up front, of course. Garrett drove across the valley and into the mountains, for his final destination was Park City. It only took about 40 minutes to cover the 31 miles to the famous ski resort.

Miraculously, he found an open parking place on Main Street and the four of them went into the *No Name Saloon*.

Everyone ordered drinks and Jessica selected a huge Porterhouse steak, grilled medium-rare, for she had worked up quite an appetite. Besides, fully aware that she couldn't eat all of it, it was her intention to share bites with Garrett.

The conversation was very warm and friendly, as if everyone had known each other for years. While Garrett tried to focus on Jessica's talents in the ring, the three women kept steering the topic towards Brody's books and especially the movies based on his best-selling novels.

Jessica beamed with affection and admiration, for she knew a great deal about the famous author, perhaps more than anyone else in the world. It was easy for her to brag about him, while trying not to embarrass him either.

"How do you come up with your character's names?" Amanda inquired.

"Most of them come from real people I've known," he answered.

"Does the name have significance to the story?" Jessica wondered.

"Indeed," he replied. "Names are not just given by chance."

"What do you mean?" Amanda asked.

"I'm convinced that first names hold special meaning and are clues to behavior and personality," he explained.

Jessica seemed quite intrigued, but rather than focus Brody's attention just on her, she said, "Tell us what you think the name Stephanie stands for."

"Stephanie comes from Greek and means crowned," Garrett spoke from memory. "You must be of noble birth from a far away land, where flowers blossom and horses gallop like the wind. You hold yourself with regal elegance and your stance communicates the willingness to seek out that which life has to offer. I imagine that you will succeed at everything you put your mind to, all the while in no hurry. That power resides in your name as well, for like a great piece of art, Stephanie expresses more than the eye can see."

None of the women said anything, but stared at the speaker.

"Jessica told me you were a writer, but I never imagined you would have such a gift with words," Stephanie said.

Garrett shrugged. "I am fascinated by the history surrounding names and since I think all forms of successful communication originate with the effective use of words, I do my very best to select the proper ones."

"I don't think there's any doubt of that," Amanda interjected. "Your description of Stephanie was quite beautiful, as well as accurate."

"So what does the name Jessica mean?" Stephanie then asked.

"The Hebrew translation means a woman who sees," Garrett replied without hesitation, looking directly into the eyes of the woman he loved. "Shakespeare wrote that Jessica was a woman of wealth, much blessed by God, a precious gem with character and color and vibrancy. She always stands out and is measured by her convictions. Her beauty is more than physical, but emanates from the very center of her soul, where passion and truth reside. She is independent, headstrong at times, but very compassionate and tender too, with a great capacity for love."

"Wow," Amanda spoke up as soon as he had finished. "Tell us what Amanda means, please?"

They all chuckled again.

"Amanda is Latin in origin and means lovable," Garrett answered.

"How can you possibly know these things off the top of your head?" Stephanie demanded.

A sly smile crossed Brody's face and he said, "I cannot tell a lie. I looked up the meanings for the names Amanda and Stephanie, shortly after Jessica told me who her friends were. I like to be prepared."

He received a punch in the arm from Jessica, while the other two women laughed hysterically.

"Well, at least I confessed," he said in defense.

The evening's festivities continued into the wee small hours of the morning, as Garrett entertained his guests with humor, stories and dessert. When last call was announced, Brody made certain everybody's glass was full.

"Here's to **Temptation**," Garrett toasted. "May she forever rule the ring, master the males, and leave the crowd breathless with admiration and desire."

"Here, here," the women replied in unison.

Then, as if by cue, they all yawned.

"It's been a very long day," Amanda commented.

Rather than traveling back to Albuquerque that night, Garrett suggested they all spend the night in Park City. In spite of their attempts to refuse his generosity, Brody paid for rooms for Amanda and Stephanie, while Jessica remained with him.

Once in their hotel room, Garrett and Jessica kissed for a long, long time, making their way to the shower, where they made love under the steaming hot water. After that, the lovers climbed under the cool, clean sheets and snuggled.

Garrett held her very close and ran his fingers through Jessica's luxurious black hair, whispering his love. In a matter of minutes, she fell asleep, not only exhausted by the wrestling match, but also very relaxed by Garrett's gentle affection.

Her head lay on his chest and Garrett too was very content. It seemed as if they didn't have a worry in the world.

In fact, nothing could have been further from the truth.

CHAPTER 17

COVERT AGENDA

THE DIRECTOR OF THE University of New Mexico's English department, Dr. Cynthia *Wolf's Robe* Mendez, welcomed Brody into her office. "Come on in, Garrett. I so look forward to our meetings."

"Thank you, Dr. Mendez," he said. "I truly appreciate the time you spend with me."

Cynthia pointed to an open chair. "Make yourself comfortable. So how are things? Do you enjoy teaching as much as your students enjoy your class? I've received a great number of enthusiastic reports about your teaching and how much they're learning."

Brody smiled as he sat down, but it was obvious that something serious was on his mind.

Dr. Mendez noticed immediately. "What's wrong, Garrett?"

Brody sighed heavily and looked up at the ceiling for a minute to collect his thoughts. "I'm afraid I might be in a spot of trouble and I'd like to resign my guest lecturer position, before I bring discredit on the University."

Even though his pronouncement shocked the director, she remained calm on the outside. Dr. Mendez didn't say anything at first, but studied the man sitting before her.

Then she asked, "What's this really all about, Garrett?"

He wondered if he should lie and use his torrid romance with Jessica as an excuse. After all, he was having an intimate sexual relationship with a student and she was significantly younger than he was. In the end, however, Garrett knew he could never lay the blame at Jessica's feet, because he had fallen deeply in love with her and had serious plans for their future together.

"As you're aware, while backpacking in Bandelier National Monument, along with Professors Todd Everett and Alice Coleman, we came upon a man who had been murdered," he recounted.

Dr. Mendez nodded. "Yes, I'm sure it was difficult to come to terms with."

"Well, I believe I'm onto something that has the potential of creating bad publicity for the University and I don't want to do that," Garrett said.

Cynthia Mendez leaned back in her chair and smiled. "When I first met you, Garrett Brody, you were lecturing at the American Booksellers Association National Convention in Chicago. Do you remember that?"

"Yes, I remember fondly."

"You were promoting *Afterburner* and the entire presentation was about the author's responsibility to be passionate about his craft," Dr. Mendez continued. "After your session closed, I knew I wanted to invite you to lecture at the University of New Mexico. Do you know why?"

"Only what you told me at the time," Brody replied.

"Well, beyond what I told you, it was because of your overwhelming desire to seek justice," she said. "Your books are not just entertaining novels full of violence, edge-of-your-seat action and hot sex."

In spite of himself, Garrett blushed, but managed to say, "I think my publisher prefers the terms action, adventure, and romance."

They both laughed.

"No matter what words one might choose to describe the genre, there is always an underlying message in every one of your books," Dr. Mendez went on. "You are an advocate of change, as you hold up for examination some of the historical injustices that haunt this nation and the world to this day."

"I should get you to write advertising copy for me," Garrett interjected. "But seriously, thank you. Such remarks from you are incredibly important to me."

She waved him off. "So if you're onto something, then it's probably quite important. If your research uncovers some miscarriage of justice or you uncover who committed the murder, how can anyone hold you in judgment?"

"I might be up against the Federal Government," he cautioned.

She clapped. "Well, bravo then. I cannot think of any institution that needs your style of attention more. The bigger they are, the harder they fall and perhaps it will do the public good to know that their government isn't always looking out for the best interests of the many, but instead the pocketbooks of the few."

Brody's eyes were wide and he had to refrain from applauding as well. Then his eyes narrowed and he asked, "You're not planning on running for public office, are you? If you are, I'll be very disappointed."

She emphatically shook her head. "Not on your life."

"Good," he said.

"So, in conclusion, I will not accept your resignation," Dr. Mendez stated. "I supported bringing you here in the first place and if you happen to create headlines, then a little excitement will only reflect well on the University. We've never been very conservative down here, so you'll just be another crazy liberal to many."

Brody stood up and offered his hand. "Thank you, Cynthia. I'm truly honored to be a part of this school and to have gained your confidence and support."

Dr. Mendez came to her feet and shook hands with him, saying, "We're just as thrilled to have you here, Garrett Brody."

He turned to leave, but never reached the door.

"So, are you going to tell me how I can help you?"

Brody turned around slowly and looked at her.

"I know a lot of influential people in New Mexico," she said.

Garrett suspected that was the truth and said, "I'd like to talk to someone with the Navajo Nation, Cynthia. Someone who won't just think I'm another white man out to screw them."

Dr. Mendez considered his request for a few seconds, before she replied, "I will arrange a meeting for you this afternoon, if that's okay?"

Brody nodded.

"His name is Diego Ruiz and he's pure Navajo," she added. "However, I should warn you. Once you've been seen talking to him, you'll be on somebody's list."

Garrett liked the sound of that. "Excellent."

"Why are you in such a hurry to leave?" Dr. Mendez then asked.

Brody immediately felt uneasy, coming back to the chair he had been sitting in. "I'm not really, I just thought…"

"Well, there's something else I need to talk to you about," she said quite seriously.

He sat down and looked at her, but his stomach was doing summersaults.

"I received your letter regarding your selection for a research assistant," Dr. Mendez said. "It seems that you're not the only one who wants Jessica Lawver."

While Garrett's stomach settled down a little, he also had to be careful how he handled this situation. "Well, I guess I could find somebody else, but Ms. Lawver has some very credible research capabilities and is a pretty gifted writer in her own right."

Cynthia's eyebrows went up. "I detect a note of respect in your voice, Garrett."

He nodded. "Jessica is going to be a published author one day. She's a voice that needs to be heard."

Dr. Mendez saw something else, but instead of asking a possibly embarrassing question that might cause hard feelings, she said, "I do have to consider certain political ramifications regarding Ms. Lawver's availability in this regard. Professor Strong has also submitted his choice for Ms. Lawver as his assistant, so I must weigh the pros and cons."

Brody felt his blood pressure elevate a little. "Oh, I see. The tenured professional gets his choice, because the other guy just makes millions of dollars writing cheap action novels?"

Dr. Mendez pushed back her chair again and took off her glasses. "I don't like what you're insinuating, Mr. Brody."

Garrett sighed, rubbed his forehead and said, "I'm sorry. You'll do whatever you think is best for Ms. Lawver and for the University. Forget what I said just now."

Cynthia had been carefully studying the man seated before her. Certain signs were starting to paint a picture, leading to the same conclusion Dr. Mendez had tried to avoid earlier. "Garrett, there's something more to this than meets the eye. You are never this passionate about anything, unless you really care."

He looked up. "I do care."

"That's obvious," Cynthia said. "However, what concerns me is who or what you care about. I think you have some very strong personal feelings for Ms. Lawver."

He didn't answer her.

His silence confirmed her suspicions after all.

"So, how long had this been going on?" she asked.

"Since the first day of class, actually," he replied.

Cynthia frowned. "Well, of all the men in my department, I least expected such behavior from you!"

"I've fallen in love with her," Brody said.

Dr. Mendez opened her mouth, but then snapped it shut. She could see the sincerity in his eyes and heard the dedication in his voice. "I see."

"Actually, when the opportunity is right, I plan to ask Jessica to marry me," he went on. "If she'll have me?"

Dr. Mendez shook her head in wonder. "No woman in her right mind would turn down such an offer, Garrett. You're dynamic, good-looking, masculine, compassionate, and quite wealthy. Not to mention that you're a best-selling author and passionate about everything you do. That poor woman never had a chance."

Brody tried to smile. "Now that you know, are you sure you won't accept my resignation after all?"

"There are all sort of issues involved here, Garrett," Dr. Mendez said. "And I'm not just talking about ethics. I imagine that affairs between professors and students go on all the time, right under my nose. Yet this is different. You're a guest lecturer and can terminate your contract for any reason. You aren't seeking tenure and I suspect you would hardly even notice if your salary from the University suddenly vanished."

"That's not true," he replied. "It's far more consistent than royalty checks, no matter how big they are."

"So if I approve your request for Ms. Lawver as your research assistant and your relationship becomes public knowledge, I might be accused of favoritism," Dr. Mendez stated. "If instead I assign her to Professor Strong, I might be getting in the way of a serious romantic relationship."

Brody shook his head. "No, Cynthia, I don't want you to do anything based on my needs, or Professor Strong's, for that matter. I want you to decide for Jessica's benefit, since she has the most to gain or lose."

"She's a Professional Writing major," Dr. Mendez said after glancing at Jessica's file again. "To be honest, she would benefit from an association with either of you."

Garrett leaned forward. "I'd like to suggest that you interview Ms. Lawver regarding both offers. The professor and I have outlined the required duties and expectations of our specific research projects, so let Jessica decide."

"She'll be biased on your behalf," Dr. Mendez objected.

"I don't think so," Brody countered. "Ms. Lawver isn't your typical star-struck coed, in spite of her incredible good looks. She's serious about her education and even more serious about her future. I think she'll make the choice that benefits her most, from every possible angle."

"Very well, Mr. Brody, I think I'll pursue your advice," Dr. Mendez said.

Garrett stood up. "Well, that's settled then."

Cynthia Mendez offered her hand again. "You better do right by that woman, Garrett, or we'll have a meeting of a different kind."

Brody smiled and nodded as he said, "I'm very much in love with Jessica, Dr. Mendez. I would do anything for her."

As Garrett left the English Department building, he was quite concerned about whether he handled that delicate situation effectively. Now it was up to Jessica to make her choice.

About two hours later Brody met up with Jessica at her apartment. She made it clear that her preference was to spend the rest of the afternoon at his place.

"We really didn't get much of an opportunity to talk about all your reactions to the wrestling match," Jessica said as he drove.

"You were simply amazing," Brody said emphatically. "I have never been to a professional wrestling match in my life and to watch you, the woman I love, execute some of those moves, was just plain incredible. It was very difficult at first, because I wanted to rescue you from the bad guys, but later I accepted that you could take care of yourself. I managed to enjoy myself by the time you pinned nasty old *Ajax*."

"You really did like it, didn't you?" she asked with delight. "I can see the excitement in your eyes and hear it in your voice."

"I'm not kidding, Jessica," Garrett said. "My throat is still sore from shouting and I've never seen such athletic prowess before from a man, much less a woman. That backward double flip and twisty summersault thing with the cartwheel was breathtaking."

Jessica was convinced. "You're so cute."

At the traffic signal, she leaned over and they kissed.

"Would you ever consider using some of those moves on me?" Garrett asked after they parted.

Jessica said, "If you ever truly misbehave, I'll kick your ass."

"I promise I'll be good."

"Not too good, mind you."

They both laughed as he pulled into the driveway of his condominium.

As they climbed out of the car and made their way through the garage, Garrett gently patted her perfectly shaped muscular bottom, before saying, "I would willingly be on the receiving end of some of those falls."

"Be careful what you wish for, Garrett Brody."

"Right now I'm hoping we can have crazy insane sex upstairs."

"Oh, you men," she said with exasperation. "Is that all you think about?"

He shook his head. "Well, not exactly. I have an agent who hasn't let me think about anything other than writing best-selling novels for several years now. I'm sorry, but you're not only a distraction, you're far more interesting than my laptop right now. I'm just like the kid in the candy store. You're delicious and I want to overindulge myself."

"So I should take pity on you?" she asked, puckering her lips. "You poor baby."

Garrett put his arms around her again and kissed her under the left ear, while whispering, "I'll be especially obedient and do anything you say."

"Anything?" she asked with anticipation.

He just nodded.

"Oh, goody," Jessica said, pulling him towards the master bedroom.

They made love for the rest of the afternoon and well into the evening, only taking time to eat dinner and take a shower. As they cuddled up on the sofa, both of them checked their cell phones for messages.

"I had one message from Dr. Mendez," Garrett said. "She's arranged a meeting between me and Diego Ruiz, the leader of the Navajo Nation."

Jessica cocked her head to one side. "That's interesting. I had a message from Dr. Mendez too. She wants to meet with me regarding the position of research assistant. Do you know why she needs to talk to me?"

The doorbell rang, saving him from having to answer.

It was the delivery of an overnight package.

When Garrett opened it, an eagle's feather fell out, drifting to the carpet.

"What's that?" Jessica asked.

"An invitation, I presume," Garrett replied as he picked up the feather. "Eagle feathers represent justice and balance in Native American culture."

"Someone must know your propensity to seek right from wrong," Jessica said.

Garrett looked at the envelope, but instead of a return name and address, only *Canoncito Navajo Reservation* was written in the upper left space allotted.

"Something strange is going on," Jessica stated.

"I agree," Garrett said. "What, exactly?"

"I imagine you're going to find out," she said.

"The game is afoot," Brody quoted.

"I'm much better looking than Watson," she said.

"Yes, you are."

"Thank you."

"I wonder if Sherlock Holmes would have solved a single case, if Watson had been as distracting and beautiful as you?" Garrett asked.

Jessica shook her head. "Probably not, but Watson wouldn't have been any good either, because she would have wanted to make love with Holmes all the time too."

"What does that say about us?"

"We're not sleuths?"

CHAPTER 18

CONSPIRACY?

FOR DIEGO RUIZ, PRESIDENT of the Navajo Land Association, the typical day included another round of fighting against the Federal Government and big industry for Native American rights. During Diego's darker moods, he despaired that it was a fight he could never win.

"I keep telling myself it will get better someday, but it only gets worse," Ruiz told Garrett Brody.

Brody had learned that a normal day also meant bitter poverty for the tens of thousands of Native Americans who lived in a barren desert region known as the Checkerboard. Many of these Navajos, referred to as *allottees*, because they resided on individual Indian allotments separate from the large Navajo Nation to the west, lived in abject poverty, can't read or speak English and have no convenient access to telephones, schools or health-care facilities.

Brody had also discovered that in the face of such stark facts were recent allegations that oil and gas companies were cheating those people out of enormous sums of money over the years, while the federal government stood idly by. In fact, Garrett learned that The Department of the Interior was the subject of the largest class-action lawsuit in US history, at $100 billion.

Ruiz, a Navajo from the Checkerboard, had battled industry and government for most of his life. So far, there had been no victories, only a series of painful defeats in the courts.

"You can prove the Federal Government is wrong," Diego said. "But the Federal Government will spend whatever it wants to and lie however it wants to, and it will go to whatever extent it can to prove that it's in the right."

Ruiz then divulged information that totally caught Brody unprepared.

"Ever since Dr. Newman was murdered, much of the critical evidence we needed to prove our allegations simply disappeared," Ruiz stated.

"What evidence?" Garrett asked.

"The day before Dr. Newman was killed, he was fired from his position at the Lab, ostensibly for destroying top-secret documents," Ruiz answered. "However, a week earlier Flavius told me he was going to sue the government, on our behalf, under the Whistleblowers Protection Act. He never got a chance to divulge what he had discovered, since he was murdered, I assume to shut him up."

Unwittingly, Brody had uncovered a possible motive.

"They totally set him up," added Ruiz. "We Navajo trusted Dr. Newman. He was very involved with Indian affairs and tried to help us any way he could. Flavius was a victim too, because he was too nosy."

Just then, a younger Native American entered the office. Ruiz stood up and introduced him to Brody.

This is Barrett Crow, Mr. Brody," Ruiz said. "He's my legal assistant and right hand man. The college education helps keep us competitive with the white man."

Crow was in his late 20's, with hawk-like features and an easy-going smile. He wore his hair in the traditional style, with an intricately beaded slide to hold it in place. Crow was a striking man, reminiscent of the braves in movies, handsome and defiant.

"Pleased to meet you, Mr. Brody," the young man said as they shook hands.

"As well," Garrett said. "I was just asking some questions about the present situation regarding mineral and energy rights."

Crow frowned. "We spend every day arguing with the Feds about Native funds, but they always have some fancy legal double-talk. I can't do much in the courts without public opinion or money. White people could care less about our plight."

Garret shrugged and said, "Not all white people. Still, you're up again the most powerful government in the world, so if they don't want you to win, you won't, without some unplanned intervention or massive public outcry."

Ruiz pointed to Brody. "That's why Mr. Brody's here, Barrett. An author of his stature might sway that public opinion you're always talking about."

Crow looked unimpressed. "Don't take me wrong if I'm a skeptic, Mr. Brody. We've had powerful people here before and nothing comes of it. You should talk to the criminals with the BIA, if you want proof."

Garret shook his head. "You're wise to stay skeptical. I can't promise anything, but I'm interested enough to snoop around and get in trouble. That usually brings the right kind of attention from the media. They follow trouble like a blood trail. I will heed your advice and drop in on the BIA. Perhaps they'll give me something to create an incident."

Crow smiled thinly and offered his hand again. "Good luck."

"Thank you for your time, Mr. Ruiz and Mr. Crow," Garrett said.

Everyone shook hands.

"Cynthia thinks very highly of you, Mr. Brody," Ruiz said as he walked with Brody outside. "I've never read any of your books, but she loaned me a copy. She says you can influence public opinion."

Brody shrugged. "Perhaps. We'll see. Regardless of how this turns out, Mr. Ruiz, I appreciate your candor and your fight. I am a white man, so I can never fully appreciate what it's like to be an American Indian, but that doesn't prevent me from telling the difference between what's wrong and what's right."

"Believe me, Mr. Brody, in my experience that's very rare," Ruiz said.

Sadly enough, Garrett knew what Ruiz said was true.

Brody pulled out the eagle's feather from his notebook and asked, "Did you send me this?"

Ruiz smiled, but shook his head. "No, but someone must think you're worthy."

They walked together to Garrett's car.

"Does the name Carla mean anything to you?" Brody asked.

"Not that I can recall."

"Take care and thank you again," Brody said. He climbed in behind the wheel, started the engine and drove away.

"*Tses-nah bilh-he-neh*," Ruiz said in Navajo as the author's car vanished in a cloud of dust. His prayer of warning would perhaps go unheeded by the likes of Garrett Brody.

Several hours later, Garrett sat on his sectional couch with Jessica and explained what he had discovered so far. "I can't find anyone who can provide a justification for Dr. Newman's dismissal, since the allegations remain unproven. However, I think the good doctor was fired, because he discovered fraudulent government auditing of oil and gas royalty payments, made by companies operating on Indian land, and systematic underpayments of other fees."

Jessica was very uncomfortable with what she had just heard. "Do you think such disclosures warrants murder?"

"I went to the Federal Courthouse here in Albuquerque and discovered an affidavit filed with the court, which charges the Federal Government helped oil and gas companies deceive and cheat impoverished Navajo Indians in New Mexico for dozens of years. If the money is significant enough, it would be pretty easy to motivate someone to kill to protect the guilty parties."

Jessica took Brody's hands in hers. "I'm scared, Garrett. I don't want you to get involved in something that's potentially dangerous. Please?"

"There's more," Brody said, trying to avoid Jessica's request. "Another report was filed with the US District Court alleging the Bureau of Indian Affairs was approving lowball deals for pipeline companies using Indian property on the San Juan Basin of New Mexico. These deals were at times ninety percent less than what private and tribal landowners were receiving for comparable rights-of-way payments.

"The report disclosed that Indian allottees on the Checkerboard generally received twenty-five to forty dollars per rod for rights-of-way easements crossing their land."

"What's a rod?" Jessica asked.

"A rod is a metric for measuring pipeline length, about sixteen and a half feet," Garrett answered. "Tribal and private landowners, however, often received compensation at rates ranging from one hundred forty to five hundred and seventy-five dollars per rod, according to the report. I talked to a rancher who said he received more than one thousand dollars per rod for three major pipelines crossing his property."

"Not only isn't that fair, it's highway robbery," Jessica stated categorically.

"That's why I have to pursue this thing, honey," Garrett said. "I just can't turn a blind eye to injustice, you know that."

"Yes, I know that," Jessica said.

"Would you like to accompany me on my next leg?" Garrett asked.

She shook her head. "I can't. I have my appointment with Dr. Mendez. She wants to discuss my nomination as a research assistant. It seems that two learned and gifted teachers both selected me to fetch their coffee."

There was no mistaking the teasing tone in her voice.

Brody laughed. "Well, I expect a lot more from you than that, young lady. I have a list of research topics as long as my arm and I would also insist that you finish your manuscript by the end of the semester. I would keep you very busy. I can make my own cup of coffee, thank you very much."

Jessica had listened and was convinced Garrett was serious about utilizing her ambition and drive, not only to benefit his agenda, but to promote hers as well. Everything about his intensity and confidence in her was convincing enough for her.

"Will you be here when I get back?" she asked.

He smiled. "I'll be right here at this laptop for the rest of the day. We will go out for dinner when you get back. Take my car."

Jessica snagged his car keys and blew him a kiss. Then out the door, she went.

Thirty minutes later Cynthia Mendez greeted Jessica with a handshake.

"Thank you for this opportunity, Doctor," Jessica said as she entered the director's office.

"Take a seat, Ms. Lawver," Dr. Mendez said, pointing to the chair across from her desk.

"Thank you," Jessica said, sitting down.

"I requested this conference, because there are two members of the English Department who selected you as their research assistant," the department head explained.

Jessica nodded. "I'm quite honored, of course, but…"

Dr. Mendez interrupted. "Both Professor Strong and Guest Lecturer Brody have outlined very convincing and compelling cases on your behalf, Jessica. I would like to hear your input regarding which instructor's proposed project best fits your agenda."

Rather than hastily blurt her emotional response, Jessica sat back and seriously contemplated both her attachment to Garrett, as well as her professional goals after graduating. While the future was unknown, she actually felt torn by the very different opportunities that each man offered.

With Professor Strong, Jessica would be able to pursue various writing genres, from periodical and magazine articles to journalism and even screenplays. Evan Strong was one of the foremost authorities on historical research and was himself a published nonfiction author.

Then, of course, there was Garrett. Being his assistant meant she could be close to him as much as she wanted. They were lovers and this fact was like a drug to her, intoxicating and habit-forming. Would they actually get any work done? Yet it was hard to deny how successful Brody was or would continue to be. At least for the year she would be involved in some high-focus projects with him, which might get her recognition as well, including, if it wasn't just some silly fantasy, the publication of her first novel.

"I respect both men very much, Dr. Mendez," Jessica said finally. "Based on my career plans, aspirations, dreams and goals, I think Garrett Brody offers the most direct correlation. However, I have one issue that I must share with you now, before I go ahead with my choice."

Cynthia Mendez said, "Certainly, Ms. Lawver. What would you like to tell me?"

"Garrett Brody and I are having an intimate relationship," Jessica just said it straight. "I've fallen in love with him and I believe he feels the same way about me. I just wanted you to know that my feelings for Mr. Brody have influenced me in ways that couldn't be overcome by pure logic. I may live to regret this course of action, but somehow I don't think so. Garrett has taught me some incredible things about writing and I'm now pursuing publication of my first novel. I have decided, all things considered, that I would be a fool not to chase this rainbow as far as it takes me."

Dr. Mendez leaned back in her chair and smiled. "I'm relieved you were honest with me and I can hardly argue against your decision, Ms. Lawver. I understand you are also pursuing another more physically demanding career as well."

"I'm a female wrestler, if that's what you mean?" Jessica stated proudly.

"Do you think you will continue to wrestle after graduating?" Cynthia asked.

For the first time in years, Jessica wasn't so sure anymore. Things had changed and therefore her perspective altered as well. Shrugging, Jessica said, "If you had asked me that question a semester ago, I would have emphatically answered yes."

"What has changed?"

"A gifted man has opened up my eyes to all sorts of possibilities," Jessica answered. "I have discovered a love for writing, adding another true passion to my life. The role of women in the world of professional wrestling has been challenging, to say the least. The political situations, which go hand-in-hand with being a female wrestler during a time of continued male chauvinism, have supposedly been addressed, but I still have to listen to all the degrading insults and comments about the weaker sex."

"So why do you continue to do it?" Dr. Mendez asked.

"It's just something I love to do," Jessica replied. "Do you know what I mean?"

Cynthia grinned. "Yes, I do. I'm very impressed with your convictions, Jessica. At this time I heartily approve Garrett Brody's choice for you as his research assistant for the year."

Jessica sighed with relief. "Thank you, Dr. Mendez."

Both women stood up and shook hands.

"I would like to see you wrestle one day," Cynthia said.

"I'd be honored," Jessica said. "There's a match here in Albuquerque before the semester ends, so I'll make sure you get tickets."

"I look forward to it," Dr. Mendez said. "Good luck."

An hour later, Jessica was in Garrett's arms, as they passionately kissed just inside the doorway. After her meeting with the head of the English department, Jessica had stopped at her apartment to change clothes, before driving to Brody's condo. Her greeting had been warm and enthusiastic.

When they parted, she said, "I really love kissing you. I could do it for hours."

"Okay," he said, pushing her towards the sofa. "Let's get started."

She giggled, but stopped him with her hands, saying, "I'm really hungry, Garrett. Can we get something to eat?"

"While you were gone, I snuck out and went grocery shopping, so the frig is loaded," he informed her.

"Yippee," she mimicked the voice of a little girl, skipping into the kitchen. "I can't wait."

With sheer delight, Jessica pulled out all sorts of food, while giving delicious details of the meal she had in mind. Garrett kept her company as she whipped up an impressive meal for both of them.

"Presto!" she announced. Just like a magician, Jessica waved her hands over the plates and followed it with, "Poof! Here is a feast fit for kings."

When she turned around, Garret was standing close by, an envelope in hand.

"Here," he said, handing it to her.

"What's this?" she asked.

"Just a card," he replied.

Jessica slit it open and pulled out the greeting card. A folded piece of paper was inside, which she opened. Written on it was a poem. After reading it, Jessica looked up and kissed him. "This is so sweet, Garret. I assume you wrote this poem?"

He nodded, but then the most serious expression crossed his face.

"What is it, honey?" she asked.

"I want you to promise me you'll keep that poem handy," he said.

"Of course I will. I'll cherish it, like everything else you've given me."

"Promise me you won't forget what I wrote."

"I promise."

"Thank you."

Jessica kissed him and his smile returned.

"Let's eat!" she said.

After a few minutes of silence while they both ate ravenously, Garrett asked, "So, how did the meeting go?"

Jessica quickly swallowed and replied, "Oops, I forgot. Dr. Mendez approved your request. I'm officially your research assistant as of today."

It was obvious that Garrett was more than pleased. In fact, shortly after finishing dinner, they ended up in the hot tub out on the deck. There, with glasses of wine, they played and laughed and made love. It had been a long day for both of them, so Jessica fell asleep. Rather than taking the risk that they both might drown, Garrett carried her to the bedroom and slipped her under the covers. He joined her and they both slept soundlessly through the night.

The next day, upon Barrett Crow's recommendation, Brody made an appointment at the regional headquarters of the Bureau of Indian Affairs Shiprock Agency in Albuquerque, to interview the chief director of operations. Ostensibly, Garrett was conducting research about the early days of the BIA, but his motives were more covert. The author hoped to uncover some useful information about present policies regarding the use of natural resources on Indian land. Jessica accompanied him to take notes and watch Brody in action. She was very excited to be included in Garrett's typical process.

Upon reaching the Bureau offices, they were politely escorted to meet with the senior manager on site. As Garrett stepped through the doorway, a towering giant of a man greeted him.

"I'm Terry McNab, Regional Director," the man introduced himself. "It's a real honor meeting you, Mr. Brody. I've read all your books."

However, McNab didn't seem to even notice Jessica, which Brody found very strange, since just about every man reacted to her intense beauty.

"Well, thank you, Mr. McNab," Garrett said. "This is my research assistant, Ms. Jessica Lawver, a student at UNM."

"It's a pleasure," McNab said to her.

The director was smiling, but there was an underlying tone in his voice, which communicated something other than polite indifference. It was almost as if Jessica represented some kind of threat to McNab.

Just the same, everyone shook hands.

"Please, be seated," McNab said, pointing to the chairs. The bureau chief had an easy-going manner and jovial expression that seemed the byproduct of a healthy appetite. Brody was certain the man could convincingly play Santa Claus at holiday parties, with a white beard and no padding required. He was enormous, weighing well over 300 pounds, yet much of it looked like muscle. Garrett assumed the director had once played football, if not professionally, then certainly at the collegiate level.

"So what can I do for such a famous author?" McNab asked with the same warm mannerisms. "I hope this doesn't mean the Bureau of Indian Affairs is your next target?"

Brody grinned. "That depends."

McNab never lost his smile. "On what?"

Garrett was impressed. The bureaucrat never flinched and honestly looked like someone who could handle all the negative press the agency has been receiving lately. "It depends on how evasive you are with my questions." Brody too never let his grin waver.

McNab laughed. "Touché!"

Of course, Jessica observed this with complete and utter fascination, because she had never seen Garrett in action before as interviewer.

Brody made a little exaggerated bow with his head and said, "At the moment I'm researching a new novel, but the plot revolves around the Lincoln County War, over a hundred years ago."

There was just the slightest sign that McNab was relieved at what Garrett had just divulged. He relaxed a little more and sat back. "I wasn't aware Native American policies played any part during that conflict."

Jessica thought to herself, 'Oh, how politically correct you are, you jerk.'

Brody said, "Well, for the most part that's true, but the cattle that initiated the war were supposed to be supplied to the Indians on the nearby reservation. The evidence points to several cattle barons gouging the US Government on beef prices, while rustling other herds to fill bogus orders and sell the herds yet again. Caught in the middle were the Navajo, who as usual came out on the short end. I was just wondering if you had any historical information regarding these incidents?"

McNab leaned forward, his hands open before him. "I will certainly look into it, Mr. Brody. I suspect most of the historical data you're looking for, if it exists, resides in Washington DC, but I will make inquiries on your behalf here as well. It sounds like interesting research."

"So far I've discovered all sorts of things I didn't know about New Mexico, the Navajo Nation, and the Bureau of Indian Affairs," Garrett said pointedly.

It was obvious by McNab's slightly pained expression that the bureau chief could surmise what Brody was implying. "We've been having some incredibly bad press lately, but most of it is deserved. There have been many questionable decisions made, most of them before I came on board. The present administration is trying to make amends and prevent such oversights from happening again."

"As in misplacing billions of dollars?" Jessica spoke up for the first time.

Garrett grinned. She had done her homework.

McNab frowned, but nodded. He stood up and once again, Garrett appreciated the man's incredible size. The director lumbered over to a filing cabinet and slid open one of the many drawers, rifling through the folders.

However, it was a sheet of letterhead lying on McNab's desk, which suddenly caught Brody's eye. Written in pencil along the margin was a name he recognized.

Dr. Flavius Newman

Garrett carefully and quietly picked up the sheet of official government letterhead, surreptitiously slipping it into his notebook. Then he leaned back in the chair and forced a yawn.

McNab hadn't noticed this sleight-of-hand, but Jessica couldn't have missed it.

Her eyes were huge with amazement.

"The Bureau of Indian Affairs can't account for $2.4 billion, or one out of every seven dollars that flowed through tribal trust funds in the last 20 years," Brody stated loudly to cover for his pilfering.

"The money isn't necessarily missing, but documents cannot be found to show where it came from or where it was paid," McNab said over his shoulder as he continued flipping through the files. "The tribes are likely to ask Congress to restore some of it and rightfully so."

Garrett was impressed with McNab's response, but followed up with, "The Bureau has been under criticism for years for alleged mismanagement of trust funds, but isn't it correct to say that the extent of the problem only became clear with completion of a five-year independent audit?"

McNab nodded. "Congress ordered the audit to figure out how much money should be in the 2,000 tribal accounts, set up over the years to handle receipts of tribal income from timber, minerals, water and land claims."

"Don't forget gas and oil," Brody pointed out.

"To be perfectly honest, Mr. Brody, what we've got here is a colossal mess," McNab admitted as he returned to his desk. After briefly looking over the documents he had retrieved, the director continued, saying, "As far as I can tell it's an unprecedented disaster. The current fund totals about $2 billion. However, the independent audit firm studied all the transactions between 1973 and 1992 and found unreconciled documentation for $15.3 billion."

Garrett whistled. "That's quite a disparity."

"The problem is akin to a bank being unable to provide canceled checks or deposit receipts to back up its account statements," McNab explained. "For the present, the funds have been put under a special trustee independent of the Bureau."

Brody looked at his notes and said, "Over the years, dozens of audits by the General Accounting Office and the Interior Department's inspector general have criticized the bureau's management of the funds. Problems cited included unreliable accounting systems and lack of security controls and competent personnel."

"Washington can't confirm that all the money that should have been collected was actually collected," McNab said. "They can't prove that money that was collected was deposited. They can't even prove that the money that was deposited was invested properly."

"If this were a private bank trustee, they'd be in jail right now," Jessica commented.

McNab nodded. "That's going to be something Congress must come to grips with. The Senate has set aside three million dollars to reimburse tribes that are missing money."

"I would expect the claims to far exceed that," she countered.

Garrett enjoyed witnessing Jessica think. He just watched and listened.

"All the tribes are going to be entering claims," said McNab. "Many tribes will withdraw their funds from government control under a 1994 law that allows them to do so."

"What about private accounts?" Jessica inquired.

McNab grimaced. "There are also 300,000 accounts, totaling $400 million, belonging to individual Indians. No attempt will be made to reconcile them, because the cost of doing the work was estimated at up to $250 million."

"So they're screwed?" she reacted.

The bureau chief shrugged. "They can withdraw their money as well, but there's no way to account for how the money was managed. Like I said, it's a mess."

"Sounds like the same old story, Director McNab," Jessica said with noticeable hostility in her voice. "Once again the Native American gets shafted by the white man, who hides behind the law and gets away with it."

McNab looked genuinely hurt by her accusation, but said, "I know it appears that way, Ms. Lawver and there is certainly evidence to suggest you're correct in your summation. However, there are some of us who have a conscience and will do whatever they have the power to do to rectify the past."

Jessica nodded. "I certainly hope so."

Garret closed his notebook and stood up. "Thank you for your time, Director. We appreciate your busy schedule, so we'll not take up any more of your day."

McNab came to his feet as Jessica did and offered his hand to her first. Somewhat reluctantly, she shook it, but then went to stand by Brody.

"I will make sure to request Bureau information regarding the Lincoln County War timeframe for you, Mr. Brody," McNab said.

"That would be great," Garrett said, handing over his business card. "You can email any information, as an attachment, to that address."

McNab walked with them to the door. It was then that Garrett truly appreciated what a big man the bureau chief really was. He towered over them and reminded Brody of a Brahman bull at the rodeo.

"Thanks again for your time," Brody said as they exited his office.

"I enjoyed it," McNab called out after them. "Stop again."

On the drive back to his condo, Garrett noticed Jessica was unusually quiet. He had expected lots of feedback and questions, but instead she just stared out the window.

As he pulled into the garage, she was still acting strange and Brody hoped it wasn't something he had said and done, or not said and not done. Jessica went into the kitchen and grabbed herself a cold beer out of the refrigerator.

"I'll take one too, please," he said.

She handed him a bottle and slipped past him to the den, where she flopped on the sofa. General Sherman bounded up and immediately curled up in her lap. Jessica pet the cat and made smoochie sounds.

"Are you okay, sweetheart?" he asked gingerly.

She smiled half-heartedly. "I'm fine."

"Can I get you anything?"

"You could stomp that jerk's head in for me."

Garrett recoiled from the hostility in her voice. "Which jerk is that?"

"Bureau of Indian Affairs Regional Director Terry McNab," she replied with attitude. "What a pompous, conceited asshole."

Garrett's eyebrows went up. "So tell me how you really feel."

"He's an arrogant, slimy…"

"Okay, I get the point," he interrupted. "Why didn't you like him?"

"I just didn't like him," she said.

"Perhaps you don't like what McNab represents," Garrett observed. "The Bureau of Indian Affairs has never enjoyed a positive public image."

"Deservedly so," she reacted.

He put his arms around her and gave Jessica a gentle hug. "I love you very much, you know, and one of the reasons is because you care about things so passionately. I see and hear the intensity of your convictions."

She looked up at him and said, "Did you know I'm part Tonkawa-Comanche?"

"I guessed you have Native American blood in your veins, from your book, but I didn't know the details," he replied. "I just figured you'd tell me when you felt ready."

"My father met my mother while he was stationed at Tinker Air Force Base in Oklahoma," Jessica related. "At the time he was an officer, very bright, handsome, and could offer a better future for her. My mother was a restless spirit and wanted to leave the reservation, the Fort Oakland Reserve, which is the present day home of the Tonkawa Tribe. It's in northern Oklahoma, near the towns of Tonkawa and Ponca City."

"You obviously inherited your beautiful black hair from your mother," he said.

"Yes and my rebellious spirit too," she replied. "Sometime in the 1800's the Comanche and Tonkawa blood was mixed, probably as an act of self-preservation. The Tonkawa name for themselves is *Tickanwatic*, which means Real People."

"Well, you certainly are that," Garrett observed.

Jessica smiled and they kissed. When they parted, she leaned back with another big sigh. Garrett interlocked his fingers with hers, but didn't say anything. It was obvious to see there was a lot on her mind just then.

Then she turned and looked at him. "I refuse to wear any stupid Indian princess costumes or assume a Native American stage name when I wrestle. I will not defile my ancestry with such ridiculous Hollywood stereotypes."

"I don't blame you," he said.

"My former manager actually wanted me to dress up in a beaded-leather miniskirt, with moccasins and war paint," she went on. "Then I was supposed to go around hooting and whooping it up, flashing my tits and acting like some idiot."

Garrett quickly said, "Well, I guess that's why he's your former manager."

Just that little bit of lightheartedness made Jessica laugh and dispelled her lingering feelings of bitterness. She cuddled up against him.

"That's also why you don't like McNab," Garrett concluded. "He reminds you of your old manager, doesn't he?"

Jessica just said, "Bigot."

"I am not."

"Not you," she said. "You're wonderful."

"Thank you."

"You're welcome."

He kissed her.

"Why did you steal that sheet of paper from McNab's desk?" Jessica suddenly demanded.

He shrugged. "I was merely borrowing it, but it turned out to be pretty useless. There was only a handwritten statement, unsigned and nothing more. A different hand wrote Doctor Newman's name, almost carelessly. I don't think the two had anything to do with each other, but was just some idle doodling."

"Perhaps," she said. "May I see it?"

"Of course," Garrett replied. He got up and retrieved the piece of paper.

The printed letterhead read:

THE BUREAU OF INDIAN AFFAIRS
SHIPROCK AGENCY, NEW MEXICO

Below that, in black pen, was another sentence.

"I can no longer remain silent, as others do at the Interior Department and the Justice Department, about this criminal misconduct."

"This was written by a woman," Jessica stated.

Garrett looked over her shoulder. "I think you're right."

"Of course I'm right," she quipped.

"It's strange it's handwritten," Garrett said. "It's not part of a longer note or letter, but stands all by itself."

"As if someone was being quoted," Jessica said.

"Perhaps it was taken out of context, from some other document or a speech?" he wondered allowed.

Jessica pondered the sentence again for a moment. "These are pretty powerful words. I think whoever wrote this was making sure the impact was strong enough."

"Do you think this was part of a scripted statement?" Garrett asked.

"Possibly," she said. "I think it's more likely that this line was the crux of someone's explanation for their actions. Criminal misconduct would seem to give the writer the justification for breaking their silence."

"Since Dr. Newman was murdered, this might be something he was dictating to his secretary," Brody suggested.

"How did it end up on the BIA director's desk?" Jessica asked. "That seems strange itself."

"Well, you did say you didn't like the man," Garrett pointed out. "He might be involved in all this. We are talking about lots of money, after all. No telling what somewhat might be capable of."

"What should we do next?" she asked.

"You, young lady, are going to your next class," he informed her directly. "I'll investigate this more and fill you in later."

Jessica pouted, but knew he was only thinking of her behalf, so she gave him a kiss and headed for the door.

"Take the other car, so you won't be late," he called after her.

"I'll see you tonight," she said over her shoulder. "I love you."

"I love you too," he said as she went out.

CHAPTER 19

EDGE OF THE SEAT

"MOST OF YOU ARE aware that I don't actually write novels filled with action, adventure and romance," Brody began his lecture. "While critiques of my books have ranged from rave reviews to thumbs down, I think avid readers have come to expect certain things from those novels. In reality, as one reader recently pointed out to me, my books are actually filled with violence, suspense, and hot sex."

Everyone in the room laughed, perhaps Jessica even more.

Garrett raised his hands to silence them.

"However, I've aggressively promoted to all of you that you must pursue the genre you feel the most passionate about, regardless of whether that's considered publishable or not. Few, if any, trends can be tracked in the publishing world. If it's good, it will find its way into the public's hands, even if you have to publish it yourself!"

A hand shot up.

Brody recognized the student. "Go ahead, Gary."

"What about print-on-demand and vanity publishing?"

Garrett stepped closer and replied, "Less than two percent of the writers in the world ever get published by the traditional houses. That is hardly a fair representation of the ability or salability of those authors. Many publishing companies make ridiculous advances for big names and the subsequent books are incredible flops, while others don't want to commit the time, spend the money, or assign the personnel to promote a new talent. Most of you wouldn't know this, but before I landed a traditional contract from a New York house, I pursued my passion through POD titles. They sold well and I established a loyal readership, before my agent hooked one of the, quote acceptable, companies. I would never admonish or belittle an author for pursuing their passion through any means possible, as long as it was legal."

Laughter.

"Yes?" Brody said as he pointed to the next raised hand.

"You've written screenplays for some of your books," the student said. "Why and how is it different from writing your novels?"

"I've always been convinced my novels would make great movies," Garrett replied. "So, I decided to try my hand at converting one into a screenplay. It's a very difficult process, because so much of the descriptive writing is deleted, with dialogue and action being the focal point. It was quite a difficult learning process, but rewarding too. If you have an interest in writing for Hollywood, there are screenwriting courses offered here at the University. I wish I could devote more time to screenplays. In fact, I'll drop everything I'm doing, the next time a studio executive offers to pay me to write one."

Laughter.

Another hand shot up.

It was Jessica. She was holding one of Brody's books in her hand.

Brody quickly assumed a defensive pose, but his smile was very pronounced. "Uh, oh."

This time everyone howled with delight.

Jessica was blushing, but saw it was all in jest and said, "I promise not to throw this at you, Mr. Brody."

He took a more relaxed stance and said, "Okay, I guess I'm safe for now."

The students responded with more laughter.

Jessica wanted to jump up, throw herself into his arms, and kiss him in front of everyone, because she just plain adored him. Instead, she asked, "How do you create so much tension and suspense in your novels?"

Bang!

Everyone jumped.

All Garrett had done was simply slap his hand down on one of the tabletops.

"One technique is to do the unexpected," he replied to her question. "Keep the readers guessing. Then, write sentences that are short, to the point, and delivered in increasingly dramatic style."

Brody snapped his fingers in rapid succession.

"Like this."

Another hand shot up.

This time, much to Garrett's delight, it was one of the more quiet and reserved students in his class. "Yes, Daryl, what's on your mind?"

"In the climax of *Afterburner*, I found myself reading so fast that I was afraid I was missing something, so I read the pages over again," the student said. "Was that your intention or was it just me? I felt exhausted and a bit confused."

Brody was intrigued. He had never heard that criticism before, but that didn't mean it wasn't a valid complaint or concern. "Now you've just thrown me a poser, Daryl. I do want the reader to get so wrapped up in the flow of the story that he's turning pages as fast as possible, but I don't want him to miss anything either. The exhaustion part you described is a great side effect, but did your confusion go away once you finished the book?"

"Yes, it did," Daryl replied.

"In that case, it's okay that I made you confused at that point in the plot," Garrett said. "If you remained baffled after finishing the book, then I failed to pace the resolution or solution effectively. That was a thought-provoking question, Daryl. Well done."

The typically shy student just beamed. "Thank you, Mr. Brody."

Garrett cast a quick glance at Jessica, who was also smiling with approval. There was no doubt who his biggest fan was in that room.

"All right, that's it for today," he said. "Remember that we're getting pretty close to the end of the semester. Everyone has met with me and I'm completely up-to-date with all of your assignments and projects. I'm very proud of you and you've all worked very hard, because I can see it in your writing. All that remains is completion of your edited and finalized individual manuscripts. That project will be considered your final test, if you want to think of it that way. My goal is to get your work into the best possible shape for eventual publication. The rest is up to you. I told you that our working relationship would go beyond the confines of this class and I meant it. I want to give you every possible edge on the road to publication, regardless of the format. Class dismissed."

Instead of the usual after-class rendezvous, both Garrett and Jessica agreed to focus their energies on a list of chores and responsibilities until dinner. Then they would spend the evening together and sleep with each other, before Jessica had to leave for her next wrestling match.

Jessica went directly to the gym to work out. There were some new moves she needed to perfect, as well as going through her usual routine.

The upcoming match was in Des Moines, Iowa, of all places, but Jessica went wherever and whenever she could get a chance to wrestle.

Garrett, on the other hand, was feeling very guilty over his lack of productivity on his latest contracted book. It wasn't that he had lost interest in the historical piece. On the contrary, Brody was very intrigued. He had just been wrapped up in other things, namely his love affair with Jessica Lawver and the not-so-amateurish investigation into Dr. Newman's alleged murder. The evidence so far was pointing to some disturbing possibilities and Garrett couldn't just walk away.

After feeding General Sherman, Brody decided he would spend the entire afternoon dedicated to *Decision at Enchanted Mesa*. He gathered up his reference material, sat down at the desktop computer and began fiddling with an opening chapter.

However, his mind wandered, first, to how much he wanted to make love with Jessica and then to the other book he had been writing on the side. Garrett had never written a murder mystery before and it was a new and exciting genre for him, especially since he was basing the entire thing on his present investigation. Not only that, but he had decided to make Jessica the model for his female lead character.

With all of this rattling around in his mind, it's little wonder that Brody once again lapsed into a productive writing session that had nothing to do with the project that really required his attention. Eventually, if he missed another deadline, Brody was in danger of not only losing a lucrative relationship with his publisher, but also forfeiting a sizeable monetary advance, not to mention the commissions from proposed sales. Yet, with all these possibilities lingering in the background, he didn't seem to care. In fact, Garrett had moved on to think about engagement rings and honeymoon getaways. To any casual observer, Mr. Brody was simply acting irresponsibly.

Suddenly his cell phone rang and Garrett quickly snatched it up. He didn't recognize the number, but it was long distance. "Garret Brody, how may I help you?"

"I want to make this very clear, Mr. Brody, so there will be no misunderstanding," a deep muffled male voice said. "If you continue to pursue your present course of action, somebody's going to get hurt."

"Who is this?" Garrett demanded.

"It isn't important," the man replied.

"Are you threatening me?" Garrett asked.

"No, it's a promise," the voice said. "Just stick to lecturing. It's what you're good at."

"Well, I don't scare too easily," Garrett said.

"Consider your words carefully, Mr. Brody," the voice went on. "It would be your fault if anything nasty happened to that foxy little coed. Jessica is her name, right?"

Click.

"Damn it!" Brody swore, hurling the cell phone at the sofa. It almost hit General Sherman, who vaulted into the air, startled from his catnap.

"I'm sorry, big guy," Garrett apologized as he tried to calm the cat by petting him. General Sherman meowed and stretched to signify how much he enjoyed the attention.

Perhaps for the first time since undertaking his own private investigation into the death of Dr. Flavius Newman, Garrett stopped to consider how his actions might affect other people. He sat down on the sofa and stared at the cell phone. Whoever the caller was, the person sounded deadly serious.

Then the memory of his Carla flashed again in his mind. A person bent on punishing Brody for pursuing a certain investigation had killed her. Garrett had lost the most important person in his life, because he had been too stubborn to quit. He had held Carla in his arms, as she was dying, when she still managed to tell him how much she loved him. That moment was a turning point in his life. He resigned from the agency and took up a career as a writer, holding part-time jobs and barely making ends meet. Financially things had definitely turned around, but Jessica had only recently healed the void in his heart and soul.

Now was history about to repeat itself? In his damn-the-torpedoes drive to solve the mystery surrounding Newman's murder, Brody might actually force another killing.

This train of thought was not only disturbing, it also preyed upon Garrett's very soul. There was no way he would endanger Jessica's life, but he also knew he couldn't just ignore what facts he had discovered surrounding the crime. Brody had tried before to walk away from injustice, but unsuccessfully.

His cell phone rang again.

This time he recognized the caller ID. It was Jessica.

Yet he didn't answer it.

Garrett felt very strange indeed, as if he was committing an act of betrayal.

It stopped ringing and shortly afterwards, the cell phone beeped with a message.

Impulsively, he deleted it without listening to it.

Something was happening to him and it wasn't good.

Garrett had to make a choice and no matter which way he looked at it, somebody was going to get hurt, just as the unidentified person on the phone had implied. Except that if Brody acted first, he could prevent anything physically bad happening to Jessica. She was all that mattered to him. To protect her, he would do anything.

Anything?

Brody got up and poured himself a whiskey. Swirling the brown liquid around in the tumbler, Garrett suddenly saw himself reflected in the worst possible light. His past life had collided with the present and he didn't see any other solution. Somehow, he had to get rid of Jessica.

Shaking his head, he said to himself, "But how can I do that? I'm so in love with her it hurts."

Yet the alternative was too devastating to even contemplate. She was already in danger. Garrett was certain it was no idle threat.

"How do I make her stay away from me, without ruining the most wonderful relationship I've ever known?" he asked himself with dismay.

He knew there was no such solution available.

About an hour later, the front doorbell rang. Garrett jumped, before rubbing his forehead as he screwed up enough courage to proceed with his desperate plan. His stomach was doing barrel rolls as he went to open the door.

Jessica was very pleased to see him. "Hey, honey…"

Garrett turned and walked away.

She was shocked by his behavior, even though she had seen him act this way once before. Deciding not to let it ruin her mood, she closed the door behind her and scampered after him.

"I called earlier, but I guess you were out," she said.

"No, I was here," he said glumly. "I just didn't want to talk."

"Busy writing, huh?" she surmised. "That's okay. I wouldn't want to disturb a genius at work."

"What did you want?" he asked.

His voice, his mannerisms, and everything about him were very negative, so Jessica tried to tread carefully. "I just wanted to see you."

"Why?"

"Because I missed you."

"That's nice."

She sighed. He certainly wasn't making it any easier.

"I was worried about you," Jessica said, trying to kiss him.

Garrett pulled away and went over to the desk.

"What's wrong, honey?" she asked worriedly. "You look so upset."

"Nothing."

"Well I can see something is bothering you. Did I do something wrong?"

He shook his head.

Jessica closed the distance again, hoping to bombard him with her love.

It was a physical change that took place right before her eyes. Garrett assumed a very unfriendly stance and his face was etched with serious intent. "Look, this isn't easy for me to say, but from now on, you need to focus on someone other than me."

"How can I do that, honey?" she asked incredulously. "You're onto something big and I want to help you nail the bad guys."

"I can handle it from here on out," he said.

"I can help."

"You've got finals to study for."

Jessica reached out to take his hand, but he pulled away.

"Garrett, there's something you're not telling me."

"No, that's all," he lied. "It would make me feel better if you focused on being a student for awhile, instead of some two-bit detective."

"I resent that," she said light-heartedly, still trying to keep her sense of humor. "I'm at least a five-bit detective."

Brody grunted and said, "You know what I mean."

Jessica rolled her eyes. "Okay, my joke was pretty lame, but you don't have to get so surly about it. I just don't understand why you're so adamant about it now."

"I don't want you to get hurt!" he suddenly shouted. "Don't you understand?"

"I guess so, but that's not really the point," she shouted back. "I've been involved with you in this every step of the way. I can't sit back and take the chance you might get killed or something."

"It's what I do, Jessica," he countered.

"No, you're a published author," she said. "I thought that other life was in the past."

"It's never in the past," he yelled. "It's always there, reminding me of how I failed to protect an innocent life. Carla died, because she trusted me. I carry that with me every moment of every day. I loved her more than anything in this world and I failed her."

"But it wasn't your fault, was it?" Jessica asked.

His anger boiled over. Garrett took one step forward, pointing a wicked finger. "How the hell do you know what's my fault or not?"

Jessica didn't retreat. "Because I know you, Garrett. You're kind and loving and…"

"Oh, bullshit!"

"It's true."

Brody turned his back on her, shoving his hands deeply into his pants pockets.

She carefully put a hand on his shoulder and said, "Please Garrett, don't torture yourself so. Let me help you."

"No," he said, without facing her.

"Why not?" she asked.

"Because I said so."

"Oh, that's a good one," Jessica reacted. "Is that what your parents used to say?"

This time when he turned around, his face was contorted by barely controlled emotions. "I have nothing more to say to you, Ms. Lawver. You are a university college student and my research assistant, nothing more. If you don't do what I say, then I will have to terminate that contract."

Jessica was stunned, but still said, "I don't care about some stupid research assistant job description. I care about you. I don't want to lose you over this."

Brody was tight-lipped when he said, "I want you to leave and don't come back."

"What?" she asked, startled by his callous words.

"You heard me," he said coldly.

Jessica didn't move. She just stared at him, eyes suddenly wet with tears.

Garrett had to drive her away. It was the only way to keep her safe. If that meant hurting her emotionally, then so be it. Perhaps later he could pick up the pieces and start anew. Until this murder case was solved, Brody couldn't take the risk of further endangering her life.

Brody put his hands on his hips and said, "Look, Jessica, you have no right to muscle your way into my business, my affairs, or my life. You're a hot babe and I've never had such awesome sex, but that doesn't mean that we're headed for something more serious. I mean, really, you can't seriously expect me to take a female wrestler to the altar."

Jessica reached out and slapped him. "You fucking bastard!"

His face burned from the impact, but he said nothing more.

Jessica moved to just inches from him, her eyes now flashing with pure passionate rage and hurt. After everything they had done together, after all the wonderful lovemaking and all the promises of his undying love, he was just another lying jerk. How could she have been so stupid?

She wasn't through yet.

Taking another dramatic step, Jessica slapped Garrett even harder, from the other side.

Whack!

This time the blow brought tears of pain to his eyes, but he still didn't retaliate or say another word. He had to make her go away, even if it meant losing her forever. It was the only way to make sure she wouldn't get hurt. People had a habit of ending up dead when they were associated with him.

A steady stream of tears ran down her cheeks. "I can't believe you turned out to be just another asshole, like all the rest. I thought you were different. As long as I gave you a piece of ass, everything was fine, but as soon as you discovered who I really was and what I'm all about, you treat me like this? How dare you!"

Jessica turned and started heading out of the room.

However, before she reached the doorway, she stopped. With perfect execution, Jessica vaulted backwards, executing a perfect series of flips.

Brody saw it coming.

It was like slow motion.

Yet he didn't move.

He didn't even try to protect himself.

He just waited.

Jessica's feet hit him square in the chest.

Garret went flying into the wall.

The impact knocked him out cold.

Jessica dusted off her hands and said, "I told you I could kick your ass, you conceited shithead."

She stormed out of the room, the front door slamming to signify she had left.

Garrett regained consciousness about an hour later. He groaned as he got up, gingerly feeling the bump on the back of his head. Making his way to the sofa, he lay down. Brody stared up at the vaulted ceiling, before closing his eyes.

General Sherman came out from under the desk and hopped into Brody's lap. The cat purred and rubbed, bumping for attention. Garrett sat up and absentmindedly pet the cat, before his head fell into his upturned hands.

"Oh, Jessica, forgive me," he prayed aloud. "I just couldn't let anything happen to you. I love you so much. I just couldn't let them do to you, what they did to Carla. I just couldn't."

Then he completely broke down.

Poor General Sherman tried his best to comfort his owner, but to no avail. In the end, out of instinct, the cat bit Garrett, but that didn't help any either. For all his trouble, the cat got tossed to another chair.

Across town, Jessica stood in the middle of her apartment bedroom, her hands clenched, her body shaking with anger and the feeling of betrayal. Garrett Brody had been so romantic, attentive, and wonderful, when all he wanted was to screw her. He was like all the rest of the dogs she had ever known, without scruples or morals or decency. He was a jerk, a scumbag, a deceitful lying bastard who deserved to die.

Most of all, he had violated her trust.

She collapsed to the floor, sobbing her heart out.

Jessica cried as hard as she ever had, for in the midst of her total misery, she knew she had fallen so deeply in love with him. That's why his betrayal hurt so badly.

After awhile, she regained some composure and went around the apartment collecting everything Garrett had given her, including the beautiful necklace. In a symbolic gesture to rid herself of his memory, Jessica dropped each and every gift into the wastebasket.

As she prepared to throw away his most recent greeting card, however, Jessica stopped and opened it. A piece of paper fluttered to the carpet.

She picked it up, but couldn't resist reading the poem one more time.

No matter what appears to be happening,
Stop long enough to listen to the wind.
No matter what you think you're hearing,

Stop long enough to listen to my soul.

I will always love you.
I will always care.
Yet I must protect you.
You must decide to trust.

No matter what might seem like darkness,
Stop long enough to see the light.
No matter what your mind is telling you,
Stop long enough to see our love.

I will always love you.
I will always care.
I must somehow protect you.
You must decide to believe.

In that moment, Jessica's stomach turned and she sat on the edge of her bed, rereading the poem, repeatedly, over and over. How could she have missed the significance before? Garrett was afraid, afraid of losing her like his Carla. It was obvious he was trying to drive her away, to keep her from danger.

"Oh, my God, Garrett, I'm sorry I didn't see your pain," she whispered in despair. "I love you. I am so sorry…"

Her door buzzer went off.

Jessica scrambled to the button and pressed it, before throwing open the door to greet him. She would forgive him, they would make up, and everything would be fine.

However, it wasn't Garrett who came down the hallway.

It was two men she didn't recognize, both dressed in dark clothing, with very dour and serious expressions. She felt as if she should slam the door in their faces, but did not. They stopped directly across from her.

"Ms. Jessica Lawver?" one man inquired.

"Yes," she replied. "May I help you?"

"Garrett Brody has been seriously injured, Ms. Lawver," the one man told her, flashing a badge. "He was struck by a hit-and-run driver and is in intensive care."

"Oh!" she exclaimed, before a fresh rush of tears streamed down her face. "No, please, tell me it isn't true."

"I'm afraid it is," the other man said. "Will you come with us? We'll take you to the hospital. He asked for you by name, before he slipped into a coma."

Jessica wiped her eyes and dashed inside, grabbing her purse. Before reaching the door, however, she doubled back and retrieved the necklace from the trash, putting it on as she joined the two men in the hallway.

"I'm ready," she announced. "Please, let's hurry."

The door across the hall opened and out stepped Amanda, who had heard Jessica crying earlier. She figured Jessica and Garrett had a bad argument and was going to offer her shoulder to cry on. "Are you alright?"

"Garrett is in the hospital," Jessica sobbed.

Amanda put her arms around her best friend and said, "Do you want me to come with you?"

Jessica shook her head. "No, that's okay. I'll be fine. I'll call you later, once I know how he is."

Amanda walked with her to the door. "I'll call Stephanie to let her know. Just take care of yourself. Garrett will be fine, you'll see."

"Thank you, Mandy," Jessica said as she hurried to catch up to the men waiting impatiently by parking lot. "I'll call you."

As they drove her towards the hospital, Jessica fervently prayed Garrett would come out of the coma. Now, she swore she would stay at his bedside until he recovered from his injuries. She loved him more than anything and now that she understood his behavior, she forgave him.

It was then that Jessica realized the SUV hadn't exited where it should have, but continued on past the ramp. As she leaned forward to point out this fact, the barrel of a gun was suddenly shoved against her chest.

"Now just sit back and relax, Ms. Lawver," the man on the passenger side warned her. "That way you won't get hurt and you might live long enough to see another day."

Back in Brody's condominium, Garrett paced back and forth around the living room, decidedly not in the mood to write, or anything else for that matter. However, he was determined to go through with his

However, once again Garrett wasn't really listening. He was staring at the open seat that had always been occupied by Jessica Lawver. Instead of trying to hide his disappointment, Brody slowly turned and faced the class. "Does anyone know why Ms. Lawver isn't here today?"

For just about every member of that class, his question came as something of a surprise to them, but for reasons he wasn't aware of. Throughout the semester, the chemistry between Jessica and Garrett was more than obvious and when it was announced that she had been chosen as his research assistant, no one had been surprised. It was just naturally assumed they were having an intimate relationship. The rumor mill being what it was, many people accepted that the best-selling novelist and the gorgeous female student were sleeping together. Therefore, to hear Garrett Brody openly ask where Jessica might be, came as a shock.

Unfortunately, none of them knew anything about her whereabouts. They all shook their heads. Not that this lack of knowledge was really a surprise to Garrett, but he was nonetheless very disheartened.

"Well, I assume she has a good reason to miss the final class," Brody said. "If you happen to run into her on campus, please let her know that..." His voice just trailed off.

Rick stood up. "I can find out where she lives, Mr. Brody and see if I can get in touch with her, if you'd like?"

"No, that won't be necessary," Garrett replied. "Ms. Lawver will just have to get in touch with me at her earliest convenience. Now, let's get on with the agenda at hand."

Garrett handed out all the written exercises they had turned in over the semester, with comments and recommendations. He then praised them for their participation and without exception, let the students know he had seen marked improvement in their writing.

"I want to stress that writing is an ongoing learning process," Brody said. "When each of my novels comes out, I'm convinced it is better written than the previous one. It takes hard work, perseverance, and studying the craft. I would wish you all good luck, but you know luck has nothing to do with it. Don't be afraid to keep in touch and I would enjoy reading your projects from now on. Thank you."

All the students came forward and Garrett took the time to shake hands and talk to each of them, even though his stomach was tied up in knots. His imagination would have run wild, but he forced himself to keep focused on the business at hand.

Immediately after the last student said goodbye, Garrett literally sprinted to the faculty parking lot and then drove to Jessica's apartment. Brody was doing well over the speed limit, but he seemed oblivious to his law-breaking ways. Parking on the front curb this time, he jumped out and hurried to the building entrance. Garrett buzzed her apartment several times, but there was no answer. When he asked several tenants if they had seen Jessica, no one told him anything encouraging. He even walked around to her patio sliding door and rapped on the glass, but no one came to investigate. Brody tried calling her home telephone number and her cell phone, but just got voicemail in both cases.

"I know we parted ways on bad terms, Jessica, but I was very alarmed when you didn't come to the final session of class," Brody left the same message at both numbers. "I took the time to check with your other professors as well and they all reported you missed your finals. No matter how much you despise me, you cannot risk your education in this manner. I will try to negotiate leniency from those same professors on your behalf, but you must follow up in good faith. Based on your overall performance, I don't think there will be any difficulties. If you can't respond to me directly, please contact your other teachers as soon as possible. Regardless of our personal relationship, you will receive an A in my class, because your novel is such quality work."

He hung up, but was quite dismayed at Jessica's irresponsible behavior. He had convinced himself she would consider him a colossal jerk and get on with her life. Missing her final exams was so uncharacteristic of her, that Garrett began to worry that she might have done something irrational.

When Brody got back to his condo, he checked his university voicemail, but there were no messages. He checked every possible email and tried his private cell phone number, but the only call was from James Tagget. In no mood to talk to his agent, Brody paced back and forth, ignoring the constant meowing and bumping from General Sherman.

No matter how many times he tried to sit down at the laptop and write, it was pointless. Frustrated by his total lack of concentration, Garrett poured himself a tumbler of whiskey, but the alcohol didn't help calm him down either.

"Jessica," he shouted to the empty room. "Where are you?"

For several hours, Brody battled all sorts of negative thoughts, until he couldn't stand it any longer. Garrett jumped into the Jaguar and drove back to her apartment building, where he vowed to camp outside until she returned. Then he would confront her.

As luck would have it, just as he pulled into the complex parking lot, he spotted Jessica's friend Amanda. He honked his horn to get her attention, before parking and climbing out.

"I'm sorry to be so rude, Amanda, but have you seen Jessica?" he asked.

Amanda was indeed startled. "Actually, Mr. Brody, I saw her leave with two men several days ago. They looked like detectives or something like that. She said you were in the hospital. How are you feeling?"

"What?" Garrett reacted with shock. "I'm fine. Nothing is wrong with me."

"Well, that's what she said," Amanda reacted with sudden emotion. "Jessica was very distraught. I haven't seen her since, so I thought she was staying by your side at the hospital, or had gone home with you."

"Damn it!" Garrett swore.

"Do you think she's in some kind of trouble?" Amanda wondered, her voice quivering.

Exasperated, Brody replied, "I don't know, Amanda. Can you think of anything else? What kind of car they were driving, or what those men looked like?"

Amanda shook her head and started to cry. "Oh, my God, what if she was kidnapped? They might rape her or kill her."

Brody grabbed the woman by the upper arms to steady her. "Everything will be okay, Amanda. Don't think like that. Besides, if they're stupid enough to mess with her, you know Jessica will kick their heads in. I bet they don't know they've got a professional wrestler on their hands, eh?"

Amanda smiled. "No, you're right. She can take care of herself."

Garrett sighed and forced a smile. "Now think, please. Try to remember anything you can."

"There were two men wearing dark blue or black suits," Amanda recalled, closing her eyes to concentrate. "One was blond, the other had dishwater colored hair. They took off their sunglasses, but didn't really look at me, so I didn't get a glimpse at their eyes. I walked with Jessica to the door. They all climbed into an American-made, four-door SUV, which was black and looked brand new. It had totally darkened windows."

"Did you get a look at the license plate?" Garrett naturally hoped.

Amanda shook her head. "Not really. But I do remember thinking it was odd the plates were US Government."

Now Garrett had not expected to hear that piece of information. He took Amanda's hand and said, "I'll call the police and file a missing person report. If Jessica calls you, please find out where she is. They might have mistaken her for somebody else or some other unexplained mix-up. Here's my business card, which has my cell phone number on it. Day or night, you call me, no matter what you find out. Okay?"

"Please find her, Mr. Brody," Amanda sobbed. "She's my very best friend in the whole world. We've been through so much together."

"I'll find her," he said. "I love Jessica very much, so there's no way I'm going to let anything happen to her."

Garrett was troubled that his words might prove hollow in the end.

Instantly Amanda stopped crying, for the conviction in his voice convinced her of his eventual success. She gave him a hug and then he ran back to his car. Before he was out of the parking lot, Brody was dialing a memorized number on his cell phone.

A familiar voice answered. "Well, this is an unexpected surprise."

"Hello, Lucas," Garrett said. "I need to arrange an emergency meeting, just you and me."

"For what reason?" Perret asked suspiciously.

"It's too complicated to go into over the telephone," Brody replied. "Let's just say it's important enough for you to hear me out, before I take the matter into my own hands."

"If you think it's that important, then I'll be there as soon as possible," Perret said. "I was going to catch a flight to Los Angeles anyway, so I'll make some itinerary changes and detour to Albuquerque."

"I think you know I wouldn't be calling you, if I didn't consider this to be of vital importance," Brody said.

"I know that, Garrett," Perret said.

"Tomorrow then."

"I'll call you when the plane lands."

"Thanks,"

"Don't mention it."

Click.

Brody's cell phone rang. It was long distance again, the area code from Arizona.

"This is Garrett," he answered.

"Listen very carefully, Mr. Brody," a muffled and distorted voice instructed.

"I'm listening," Garrett said.

"I'm assuming that you care about what happens to the person now in our possession," the voice went on. "Would you like her returned to you, alive?"

"Yes, I would," Garrett answered.

"Good. Then you'll do as you're told?"

"Yes."

"I assure you that no harm will come to her, as long as you cooperate."

"What do you want me to do?"

"Drop your investigation immediately."

"It's not quite that easy."

"And why not?"

"Because someone was murdered."

"And what business is that of yours?"

"Murder is a crime."

"Not if the person was eliminated to protect our country's security."

Garrett couldn't help but roll his eyes in disbelief. "Oh, please, you're not going to use some lame-ass excuse about protecting America's national security?"

"Are you belittling the rights of American citizens to be protected, Mr. Brody?"

"No, I'm belittling you, you idiot."

"Does that mean you refuse to save your little friend's life?"

Garrett paused and then very quietly answered, "No, I'll do whatever you ask."

"Good boy. We'll be in touch."

Click.

CHAPTER 21

A LIFE ON THE LINE

GARRETT ONCE AGAIN MET Lucas Perret at *Weck's*. Brody was already seated at his favorite table, but the cup of soup sitting in front of him had gone cold. He had lost his appetite ever since discovering Jessica had probably been kidnapped. Things were just not turning out the way he had planned.

Perret walked up to the table. "So what's so important to bring me all the way to New Mexico, again?"

"Have a seat, Lucas, before I knock you on your big fat ass," Brody said.

Perret didn't have to be told twice. He hadn't heard such a cold, threatening voice from Brody in a long, long time. Something was very wrong and Perret was astute enough to not provoke the man. He grabbed a chair and sat down.

Garrett leaned forward and in a low tone said, "Jessica Lawver, my research assistant, best student, and my lover, has been kidnapped."

Perret was surprised at Brody's candor, but took a moment to reflect on the news. He knew Garrett wasn't joking. "Any ideas as to who might have done this?"

"I warned you once already Lucas, if anything happens to Jessica, I'll kill everyone associated with you," Brody promised.

Perret was convinced it wasn't an idle threat, but he still said, "I have nothing to do with this crime, Garrett. I'm as clueless as you are."

Then with an exaggerated look of confusion, Lucas Perret tipped his eyebrow with a Boy Scout salute and said, "Now imagine that."

Then the man just walked away.

"Bastard," Garrett said under his breath.

It was several hours later when Brody returned to his condominium to take a shower and get something to eat. He had spent several hours on his cell phone, calling many former contacts and cashing in certain markers. Garrett intended to use whatever advantage he had to locate Jessica as soon as possible. Brody turned on the TV while trying to decide on his next move. He had to keep active or worrying about Jessica's fate would drive him insane.

"Damn it!" he shouted at the mirror.

The cable news network suddenly interrupted the usual headlines recap to announce a late-breaking development. Garrett's ears immediately perked up.

"*The Justice Department, based on serious allegations, has announced it will investigate claims that the Bureau of Indian Affairs was approving lowball deals for pipeline companies using Indian property on the San Juan Basin of New Mexico,*" the reporter said.

"*According to Attorney General Deborah Carlson, a federal undercover agent unearthed these practices while conducting a four-month assignment as acting regional appraiser at the Navajo Regional Office in Gallup, New Mexico. The agent, whose identity is still undisclosed, also found evidence of document destruction by the chief appraiser of that office.*"

Brody shook his head in amazement. "Damn, Lucas, you sure work fast. Now I just hope it works."

Carla Denato was watching the very same news report during her lunch hour. Suddenly losing her appetite, she drove back to the Lab and went directly to her office. Much to her surprise, Dr. Steve Chase was sitting at her desk.

"Good afternoon, sir," she said, forcing a smile.

"Did you hear the news?" Chase asked.

She couldn't lie, but only nodded.

"This may require some more damage control from your people, Carla," the director said. "If the investigators discover Dr. Newman's past dealings with the Checkerboard Council, it might lead them here. I won't tolerate any more bad press."

The PR Director shrugged. "As far as I know, the Lab has no association, directly or otherwise, with the Bureau of Indian Affairs. I can't see how any fingers can be pointed at us, unless you have some conflicting information I should be aware of?"

Chase stood up, smoothed the front of his tie and said, "Flavius was my friend too, Carla. He was a brilliant scientist and someone killed him for a reason. I suspect it was someone from the Reservation actually, although I would be labeled a racist for saying so."

Carla was very alarmed by what Chase had said. "Who in the Navajo Nation would do such a thing? Everyone on the tribal council admired and trusted Dr. Newman. Your theory doesn't make any sense at all."

"Unless someone was using those energy reports to falsify the true value of the energy deposits on Indian land," Chase suggested. "The Council would have more than greed to motivate such an act."

Carla Denato had never considered such an outlandish possibility. She had just assumed a white man killed Dr. Newman. The thought of a Native American murdering the learned doctor seemed highly unlikely.

"Exactly how do you want me to handle this?" she asked instead.

"Don't make any public announcement just yet," Chase suggested. "I just want you prepared to deny any prior knowledge of this scandal."

"That was what I planned to do, sir," she said.

"Have you heard again from that famous author, Garrett Brody?" Chase asked.

Carla shook her head. "No. Why?"

Chase headed for the doorway. "Well, you worked so hard to get his tour approved in the first place, so I imagine he could be pretty useful in creating positive public opinion for us. Perhaps you should give his agent a call and set up something."

"Such as?" she asked suspiciously.

Chase smiled. "He's a best-selling author, wealthy and influential. Let him come to his own conclusions. You two seemed to hit it off quite nicely. Perhaps a nice evening out, over dinner, will add to his impression that we're not all geeks and nerds."

Carla didn't have to read between the lines or guess at what Chase was implying. She defiantly crossed her arms across her chest and said, "Be careful, Dr. Chase. Your insinuations are both unwelcome and unprofessional."

Chase looked shocked and shook his head. "I'm not insinuating anything, Carla. I was merely suggesting that you use your charming ways to build an ally. Brody is famous and could prove useful."

"Oh, so you'd like me to repeat your plan for seducing Flavius, but this time on Garrett Brody?" she demanded. Her eyes narrowed and she added, "I would almost suspect you had something to do with Dr. Newman's murder, if you didn't have such an air-tight alibi."

Chase shrugged and grinned. "I would have preferred to have been with you, Carla. I imagine Flavius had quite a smile on his face."

Before she could say another word, Dr. Chase was out the door and down the corridor. Carla was fuming as she said, "Sick bastard."

She huffed and puffed, fully aware her blood pressure was up. The PR Director flopped down on her chair and glared at the open doorway. The longer she sat there, the more she wondered about Dr. Chase's motives and the possible implications.

Finally deciding on a course of action, Carla picked up her cell phone and carefully dialed a number from a business card she had been carrying with her for several weeks.

"This is Carla Denato," she spoke quietly. "I was wondering if we could get together soon, over dinner or drinks, if you have the time? I think I might have uncovered something of interest. Please call me when you get this message. Thanks."

CHAPTER 22

LITERARY AGENT'S RESPONSIBILITIES

THE NEXT MORNING BRODY'S cell phone rang while he was shaving. He jumped to grab it, hoping by some miracle it was Jessica. It was not. He did, however, instantly recognize the caller's ID.

"Hello, James," Garrett answered.

"I'm glad I got a hold of you, Garrett," Tagget said over the other end. "This call is not social. I'm really getting concerned over the apparent lack of progress on your contracted work. You missed the first deadline, which was just a simple outline. I managed to convince them you were out-of-pocket doing hands-on research, but you still haven't produced any sample chapters or anything. What's going on with you?"

"I've been busy working on a different book, James," Brody replied. "Didn't you get the attachment of the unedited manuscript? I emailed it to you several days ago."

"I don't normally question your writing skills or your plots, you know that," Tagget said. "But I'm really not comfortable with this new story, or the characters. I thought you went to New Mexico to write another historical novel, not some complicated and far-fetched murder mystery?"

Brody pulled the cell phone from his ear and stared at it for a second. For some unknown reason, Garrett sensed his agent wasn't being totally honest with him right then. He could hear it in Tagget's voice. James was trying to get Brody to agree to something, even if it was only over the telephone.

"Okay, my friend," Garrett said. "I respect your opinion. I'll just drop that project and get back to the historical piece. It's actually coming along nicely and revolves around the Lincoln County Range War here in New Mexico. The working title is *Decision at Enchanted Mesa* and it has more romance than my other books, but it's a solid project. Tell the publisher that I'll get the chapters I've written so far, off to you later today."

Brody was really stretching the truth. The project was real, of course, but he hadn't worked on it for quite some time. In fact, except for an outline and the research he had conducted with Jessica, he hadn't written more than a few pages.

"That's great, Garrett," Tagget said, his voice filled with relief. "I'll just delete this other manuscript to my trashcan, if that's okay with you?"

"No problem, James. I'm sorry if I've disappointed you or put you in a bad position with the publisher."

"Oh, never mind. You're good at giving me gray hairs."

"Thanks for calling, James."

"Take care."

Click.

Tagget had actually sounded like there was a gun pointed at his head.

Brody clicked his tongue and said, "Perhaps there was."

In fact, Garrett's supposition wasn't too far from the truth. After Tagget had hung up the phone, he turned and faced Lucas Perret. "There, does that satisfy you?"

Perret shrugged. "I guess so, for the time being. But I don't really trust Brody to fully abandon any project he sets his mind to."

"Well I don't appreciate being threatened by you or anyone else, even if you are Garrett's former employer," Tagget protested. "There are certain freedoms protected by the Constitution and freedom of speech is one of them."

Perret grunted and headed for the door. Before Lucas exited, however, he turned back and said, "If I was going to violate those fundamental rights, I would have ordered Garrett Brody's disappearance long before he wrote his very first novel, Mr. Tagget. In this case, I'm merely protecting national security."

"Oh, bullshit," Tagget spouted. "You government types always have some lame excuse for your actions. In reality, you're worried Garrett might inform the public about some new lapse of morality or ethics from the very people who are supposed to be focused on representing our best interests."

"You have a right to your opinion," Perret said.

"You're damn right I do," Tagget fired back. "Now get out of my office, before I call the police and have them charge you with assault and battery."

"I never touched you," Perret said as he stepped out into the hallway.

The door closed, but Tagget just sat perfectly still, fuming with anger. Then, his mood changed to great concern. "Please be careful, Garrett. These guys play for keeps."

Later that same morning Garrett was seated at his desk, glaring at the computer screen. He had gone through another sleepless night. With Jessica quite possibly in mortal danger, the old lurid nightmares had returned as well.

The words **C**omputer **A**ssisted **R**etrieval **L**os **A**lamos were staring back at him.

CARLA.

"Could it really be that obvious?" Garrett asked himself again.

Getting up, he flipped through all his notes for the hundredth time, trying to uncover some previously undiscovered clue. He was convinced he had missed something vital, a key piece of information that would point him in the right direction.

"Or is it really the name of a woman?"

Which woman? There were at least five women at the Lab named Carla who had direct daily contact with Dr. Newman, not to mention almost twenty more Carlas employed somewhere throughout the Los Alamos complex.

Garrett picked up the sheet of official government letterhead he had "borrowed" from Terry McNab's desk.

THE BUREAU OF INDIAN AFFAIRS
SHIPROCK AGENCY, NEW MEXICO

"I can no longer remain silent, as others do at the Interior Department and the Justice Department, about this criminal misconduct."

bent over his shoulder. She pulled back on the victim's arm in an attempt to hyperextend the elbow, which finally snapped. He screamed in pain.

However, before she could even think of escape, four men came rushing into the hallway, immediately converging on her. Jessica managed to fend them off for a few seconds, but their weight in numbers eventually overpowered her.

Not very many miles away, as Garrett was driving to Los Alamos, Brody placed a call to Lucas Perret. Unfortunately, instead of reaching a live person, he got only voicemail.

"Lucas," Brody left a message. "This is Garrett. I'm heading to the Los Alamos Laboratory with some compelling evidence as to who murdered Dr. Newman. However, it isn't who I initially suspected. I think it's higher up the chain of command. I sure could use some backup, just in case I get in over my head. If you get this message in time, would you be so kind to send some of your goons? You know, the guys all dressed in black, with Kevlar and visors and lots of guns."

Unfortunately, at that exact moment, Lucas Perret was on a nonstop flight from Chicago's O'Hare International Airport to Albuquerque, New Mexico, so his cell phone was turned off during the duration of the flight. He would not hear Brody's message until the plane landed. The average flight time lasted two hours and fifty-five minutes.

It would take a little under two hours for Garrett to reach Los Alamos. He didn't want to risk getting pulled over for a ticket, so Brody drove just five miles over the posted speed limit. Remaining a law-abiding citizen, under the circumstances, almost drove him to distraction, for the proverbial clock was ticking.

Garrett couldn't necessarily explain it in logical terms, but he felt as if time was running out for Jessica too. Brody made it to Los Alamos without incident and headed directly for the famous laboratory.

By the front gate sat the cluster of two-story buildings, the entire complex surrounded by a simple boundary fence. The Lab never overtly appeared protected by the layers of complicated and technologically superior security, but Garrett knew eyes and ears were everywhere. Or at least that's what he had come to believe. He parked in the guest area, and then walked casually to the Visitor's Center. Once inside the entryway, Brody approached the main security desk.

"May I help you, sir?" one of the guards asked. His voice was neither friendly nor hostile. It was without emotion.

"I don't have an approved appointment," Brody told the guard. "Is there a telephone I can use to contact someone inside the Lab?"

The security agent pointed towards a white courtesy phone on the wall. "You can call senior personnel only on that phone, sir. However, I still can't give you access without prior clearance."

"I know that," Garrett said. "It's okay. I just want to talk to Ms. Carla Denato."

"Her direct number is available through that phone, sir," the guard said. "Just dial the first three letters of her last name."

"Thank you," Brody said.

He stepped over to the telephone, where he punched in 336.

A recorded voice came over the line and said, "If you have selected Carla Denato, please hit the pound sign."

Garrett did so.

On the third ring, someone picked up.

"Hello, this is Carla Denato. How may I help you?"

"Ms. Denato, this is Garrett Brody. I'm standing in the lobby of visitor's center."

She didn't say anything right away. Then, finally, she asked, "What can I do for you, Mr. Brody?"

"I need to talk to you in private," Garrett spoke into the receiver.

She responded in a most belligerent tone, "You haven't been authorized."

"I know, that's why I'll be waiting right here," Brody said.

"What do you want?" Carla demanded.

"I want to talk to you about Dr. Newman," Garrett replied.

"I have nothing to say to you, Mr. Brody," she said. "I told the police everything I know already."

"Really?" Garrett asked. "Then what about a certain interdepartmental memo you wrote, and I quote, 'I can no longer remain silent, as others do at the Interior Department and the Justice Department, about this criminal misconduct,' end of quote."

Silence.

"Ms. Denato, I think you should talk to me," Garrett said. "Otherwise I'll turn this over to the proper authorities. Is that what you want?"

More silence.

Brody shrugged and started to hang up.

Her voice startled him and he almost dropped the phone. "I'll be right there."

CHAPTER 23

CARLA

"It's all rather simple, really," Carla Denato said. "I was having an affair with Dr. Newman and I just didn't want anyone to know."

Garrett shook his head. "Nope. I don't buy it."

"Are you calling me a liar?" she was shocked.

"Well, not exactly," Brody said. "I do believe you were having an affair with Dr. Newman. I just refuse to believe that his dying words had anything to do with that. He would have said how much he loved you or how sorry he was for being such a jerk. Something like that. Instead, he was giving me a clue to identify his killer."

"I didn't shoot him," Carla said emphatically.

"Then who did?" Brody asked.

She didn't answer, but Garrett could tell she had someone in mind.

"Dr. Newman was murdered, Ms. Denato," he stated. "He uncovered something illegal going on and somehow tied it to the Lab, didn't he? Silencing him prevented yet another scandal from hitting you people. As the public relations manager, you must be painfully aware of how much bad press Los Alamos has been receiving lately, what with secret files missing and security breaches every other day?"

Carla nodded.

"So what's going on?" Brody asked.

"Perhaps I should call my lawyer, before I answer any more of your questions," she said.

"Why, do you have something to hide?" Brody wondered.

"I might say something that would incriminate me."

"Not unless you killed him."

"I told you already. I didn't shoot Flavius!"

"Then who did? I can sense when people are telling lies, Carla and you're telling one of omission right now. What did Dr. Newman discover that would warrant his murder?"

Carla sighed. "It was **CARLA**."

"**C**omputer **A**ssisted **R**etrieval **L**os **A**lamos?" Garrett asked.

She nodded. "Flavius didn't like what **CARLA** was being used for."

"What *was* **CARLA** being used for?"

"The system was designed to gather all the pertinent data on fossilized fuels on Navajo land," Carla explained. "As part of the ongoing research into energy conservation, the program would bring breakthrough technological analysis to enhance production. With the best intentions, Dr. Newman had designed **CARLA** to give Native Americans increased earnings and substantial documentation about previous land usage."

"Did Dr. Newman create the acronym in your honor?" Garrett had to ask.

Carla smiled sadly and nodded. "Flavius was quite flattering."

"I should say so," Brody said. "So what went wrong?"

"Flavius discovered that the Bureau of Indian Affairs was gouging the Checkerboard Navajo out of millions and possibly billions of dollars," Carla went on. "The price per rod was significantly less than reported to Washington, so somebody other than the Indians must have been getting rich."

"So Dr. Newman's dying words were a double entendre, a word or phrase that might be understood in two ways," Brody concluded. "He meant Carla was the key for both the computer and you."

She nodded. "I think so."

"I'm all ears, Carla."

She sighed.

Brody waited very patiently.

"Dr. Newman notified several of his superiors about his findings," Carla said. "After two years of being ignored, Flavius scheduled a meeting with certain Navajo Indian leaders to share with them what he had discovered."

"So you killed him?" Brody asked.

She started to cry. "I said I didn't shoot him."

"But you arranged his murder?"

"No, I wouldn't do that. I was…" She didn't finish.

who could manipulate the Navajo into believing they were getting fair payment for their gas and oil."

Neither Chase nor McNab said anything, but Brody maintained his suspicion.

"Why did you have to kill Flavius?" Carla asked Chase, tears dribbling down her cheeks. "He was a wonderful man and a kind soul."

"He was a busybody," Chase replied. "I warned him to keep his mind on Lab matters, but he couldn't just leave it alone."

Carla sobbed, "You didn't have to kill him. He had agreed to cancel his meeting with the Navajo. Oh, Flavius, I'm so sorry."

Dropping to her knees, the woman cried hysterically. Brody knelt beside her and just held her trembling body.

"Terry took the good doctor out into the woods and shot him," Chase said, his voice quivering with barely contained excitement. "Carla had unwittingly placated him with great sex, so at least the old fart died with a smile on his face."

"You sick bastard," Carla screamed.

Garrett held Carla even tighter.

Chase pretended to grimace in shock. "I'm surprised at you, Ms. Denato, using such profanity. You're hurting my delicate ears."

"You shot him four times, in a diamond-shaped pattern like an elongated checkerboard," Brody said to McNab. "Why would you bother leaving such a clue?"

McNab answered, "The Navajo would know what the fetish meant. A little symbolism goes a long way, Mr. Brody. I'm impressed you figured out the significance all by yourself."

Garrett then said, "Dr. Newman must have had incredible willpower to make it cross country to Bandelier, completely naked and with four bullets in him."

McNab said, "The old man had a habit of snooping into things that didn't concern him. When we discovered he was going public with his findings, I decided to remove the problem, that's all. I made certain the damn savages would get the message, by arranging the shots in a death fetish they would understand. By themselves they weren't fatal, but he would eventually bleed to death, something those damn redskins would appreciate."

"So you're the brains behind all of this?" Garrett asked with obvious doubt. "It doesn't seem possible a moron like you could dream up this little conspiracy."

McNab turned red. "What the hell is that supposed to mean?"

Dr. Chase stepped in front of the bureau chief. "Take it easy, Terry. The famous author is just trying to provoke you."

"Now what?" Brody asked. "Are you going to shoot us all too?"

"That won't be necessary."

"Why not?"

"Because I have insurance that you'll keep your mouth shut until we're out of the country," McNab replied.

"Why should I agree to any of your terms?"

"You'll do whatever I say, if you ever want to see your hot little bitch friend again," McNab said.

Brody got to his feet and took a step forward. "What have you done with her?"

"Nothing, yet," McNab replied. "But her life depends on you."

"I'll do anything you ask," Garrett said quickly. "As long as no harm comes to Ms. Lawver or Ms. Denato."

"Ms. Lawver?" McNab asked with disbelief. "I think Jessica deserves more tenderness than that, don't you? You call out her name when you're having sex with her, don't you?"

"You lowlife," Brody said.

McNab shrugged. "To each his own. Or is that too cliché for you?"

"I told you I would agree to anything to protect Jessica and Carla," Garrett said with emotion. "And I meant it."

"I'm sure you did," McNab said. "It's because I was so certain you would cooperate, that I arranged for Jessica to be driven here, so you could see for yourself that she's just fine. Then, Ms. Lawver will go with us as a hostage, until I think it's safe. After that, I'll release her."

Brody instantly felt bile in his throat.

History was indeed repeating itself.

Those were the identical conditions Garrett had agreed to several years before, to save his Carla. Instead, a sniper shot his fiancé in the back, just before she reached Brody's open arms.

Garrett forced a smile. "All right."

His stomach was churning and a sense of panic surged through his body. He had to do something, anything, to prevent McNab from leaving with Jessica.

Because he knew.

He just knew.

If he failed, Garrett would never again see Jessica alive.

History always repeated itself.

Just then, the sound of an engine was heard coming closer. After a few minutes, a black, four-wheel-drive SUV appeared, coming up the embankment. Brody was convinced it was the same vehicle Amanda had described. It came to a stop and out climbed four armed men dressed in black fatigues, followed by Jessica Lawver.

She spotted Garrett and ran to him.

Nobody tried to stop her.

Garrett opened his arms and as she fell into his embrace, she hugged him with all her might. Much to his surprise, though, she didn't start crying.

"Hello," he said, kissing her forehead.

"Hello," Jessica spoke into his chest.

"I missed you," he added.

"Not more than I missed you," she said.

He chuckled. "Are you okay?"

Jessica decided she would give him certain details later. "I'm just fine. I can handle myself, you know."

Garrett immediately recalled being on the receiving end of her wrestling capabilities. He rubbed the sore spot on the back of his head. "Yes, I do remember."

"I'm sorry I hurt you, but you deserved it, after acting like such a jerk," she said.

"I know. I'm sorry. I just didn't want you to get hurt."

"Have you learned your lesson?" Jessica asked.

"What do you mean?" he asked in return.

"If I had been with you, instead of in my apartment, kidnapping me might have proved impossible," she answered.

"I didn't think of that."

"No, because you were too afraid history would repeat itself."

He nodded.

"Well, let's change history, okay?"

He nodded again and smiled. "You're on."

They shook hands.

"All right, you two, the nice little reunion is over," McNab said. "Get back into the SUV, Ms. Lawver."

Nearby, one of the men who had been escorting Jessica earlier, beckoned for her to return. His left arm was in a sling and when he took off his sunglasses, Brody immediately noticed the man was sporting a nasty black eye.

Garrett looked at Jessica, who looked at him a little sheepishly.

"Did you do that?" he asked her.

"He tried to cop a feel, so I decked him," she replied.

"Thata girl," Garrett laughed, just as an idea came to him. "Do you think you can pretend you're in the ring out here?"

Jessica looked down at the ground. "The terrain's a little rough, but sure."

"Good," Garrett said. "When I give the word, you do your thing, okay?"

"I'd love to," Jessica chirped.

McNab shouted angrily, "That's enough chatter, you two. Now if you please, you little slut, march your tight little ass back to the SUV. I said, now!"

Jessica began to slowly walk back towards her captors.

"Now!" Garrett shouted.

Jessica planted her feet and flipped forward, executing a perfectly timed forward flip, her feet landing dead center against one of her guard's chest. The wind was knocked out of him as he sprawled to the ground.

Perhaps understandably, Garrett didn't see to his end of the bargain right away, for he was awestruck by the gracefulness of Jessica's moves. By the time he bolted towards Dr. Chase, who was the closest, Brody had lost the element of surprise.

Terry McNab was prepared.

Quickly following up her initial success, Jessica was facing the next guard. She grabbed him around the waist with both arms, while hooking both of his legs. She lifted him up, while kneeling down and dropping him crotch first on her bent knee.

The man's eyes screwed up into his head and he passed out.

Jessica scooted away and bent forward as another one of her captors charged towards her. When he reached her, she suddenly stood up, lifting him up and over, so they landed back first on the ground. While he was still on his back, Jessica grabbed him by the legs and hooked both his feet with her arms. Then she fell backwards, pulling her victim off the ground and shooting him over her body into a nearby tree trunk. He was knocked out cold.

"Stop!" McNab shouted suddenly. "Or Brody dies."

Jessica let go of the last remaining victim and took a very deliberate step backwards, her arms raised in surrender.

The first bullet punched a hole in McNab's midsection, the second slug went clear through his chest and the third round took the man's skull apart, scattering brains and blood everywhere. The Regional Bureau Chief for Indian Affairs flopped backwards in the pine straw like a felled tree.

He was quite dead.

Garrett spun to his right and fired again.

With the same deadly accuracy, Brody killed McNab's remaining black-clad assistants. He didn't have the luxury to contemplate disarming them.

"Please, don't kill me!" Chase begged, falling to his knees. "I was only doing what Terry ordered me to do, because he threatened to kill me if I didn't."

While keeping his gun on Chase, Brody ran to see if Jessica was still alive. He feared the worse.

Garrett dropped to his knees by her sprawled form, fighting to maintain control. "Oh, God, please, dear Jessica. I love you. Please don't die. I'm so sorry."

Her eyes opened and she tried to smile.

He took her hand and whispered, "I thought I'd lost you too."

"Shh," Jessica hushed him, trying to soothe his emotional pain. "I'm okay, sweetie, really I am."

"Does it hurt?" he asked.

Jessica rolled her eyes. "Well, what do you think?"

He felt like an idiot. "I'm sorry, of course it hurts. Just take it easy, until I can get an ambulance up here."

She nodded and bit her lip as Garrett applied pressure on the wound in her shoulder, to stop the flow of blood.

"Guess what?" she asked in between the spasms of pain.

"What?" he wondered.

"Now I'll have a scar to match yours."

He laughed and kissed her nose. "Yes, you will."

"I love you," she croaked.

"I love you too," he said. "I'm so sorry for all those things I said. I didn't mean them, not any of it."

"It's okay," she said. "I figured out what you were trying to do."

"I'm glad."

"By the way, thank you."

"For what?"

"Being the hero and rescuing me, of course."

"The heroes in my books would never let the bad guys shoot the girl," Garrett said, remembering his failure from the past as well.

"Remember, honey, your books are fiction," Jessica pointed out. "Life is never so easy to manipulate."

The helicopters that first zoomed overhead circled around and came down to land, as law enforcement vehicles arrived from several directions, disgorging a veritable army of heavily armed police officers and men in dark suits. In the lead came Lucas Perret, surrounded by some fellow agents who instantly recognized Brody from past assignments.

"I need an ambulance over here, Lucas," Garrett shouted.

"One's coming up the road now," Perret replied, pointing. He was talking into a walkie-talkie and issuing orders like a general.

The emergency vehicle pulled to a stop nearby and several paramedics clambered out. Soon Brody was relieved of his immediate concerns.

"A simple gunshot wound, no broken bones," Garrett informed the nearest paramedic. "The bullet exited cleanly, but there has been significant loss of blood."

"Thank you, sir," the paramedic said. "We'll take it from here. She'll be fine."

"She better be," Brody said. "Or you won't be."

"Just let them do their work, Garrett," Jessica scolded him. "I'll be okay. It doesn't even hurt as bad as some of the falls I've taken in the ring, so stop fussing."

"Yes, dear," he replied, as one of the paramedics decided to take a look at him too.

"I'm all right," Garrett protested. "Just make sure you take good care of her."

Then Brody went to check on Carla Denato, who in the meantime had regained consciousness.

"Are you okay?" he asked.

"Yes, I'm fine, considering all of this," she replied.

Brody knelt down beside McNab's body and pulled free one of the deceased man's shoelaces. He handed it to Carla,

"Please tie Chase's hands behind his back," Garrett requested.

"My pleasure, Mr. Brody," Carla obeyed with a smile.

"By the way, thanks for your help, Carla," Brody said. "I'm glad it turned out to be someone other than you."

She smiled. "I told you I didn't kill Dr. Newman. No matter how I might have wanted to protect the Lab, preventing bad publicity isn't worth committing murder over. Besides, I really did adore Flavius."

"I'm sorry for both of you he's gone," Garrett said. "Love is difficult under the best of circumstances, but it's too valuable to lose."

Carla motioned towards the ambulance. "I think that young woman is obviously very much in love with you."

Garrett looked over his shoulder. "I'm very much in love with her as well."

"You're both lucky, then," Carla said. "Goodbye, Mr. Brody."

They shook hands.

"Goodbye, Carla," Brody said. "Take care of yourself."

As she started walking towards her parked car, Lucas Perret abruptly stopped her. They shook hands and started talking like long lost friends.

Brody instantly put 2 + 2 together and shouted, "Does Carla work for you?"

"Well, not exactly," Perret said. "Several days ago Ms. Denato decided to become a valuable informant. Her tips helped us successfully conclude our own undercover investigation. Earlier today we arrested Barrett Crow. He admitted doctoring the books and supplying Diego Ruiz and the Navajo Nation with bogus data on their oil leases. This has been going on for several years now."

Garrett was very disappointed by the news, but it also made sense. There had to be someone in a position of power and authority, who was close enough to the Navajo to pull off such a scam. He felt very sorry for Diego Ruiz, who had put his trust in the young college graduate to make things right. The temptation for easy riches must have proved too seductive for Crow.

"So how come it took you so long getting here?" Brody demanded, his arms folded across his chest. "I left you a message hours ago."

"We needed to make sure Dr. Chase and his fellow conspirators would follow Ms. Denato and you to this location," Perret replied. "Besides, based on the body count around here, it looks like you didn't need my help all that badly."

Garrett took one big step and slugged Lucas Perret right on the chin. Unlike his futile attacks on Terry McNab, this time his punch sent the man sprawling to the ground. Perret's men were poised to interfere, if the conflict escalated, but they refrained from immediately getting involved. Carla Denato couldn't help her smile.

"If Jessica had been killed, you'd be pushing up the daisies, you bastard," Garrett shouted, his wicked finger pointed in Perret's face.

"That's a bit of a cliché, don't you think?" Jessica called out from where she was lifted onto the collapsible gurney.

Brody couldn't help but laugh and said over his shoulder, "Yes, dear, I'm sorry. Even we authors sometimes revert to using worn out and overused phrases."

Garrett could hear her laughter in the distance.

The agents standing nearby helped Perret to his feet, as he dusted himself off.

"I guess I deserved that," Perret said while rubbing his sore jaw. "We weren't very far away, Garrett. I'm sorry about Ms. Lawver, but these things do happen."

"You're damn right they do, you callous idiot," Garrett shouted. "This isn't one of my books, you know, where all the major characters are never really in any danger."

"For whatever it's worth, Garrett, I've read every one of your novels," Perret stated. "Some of them are quite entertaining, even if they're all completely fiction."

"I didn't know you could read, Lucas," Brody said.

Perret chuckled, but looked over Garrett's shoulder at the woman being lifted into the rear of the ambulance and said, "She's very beautiful, my friend. I'm happy you found her, because you deserve some happiness after losing your Carla."

Brody nodded, reflecting on his past for a brief moment. "I know you had nothing to do with Carla's death, Lucas. It was just easier to blame you and the agency, since you both were so handy."

Perret offered his hand. "No hard feelings, then?"

Brody took it. "I'll think about it."

"Your chosen career suits you quite well."

"I'm passionate about being a writer."

"Just like you were passionate about being an agent."

Garrett didn't comment, but instead hurried off to catch the ambulance before it drove away.

Perret called after him, "If you ever get bored, you can…"

"Not on your life, Lucas," Brody shouted back.

Perret then asked, "By the way, what are you going to title this book?"

Garrett pretended he didn't hear Perret and jumped in beside Jessica. He held her hand the entire way to the hospital. Smiling to himself, Brody realized he always had the perfect title in mind, right from the very beginning.

WHERE DO WE GO FROM HERE?

Several Months Later

YANNI'S MEDITERRANEAN BAR & Grill was something of a see-and-be-seen spot, but the restaurant did serve delicious souvlaki, marinated grilled lamb chops, grilled fresh halibut, and rotisserie Greek chicken seasoned with garlic and oregano. What started out as a humble gyros place for cash-strapped University of New Mexico students, had matured into a rambling, airy, blue-and-white eatery with a full menu of Greek dishes, including grilled seafood and some of the best steaks in town. The menu was quite traditional, including several vegetarian dishes like spinach pie and stuffed grape leaves. Everything at *Yanni's,* from the top-of-the-line martini bar to the enclosed patio that opened to let the breezes in during warm summer evenings, was fabulous. The restaurant was situated in the heart of Albuquerque's popular walking district, where the human parade lasted all day and all night. In fact, this was the best Greek restaurant in New Mexico and even highly recommended by the local Greek population.

"I love lamb," Jessica announced as they stood in line waiting for their table.

Garrett spontaneously hugged her and kissed her passionately in front of all the other dinner guests.

"Yes, Mr. Brody," she pretended to obey, batting her eyes and acting very coy.

Garrett rolled his eyes and they both laughed.

"What about finishing your historical novel?" Jessica changed the subject. "Won't you get in trouble with your publisher, now that you've missed the deadline?"

"I refunded their generous advance and Tagget is renegotiating a later delivery date," Garrett replied. "They still want the book, of course, because I make them lots of money. Taking into account certain extenuating circumstances, I think they'll agree to new terms."

"I finished reading what you've written so far. It's very good."

"Thank you."

Jessica fiddled with her napkin as the wine was uncorked and the appetizers served. She had so much on her mind and felt rushed to cover it all, without understanding why it was necessary to discuss everything immediately.

"Here's to the most beautiful woman in the universe," Garrett said as he lifted his glass. "I love her more than any words could possible describe."

Jessica blushed, because he had announced his toast in an unusually loud voice and everyone seated at surrounding tables had not only heard him, but also politely clapped their approval.

Averting her eyes, she sipped at the delicious red wine. "Thank you, Garrett," she said finally. "You are very sweet."

Jessica's mind went back to Brody's latest manuscript, which was a really good, but didn't seem to have any indication of their relationship reflected in the storyline or characters. She was quite surprised by this discovery and a little wounded by such an omission. Jessica had tried to pass off her disappointment as childish and egotistical, but since Garrett spoke often of how his life was reflected on the pages of every book he wrote, she couldn't help but wonder why it was missing from *Decision at Enchanted Mesa*.

To fight the mood that was rapidly becoming distracting, Jessica asked, "Do you think you'll write a book about what happened with Dr. Newman's murder and everything else?"

He nodded emphatically and displayed a sly grin.

"What have you been up to?" she wondered.

"I've been busy writing that novel as well," he replied.

"You have?" Jessica reacted. "Why didn't you tell me? I haven't proofed a single word."

"No, and you're not going to either."

"Why not?" she asked, hurt by this apparent rebuke.

"Because, my dearest, you are a central character and would be unable to maintain a detached and unbiased view of the story, much less the writing," Garrett replied. "Besides, I want you to wait until it's published to read it."

Jessica thought the rack of lamb and salad arrived at the most ill opportune moment, but she accepted it as fate. However, the meal was so delicious, that she couldn't maintain her suspicious mood very long. After only a few bites of the scrumptious lamb, she was content to enjoy the evening and perhaps discuss her concerns with Garrett later.

As her mood improved, so did the conversation, until the couple was chattering away about their upcoming plans over the summer break, possible travel arrangements, and Garrett's suggestion that Jessica become his full-time teaching assistant in the future. The wine certainly helped her relax. They quickly went through two bottles and she was a bit giddy by the time dessert arrived. After a cup of coffee, they decided it was time to go home.

Later, hand-in-hand, the couple stood outside Garrett's condo, affectionately sharing their love for each other under the stars. It had turned out to be a delightful evening.

"I hope you're not going to give up wrestling," he said suddenly.

She hadn't made up her mind yet in that regard. "We'll see."

"Because I wholeheartedly approve of your passion," he added.

"Let's go inside," Jessica whispered.

She took his hand and as they stepped through the door, a cat's loud meow greeted them as usual.

"Hello, General Sherman," Jessica said to the feline as she picked him up.

"I'll open a can of food, while you pay attention to him," Garrett suggested.

The cat purred incessantly and rubbed against Jessica, making sure there was no doubt how much he enjoyed her affectionate petting. She sat down with General Sherman on her lap, but as soon as the sound of the can opener came from the kitchen, the cat leaped off and scampered away. Jessica could hear the sound of his claws clicking on the tile floor.

As Garrett came into the den, Jessica jumped to her feet and went to him.

He responded by gently wrapping his arms around her.

They kissed for a very long time, before ending up together on their favorite sofa.

"I love you," Jessica said.

"I love you too," he replied. "In fact, I think we should talk about where we go from here."

Her response was nothing short of enthusiastic. "Really?"

"I refuse to put any pressure on you to conform to some social standard," he said. "I want you to be with me, because you want to be with me. It's as simple as that."

"So what are you trying so hard not to say, Garrett?" she asked with a smile.

"Well, I love you," he replied.

"I know that."

"I want us to be together."

"I know that too."

Brody sighed.

"What's wrong, honey?" she asked with extra sweetness.

"Oh, it's just that you're driving me nuts," he responded. "I want to make love."

Jessica nodded and said, "Me too."

With a tone of exasperation, Garrett picked up where he left off. "So I want our relationship to grow into something permanent."

She wriggled up against his chest, propping her elbows on either side of his head, worriedly gnawing her soft lower lip. "Garrett, you don't have to marry me. I mean, I understand if you just want to live together. Some men just can't be married and I don't want you to feel trapped."

"That's very magnanimous of you, darling." Garrett grinned, before tumbling her back down on the sofa, his eyes holding her captive with a smoldering gaze. "I want to marry you, because I love you and I want you with me for a lifetime and…"

He paused teasingly.

"And?" she asked.

His lips touched hers, their breath mingling as one. "And so I don't have to change the dedication page on my latest novel."

"What?" Jessica's eyes widened perceptively, when from the corner of her eye she spotted a new book strategically sitting on his desk. It was *The Carla Conspiracy*, by Garrett Brody.

"It's your new book!" Jessica exclaimed, jumping off the couch and picking it up. "Why didn't you tell me it was out?"

Garrett said, "It was supposed to be a surprise. That's my advance copy."

Jessica opened the front cover and flipped through the first few pages. With a gasp of surprise, she abruptly stopped. After reading the dedication, she looked up at Garrett, her eyes filled with tears of joy. "Oh, Garrett, what can I say?"

Eight words were centered on the white page.

To Jessica - my love, my life, my wife!

He put his arms around her and they kissed.

When they parted, Jessica whispered, "I would love to be your wife."

Garrett was smiling even more, but again it was very sly.

"Now what are you up to?" Jessica wondered.

Brody broke away and walked over to his briefcase, where he lifted up the lid and retrieved another book.

He held it up for her to see.

It was a copy of *Voices in the Wind*, by Jessica Lawver.

The End

ABOUT THE AUTHOR

THE AUTHOR'S LOVE OF New Mexico, combined with his passion for writing and teaching, all came together to form the basic plot for this book. As with all Derek Hart novels, there were several people who helped the author with his craft, and **The CARLA Conspiracy** was no exception. Derek would like to take this opportunity to recognize those people in print.

First, a tremendous thank you goes to **Dixie Leigh Lohmar**, who provided her personal experiences from the world of professional wrestling. Dixie is not what the author expected to find, for she has an incredible sense of humor, is entirely entertaining and captivating, both feminine and very beautiful, smart as a whip, and possesses an awesome outlook on life. Not only that, Dixie was one of the rare women wrestlers who matched her athletic skills against men and looked amazing doing so! This book could not have been written without her assistance and willingness to share her setbacks, victories, and profound adventures.

Next, another big thank you goes to the **University of New Mexico**. Derek Hart toured the campus several times while researching and writing this book and talked to a number of students and teachers. Derek was immediately struck by the tremendous positive influence the University has on Albuquerque, the state of New Mexico, and anyone who has attended classes there. The author would especially like to thank the **Department of English Language and Literature**, as well as **Chairman Dr. Scott Sanders**, for their assistance in his research.

As fuel for nuclear power plants, uranium atoms are split to release energy. As a form of economic development, proposed uranium mining within the Navajo Nation is dividing the community, fracturing friendships and even splitting some families. The only matter on which people on both sides of the issue agree is that the "energy" being released is overwhelmingly negative, because it centers on that age-old source of conflict, money. For many Navajos, the ground water cannot be valued more, because it is one of the four sacred and essential elements of Mother Earth. "*Tó eii be'iina' át'é*" - water is life, they say, and no amount of money will change that. The author wishes to humbly thank **Billy Martin**, a 73-year-old Navajo from Crownpoint, New Mexico, who supplied valuable information regarding the economic and environmental plight of the Navajo Indians, especially the Checkerboard Navajo.

The Navajo Nation

THE NAVAJO NATION IS recognized as the largest Indian tribe in the United States. According to the 1990 Census, almost 80,000 Navajo people live in New Mexico (the Navajo Nation contests the number, believing that the Navajo people were undercounted). The Navajo Reservation is also the largest Indian reservation in the United States, covering a total of 17.5 million acres and stretches across northwest New Mexico, northeast Arizona, and southeast Utah. From low, dry desert elevations to mountainous regions, Navajo land is larger than some states.

Modern theory describes the Navajo people as semi-nomadic, having ventured throughout the Southwest before settling in their present location. Navajo belief is that The People emerged into the world, the fourth world, to escape a flood in the lower world. The Place of Emergence is located in northwest New Mexico, in an area known as Dinetah. This area still carries religious, traditional and cultural significance for the Navajo people. The boundary of the Navajo Nation today roughly follows the traditional boundary set by the Four Sacred Mountains.

The early Navajo people subsisted on herds of sheep and planted large fields of corn. They quickly adapted to the use of horses and other livestock introduced into the region by the Spanish.

In the years after 1860, tensions between the Navajo people and non-Indian ranchers and the US Army increased. In 1864, after a series of skirmishes and battles, a large portion of the Navajo population was forced away from their beloved homelands to the Bosque Redondo, an experimental reservation about 400 miles away on the plains of eastern

New Mexico. The people, under the eye of US Army, were forced to march the entire distance. Thousands died along the way, during the four years the people spent at the Bosque Redondo, and during the walk home in 1868. This episode of tragedy and human survival is known as "The Long Walk."

The leaders of the different clans of the Navajo people signed the Treaty of 1868 at the Bosque Redondo with the United States. The treaty set aside a reservation, a fraction of the Navajo's original homeland, and in exchange for peace, the US Government promised to provide basic services for the Navajo people.

In 1921, oil was discovered in northwest New Mexico and the US Government created the first form of the Navajo Tribal Council, a six-man business council, for the sole purpose of giving consent to mineral leases. In 1936, the US Government issued the "Rules of the Navajo Tribal Council," which formed the basis for the Navajo Nation's government that remains in effect today.

The capital of the Navajo Nation is Window Rock, Arizona. The Navajo Nation Council meets four times a year to enact legislation and discuss other issues of importance to the Navajo people. The 88 members of the Council are elected, based on the population of the 110 chapters. The Council is the governing body of the Navajo Nation and its meetings are presided over by the Speaker, who is elected by the membership of the Council. The speaker serves as CEO of the Legislative Branch.

The Executive Branch is headed by a president and vice president, who are elected every four years by the Navajo people. The bulk of tribal employees and service delivery programs are located within the Executive Branch. The annual budget for the Navajo Nation's government is about $96 million and 80 percent is appropriated to the Executive Branch.

The 110 chapters are the local form of government and each chapter also elects a chairman, vice chairman, secretary/treasurer, and other officials. Community meetings are held in the chapter houses and the members vote on issues such as home site leases and land use plans. The Navajo people easily adapted to the chapter system because it was simply a formalization of the traditional form of community meetings. Over 50 chapters are located in New Mexico or straddle the Arizona-New Mexico state line.

Three bands, or satellite communities, of the Navajo Nation are located in New Mexico. These are the Alamo Band, located about 30 miles west of Magdalena, the Canoncito Band, located about 25 miles west of Albuquerque, and the Ramah Band, which is located about 40 miles south of Gallup.

The Navajo Nation is engaged in major development, which affects health, education, economic development, and employment. Plans are under way to establish an infrastructure that can support job-creating enterprises, while increasing services and benefits to the Navajo people. For decades, the Navajo government has been supported by revenue from a wealth of natural resources, such as coal, oil and gas, and uranium. However, realizing that natural resources will not last forever, other alternatives to pay for services for the people are being explored. In addition, in 1984 the Navajo Nation Council established a Permanent Trust Fund, into which 12 percent of all revenues received each year are deposited. Under Navajo law, the trust fund could not be used until the year 2004.

A major area of development is tourism. The Navajo Nation is rich with scenic beauty and the Navajo people are world renown for their silver and turquoise jewelry, and hand-woven rugs. Recreational attractions exist at locations throughout Navajo lands in three states. Monument Valley, Canyon de Chelly, Chaco Canyon, Hubbell's Trading Post, and Shiprock are but a few of the beautiful and interesting sites for visitors to Navajo land.